SECRETARY

OF

FAITH

SECRETARY OF FAITH

A FICTIONAL COMPANION TO PROJECT 2025

K.C. BOYD

AUTHOR OF BEING CHRISTIAN - A NOVEL

Rebel Island Press

Secretary of Faith

ISBN (paperback): 9781662942037
ISBN (KDP paperback): 9781662963261
eISBN: 9781662942044

To the United States of America, the rule of law, the First Amendment, a living Constitution, and all who work to keep us free.

Jesus said to his disciples: "Beware of false prophets,
Who come to you in sheep's clothing, but underneath
are ravenous wolves."

Matthew 7:15

1

November 7, 2028

IN THE WANING moments of Election Day, Democratic Candidate Paul Greenfield conceded victory to Christian Nationalist, James Dorritt Alger, III. On the morning of November 8, Americans awoke to a new reality, unaware of the depth and breadth of the changes that would soon occur. Two and a half months later, on his first day in office, President Alger took an unprecedented action—one of many to follow: he established a new Cabinet department, the Department of Faith, and appointed John Christian Hillcox as Secretary. Then he added a word to the nation's name, one that told the nation and the world that theocracy had come to America.

The United Christian States of America was up and running.

2

September 10, 2001

A LOUD THUMP outside Christian's bedroom wrenched him from a dream that slammed into him with gut-wrenching pain. A thou-shalt-murder kind of pain. The loneliness he had suffered as a child was nothing compared to the betrayal that confronted him now. A lust for vengeance raged within him, the reality of her perfidy informing him he must do more, much more. But yet. . . .

Foggy from sleep, he whirled about, not knowing what or whom he hoped to find. All he knew was that he was alone, always had been, always would be. Eternally, soul-suckingly alone.

"Punish the whore, banish the bastard."

The mantra-like phrase he'd internalized the night before gave him the momentum to rise from bed. That his father's seed had swum in Darlene's womb was more than he—or surely any man—could bear. I woulda extinguished the life from her deceivin' eyes but for Him, my Lord and Savior. He stayed my hand an' kept me from squeezing the breath outta her. Punish the whore, banish the bastard. When Judgment Day arrives, Darlene, my bride of the Covenant, shall be doomed and damned to Hell for all Eternity.

3

September 11, 2001

THE PREVIOUS EVENING, Pastor John Christian Hillcox, the founder of San Antonio's famed Male Headship Church of God and of Spread the Word Broadcasting Network, or SWBN, the nation's largest and most influential Christian broadcast empire, had learned that his father, Mason, had enjoyed relations with Christian's wife Darlene, relations that resulted in the conception of John, Jr., the long-awaited son and heir whom Christian had for seven years believed to be his own. A biblical seven.

"He raped me!," Darlene wailed as Christian pinned her to the ground, striking her with the very belt Mason had used on him as a child, lashing out with all the rage and hurt a man could feel while J.J., her bastard child, cowered in the corner, looking on in terror. "Why won't you believe me?" she cried.

From the age of four, Christian had suffered his youth without a mother. Absent another parent to temper his rage, his spite-filled father, Mason, abused him at will. At age seventeen,

Christian left home for Pearsall, Texas where, not knowing what else to do, he established a small church. During Christian's years there, Mason disappeared from his life, giving Christian the space and time to heal—or so he thought. With the object of Mason's torment no longer near at hand, the drunkard had no use for him. It wasn't until nine years later, after Christian was living in San Antonio where he had established a thriving mega-church and broadcast empire, that Mason paid his now married son a visit that would deal him the ultimate blow.

At the moment when Christian's next action would have determined whether Darlene would live or die, he had pulled back. She might have destroyed his psyche, but he wouldn't let her faithlessness cause him to commit an act that would land him in prison, destroying everything he'd created. Instead, knowing the intensity of Darlene's love for J.J., he would banish the boy, threatening to expose her incestuous whoring to the world should she ever breathe a word about J.J.'s genesis.

While Darlene cared not a whit for herself, he knew she would do whatever it took to spare her son humiliation, even if that meant never seeing him again. So it came to be that Darlene Hillcox surrendered her only child and remained at Christian's side publicly, all the while despising him with un-paralleled loathing.

Still in his pajamas, he stormed to his desk to unleash some of his fury. Penning a sermon on infidelity, one he would deliver on Sunday with Darlene seated behind him, forced to keep face. An hour into working on his diatribe, he switched on the television to SWBN, his own network.

"Oh, my gracious God," shrieked Eden Justus, a reporter who, along with her cameraman husband, lived in the shadows of Wall Street. Her voice so wobbly, she reported, "We heard what sounded like a bomb, and ran straight outside. It seems a large jet has flown directly into the North Tower of the World Trade Center."

Transfixed, Christian collapsed onto the bed. He checked the other channels, all of them broadcasting the same nightmare.

Seventeen minutes later, his eyes still glued to the screen, a second plane plowed into a second tower. It took everything Eden had to continue reporting. She and her husband were by now several blocks away from the scene when, through her crackling mic, panicked screams from the masses racing past muffled her own sentiments. Shouting now, she exclaimed, "Oh, my Jesus Lord, what is happening? The first building has just completely disintegrated! In front of my eyes! I mean, it's gone! With thousands inside!"

Coughing from the ash tearing through the concrete canyon, the cameraman jerked his lens towards the powdery remains of Number 7 World Trade Center, capturing the hordes as they stampeded north in communal panic.

Christian snapped off the television. Thoughts of Darlene vanished and he set to writing a new sermon, one he would give that very afternoon at Headship. Even without evidence, he knew with the certainty of fanaticism that the perpetrators were Arabs. With the world witness to biblical prophecy playing out live and on TV, a window had opened for Christian.

So it was that America's nightmare enabled James Christian Hillcox to bury his wife's betrayal deep inside one of the many psychic coffins that inhabited his subconscious, simultaneously affording him the largest platform he had ever had.

On the afternoon of September 11, Headship's beloved pastor stormed the pulpit, his bile spewing forth: "Ladies and gentlemen, Lord knows I never in my life 'spected to see Muslim jihadis use jetliners as bombs. Never. See 'em strike at the heart an' soul of American capitalism before our very eyes, like we seen today."

"I spit on their book, for it is none but a book of hate an' of violence. America is no longer asleep. From this day on, we shall stand together as the Christians what we are."

He held the Bible high and proclaimed, "As it was on the Sixth Day of Creation, when Father God proclaimed, *'Let there be light,'* a light was lit today, an' this time it was our light, the light of revenge. With God as my witness, I swear to you here an' now that, until I draw my last breath, I will use my political connections, my resources, an' my will to do whatever it takes to drive Mohammed from our shores."

The congregation was on its feet, its communal hatred the balm he so desperately needed. Darlene be damned, today's attacks no longer left him alone: the greatest nation on earth stood with him, as one.

4

September 11, 2017

A RAY OF SUN made its way through a slit in the draperies, cutting a harsh slant across the Pastor's slack mouth and eyes, causing him to stir. In an effort to remain asleep, Christian clawed his way back down into his dream because for once it was a good one. He and Darlene were racing along the highway in a convertible, top down, the wind whipping her bountiful red hair, both of them laughing. They were young and in love.

Five minutes later, his alarm blared. A choir of Christian singers roused him with their call to arms, forcing him to surrender to the day. Still under the dream's influence, he fumbled his way out of bed and stumbled along the dim hallway to Darlene's room. The vivid reality of his sleep fantasy lingered, filling him with a kind of desire he hadn't felt in years. Yes, he had his wife whenever he wanted— after all, it was his biblical right. At this moment though, he was operating on feelings of old. Forgetting the hostility she had displayed the night before, he knocked on her door. There was no answer, so he tried the handle, expecting it to be locked. To his surprise, it swung open, exposing a recumbent Darlene. When he stepped across the threshold, an overwhelming feeling of emptiness washed over him. Tentatively, he approached the bed, the room's silence filling him with dread. A half-full bottle of vodka stood sentry on her night table, and beside it, an empty bottle of barbiturates. His hands trembled as he reached out to touch her. She was cold, so very cold.

Christian looked around. Books littered the counterpane. He turned over a well-worn volume entitled *Final Exit: Death on Your Own Terms*, and a feeling of loss slam-sucked the oxygen from his lungs. He shook her hard, slapped her face harder. She must have been dead for hours, her skin was like ice. Gently searching her neck for a pulse he knew he wouldn't find, his eyes fixed on her arms lying stiff beside her there in that lonely bed. Darlene was gone, and with her the contempt she bore him.

She had planned this. Planned and executed her death in the early morning hours, waiting until he had sated himself on her soulless body. Then, of a sudden, he relaxed. Why should he feel bad? He was the victim here. As well as Accuser and Prosecutor. And, as such, he judged her Deficient.

Still, no matter how deeply her betrayal had cut those many years ago, Christian found no relief in her death. She was the only being ever to have truly loved him. Throughout their years of estrangement, he'd held fast to the fantasy, unlikely though it was, that one day he would find the strength to move past her treachery, beyond the pain, and somehow, someway, find within himself a path back to what they used to be. That she had chosen death banished that hope, just as it dredged up memories of his own mother's suicide when he was a young boy, a reminder that he, as ever, remained unwanted.

Just as quickly, reality set in. How would he explain this to his followers? He had never let on that Darlene was anything other than loving and loyal. No one could know that the Pastor's wife had committed suicide—because of what it would say about him.

It was Sunday and, as usual, they would expect to see her at his side on the pulpit. Many a congregant came solely to see her. A glance at the calendar on her desk showed she'd had a busy week ahead, one filled with church business and SWBN meetings. He needed to come up with a plausible reason for her absence so as to buy himself time to figure out the rest.

Christian picked up the bottles and tucked the books under his arm. On his way out, he looked back one last time. The cheerfully flowered wallpaper and glazed chintz curtains of her choosing seemed to admonish her in death. He directed his gaze upon her eyes, eyes that had once looked adoringly at him, eyes that were as empty as they had been last night. He turned, closed and locked the door behind him, then pocketed the only key in existence. Back in his bedroom, he stuffed the incriminating evidence inside a dark canvas bag, dressed in his signature blue suit, and then tromped downstairs, the navy tote slung across his ample girth. A late morning for Darlene would raise no alarms, seeing that since J.J.'s banishment she often stayed locked in her room, sometimes for days on end. Though never before on a Sunday.

Downstairs in the kitchen, Christian's all but indentured servant, Cora, busily sweated up a storm, greasy strands of hair escaping her cap as she rolled out the morning's biscuit dough, the underarms of her white uniform ringed with perspiration. At another time, he might have chided her about her slovenly appearance, perhaps shared a verse of Scripture regarding cleanliness. But not today. With scarce acknowledgment, he mumbled, "No breakfast for me," slammed the door and left.

"Well I'll be daggone! An' me here at the crack a dawn makin' his dang biscuits," Cora snarled at the empty room as she hurled the whole of the dough onto the sparkling, tiled floor, "Moods aroun' here, I tell you." She set to work preparing a tray for Darlene should she call down.

Christian crossed the border of Height Park, then headed to the down-market side of San Antonio where he tossed the canvas bag into a dumpster before proceeding on to Headship. Worrying the Darlene problem over in his mind, a plan came to him. He would summon his internist, Beau Husty, and County Coroner, Cletus James. They owed him big ever since the time he had bailed these two church elders out of trouble of the child porn kind, enabling them to maintain their reputations and sparing them a lifetime of humiliation, criminal consequences, and most probably prison. It hadn't come cheap. Christian's personal attorney, Clive Tenderly, doubled his fee to grease the wheels of injustice. In the end, the public was none the wiser. These men would do as told.

In his mind's eye, Christian saw how it would play out. Husty would put a bottle of Nitroglycerine tablets prescribed in Darlene's name on her bedside table. They would change her into a fresh gown, settle her under the covers, then leave. The next morning, Darlene's maid would come to ask if she wanted to take breakfast in her room and, finding the door unlocked, enter to see the missus lying peacefully in bed. When she couldn't be roused, the frantic servant would call for an ambulance. At the hospital, Dr. Husty would pronounce her Dead On Arrival. Next, on to the coroner, where Cletus would rule Death by Natural Cause: a massive heart attack.

Problem solved, images from long ago rushed him, and for a moment he nearly succumbed to grief for whatever part he might have played in Darlene's suicide. Nearly, but not quite. All it took to dissipate the fleeting sense of guilt was the thought of his father mounting her willing body. What she had done with Mason was unpardonable. Over the years, he had told himself that he kept her with him because she was good for business, but the honest truth was that he reveled in keeping her miserable, locked inside an emotional prison without her son, forever powerless in a loveless, empty existence. No matter. Biblical authority gave him the right to do with her however he liked, regardless of how hateful or abusive his behavior.

During their years of estrangement, it had been a marvel to watch Darlene work the pulpit with him, peddling promises of Wealth in this world and Salvation in the next. On stage, they appeared as one because she too held fast to a delusion: that if she played her part well, Christian might someday accept the truth that she'd been raped, finally finding within himself the decency to set her free. She'd relinquished that hope last night.

❖

Christian slid his car into the spot marked 'Reserved for Pastor' and called home and dismissed the staff for the day. Dwight Sessions, his second in charge, pulled up beside him and climbed out of his new orange Corvette. Dwight had had a front row seat to the many ups and downs of Christian's life, yet he knew not to ask about J.J.. These days, he only saw Darlene at church, on set at SWBN, or when she performed her duties as Chairwoman of Straight On, the gay-cure ministry that Christian had founded many years ago. Privately, he surmised that Darlene must have stepped out on Christian, with J.J. the result. It was the only thing that made sense. Why else would the pastor's long-desired son and heir have vanished? Dwight didn't have a clue how close to the truth he was.

"Pastor? Where's the wife? I was hopin' to talk to her. See if she might could jazz up the set, over to the station."

Christian blew past him without a word, leaving Dwight to scratch his head. Oh well, he thought with a shrug. The boss had been in overdrive these past weeks, what with his frequent trips to Washington and SWBN's headquarters near to bustin' at the seams, so he chalked it up to the great man having too much on his plate.

Christian robed up and scowled his way down the tiled hall towards the stage, wordlessly passing long-time employees Tonya Staples, Katina Troy, and Jewel Devitt. When stagehands Conner McCoy and Elroy Hicks greeted him with their usual nods and friendly "How do, Pastor C," vacant eyes looked past them.

Love and goodwill were hardly what Pastor Hillcox was about when he made his way onto the pulpit. He slammed his

Bible atop the lectern, and without introduction, he began, "In Jesus' name, we pray!" With hardly a glance at the Book, he bellowed out a curious passage.

"Cursed be the day on which I was born! The day when my mother bore me, let it not be blessed! Cursed be the man who brought the news to my father, 'A son is born to you,' making him very glad. Let that man be like the cities that the Lord overthrew without pity. Let him hear a cry in the morning and an alarm at noon, because he did not kill me in the womb. So my mother would have been my grave, and her womb forever great. Why did I come out from the womb to see toil and sorrow, and spend my days in shame?"

The congregation stirred uncomfortably, puzzling over the passage, when abruptly, the intensity with which he had begun dropped from him like a stone. "I've nothin' to say this mornin'," and he lowered his head in what was seen as a moment of silence but was really one of grief. His face seemed to buckle from within. "In the end, it will be as it should, but for now, I leave the rest to my assistant."

A stunned young man stumbled onto the stage. With something approaching honesty, Christian announced, "Listen to Pastor Teegs here. Pray with him. I'm not myself today. Musta caught the virus Darlene got." There was a sadness in his voice to which his followers were unaccustomed, making it difficult for most to take in what the unprepared Teegs went on to preach. In the days to come, when they learned of Darlene's death, these mostly good people would be there to prop up their beloved Pastor.

Slumped and broken, Christian drifted back to the ranch. He dialed up his beholden associates, who arrived within the hour. Neither had been in church that morning and, while surprised that Christian was home so early, when he called, they came. He explained the situation and the necessity of hiding the truth, pointedly reminding them of what they owed him. With meticulous attention to detail, the three men set to work, staging Christian's version of Darlene's death and readying themselves for their roles the next day.

5

September, 2018

HEADSHIP'S PARISHIONERS provided the church and Christian with a constant stream of income, but it was SWBN, his worldwide television network, that was the real cash cow. It took just a few days a month for Christian to lay down four weeks of video. Christian historians, creationists, Islamophobes, homophobes, pro-lifers, racists, right wing radio hosts, and politicians eagerly awaited the call for that privileged interview with the "Nation's Pastor." A few minutes of screen time with Christian were enough to catapult any one of them into the televangelical stratosphere.

Twenty years earlier, Christian had founded a one-issue lobby, Christian Zionists of America. CZOA vowed a "Never Again" love for the Jewish people, all the while concealing its anti-Semitic End Times intent. CZOA's distinction was not that it was the third most powerful lobby in America, but that it was the only one with an apocalyptic agenda. After years of nurturing political friendships at home and abroad, for him the most consequential relationships Christian had were with those in power in Israel.

In reality, he didn't give a good goddamn about the Jews, but the Bible required that a set number of Hebrews relocate to Zion before the Rapture could begin. There would be a day of reckoning between Jews and Christians, but for now, Israel welcomed Christian's largesse without regard to the long-term geopolitical consequences.

For Christian, if the planet was the patient, its condition would be joyfully terminal.

6

April 2008

HE WAS A JAMES. Not a Jim, a Jimbo, or a Jimmy. Even as a child, Alger came across as a James. Strong, even hard, he was quiet. But what presented as arrogance was instead a boy's keen interest in observing people, learning what made them tick.

A bright boy, he had acquaintances, not friends. He never pulled a prank, joked, or goofed around. Always prepared with homework or the right answer in class, teachers loved him. As he grew into adolescence, when it came to things like basement parties, drinking, or tales of sex, he was never included. But as captain of the debate club, his skills were unmatched throughout the region.

Born in Charlottesville, Virginia to the ruling lumber scion of the South, Alger was raised with immense privilege. From kindergarten through high school, he was surrounded by other white, rich youth. His parents, James II and Dorothy Lobert Alger, were distant, like so many in the upper echelons of southern society. James always did as they asked. So when, early in his senior year of high school, they gave him a list of their preferred Southern colleges and universities, he dutifully applied to them, secretly adding one of his own.

He was eager to get out from under the expectation that he would work in the family business after college, something he had no intention of doing. Lumber, or industry of any kind, didn't interest him. What did was power. He had enough awareness to realize that what he wanted was to follow in his grandfather's footsteps—to become a politician so as to wield authority. James I had served four, non-consecutive terms as Governor of Virginia. No longer alive, his example held great sway over his grandson. But for a young man with no political training, James had everything to learn and felt strongly that such an education would be best achieved far from his parents. He began to spend time in his high school's Guidance Center, perusing catalogs and consulting with the school's excellent college counselor, Mrs. Dressler. In the end, the two of them decided that Pepperdine University in California would be the ideal place for him to blaze his own path.

"Good day, James," his mother said at breakfast one April morning. "We have wonderful news," and she handed him a stack of opened envelopes. "I held on to these until the last one arrived, which it did yesterday."

Through email, he obviously already knew of his successes, but Dorothy, who'd never taken to computers, hadn't had a clue. At school, his peers had gone on and on about their acceptances, but James didn't join in. He simply didn't care about anyone other than himself.

His mother had made it her business to get to the mail each day as soon as the housekeeper placed it on the hall table.

Knowing this, James watched for the one envelope whose return address would come from the only school of which they were unaware. It had also arrived yesterday, and as he heard his mother head toward the hall, he snatched it from the table and dashed upstairs.

"You were accepted everywhere. That's quite a testament, don't you think?," she said, more effusively than she'd ever spoken to him.

"Yeah. Sure." His expression was as dour as his voice was flat.

"We think it is. We can't wait to see which one you choose." Compliments from his parents were rare and this one meant little. In truth, it meant nothing.

"Our preference, of course, is that you follow in your father's footsteps and choose Washington and Lee. We realize you are a grown man, so we'll leave the decision to you. You can't go wrong with any of these."

His father nodded.

"I appreciate your trust, but you may not feel the same when I share my choice." James II's usually stern face became all the more so. "I've emailed my acceptance and deposit to Pepperdine, a Christian university in California. I didn't tell you I applied there because I knew you would disapprove. My guidance counselor suggested it, and the more I looked at what it has to offer, the more I knew it's where I want to go." He tossed the school's catalog and glossies onto the table. "Take a look at these. Maybe you'll feel better."

His father broke his silence, "I'd expected that if you chose to dishonor me by spurning my alma mater, you would have at least stayed in the South. But California? And a *Christian* school? It won't do you a bit of good in my business, I hope you know." His mother, Dorothy, a subservient slip of a woman, had been raised a Southern Baptist, so the school's religious underpinnings didn't bother her.

"Father, I've made my decision and as Mom said, it's mine to make. I'd like your support, but with or without it, I'm going to Pepperdine. As for your business, I've never had the slightest interest in any part of it. I plan to go into politics like Grandfather James."

Making this declaration to his parents was the first sign he'd allowed them to see of his growing self-confidence.

Further infuriated by his son's disparagement of the business that had given him his every opportunity, James II held himself in check. He was not a physical man, simply a withholding one, a man who resented his own father all the more for the attention denied him but lavished upon his son.

Dorothy sat quietly by as her husband threw down his napkin with force, rose from the table and, after a cursory peck atop her head, stormed from the house.

"Try not to worry," she told her son. "Your father will come around. This came from out of the blue, you know."

"Thanks Mom, but it makes no difference. I won't change my mind."

7

August, 2008

FROM THE START, James flourished at Pepperdine, not only because of the freedom he felt being far away from his parents, but also thanks to the structure which the school's Christian core gave him. Seen through the Bible, life made more sense to him. He discovered the kind of fellowship with other men that he had never had before, so much so that he decided to take a chance and run for Class President. Tall and whip thin, he projected an aura of patrician nobility as evidenced by the cut of his clothes, the way he carried himself, and the persuasiveness with which he spoke. The campaign posters his team plastered across campus conveyed strength, authority, and the certainty of a man born to lead.

His running mate turned out to be the dazzling blonde, Peacock Allyson Tremont, who, like James' mother, hailed from San Antonio. Thrown together during the campaign, it did not take long before they began to date. From the outset, Peacock saw something in him, something she was certain would one day make him a great success at whatever he chose to do. Equally ambitious, she was determined to hold onto him. At Christmas, he took her to Charlottesville to meet his parents, and after seeing the true extent of their wealth, she conceived a plan. If what she felt wasn't exactly love, it was enough for her. Several months into their courtship, James had not so much as hinted at a future together, so when she started to notice the girls who flirted with him and, if he thought she wasn't looking, that he'd flirt back, she pulled him closer.

One January afternoon, she and James took his car to Van Nuys to hear her hometown pastor, Christian Hillcox, guest preach at Deliverance Bible Temple. That Male Headship was her church of origin, and Christian, her pastor, beguiled James all the more.

He often thought about the times growing up when he used to visit his maternal grandmother in San Antonio. A founding member of Male Headship Church of God, she and Pastor Hillcox were dear friends. His grandmother, one of the kindest people in his young life, was a deeply religious woman. It is probable that her influence factored into his decision to attend Pepperdine. In fact, it wasn't hyperbolic to posit that Grandma Eunice and Pastor Hillcox had each, in their own way, shaped the course of James' future. Now, years later, he was seeing a girl who had grown up with the words and ways of the man James saw as his spiritual mentor, a man who also shared a deep connection to the most meaningful familial relationship of his youth.

After the service, James took Peacock by the hand and they approached the pulpit in hopes that Christian would notice them. The moment he saw James, he stopped dead in his tracks. "Lordy be, if it ain't Eunice Lobert's boy! Am I ever delighted to see you! You get on up here!"

"Pastor! I'm honored you remember me."

"Remember? Eunice's grandson? As if I'd forget!"

"Do you know my girlfriend, Peacock Tremont? She's from San Antonio and her family belongs to your church."

"Do I know Peacock?," and he let out a hearty guffaw. "Why sweetheart, you come on over an' give your ole pastor a great big Texas hug. Do tell. How is it the two of you are here, together in Californ-i-a? James, if I recall, you're a Virginny boy, ain't that right?"

"That I am, Pastor. I'm in college now. At Pepperdine. That's where Peacock and I met."

"Ain't that somethin'! Peacock, darlin', you're a lucky girl. D'you know how fine young Alger's family is? Keep a hold on this one," he said with a wink, his finger pointing to his ring finger. "If'n you get my drift."

Before she could answer, he turned to James. "I miss your granny somethin' powerful. Many's the time I reach for the phone or point my car in the direction of her house, only to remember she's gone to God. Eunice was 'bout the finest woman I ever known."

"She was, Pastor. I often think it's because of her friendship with you that I ended up at Pepperdine," and James gave Peacock a squeeze around her waist. Watching this small but intimate gesture sent a shiver through Christian's nether regions.

Twenty minutes later, James and Peacock were in the car headed back to school, both exuberant from the experience. Driving along Malibu's coastal road, the sun had begun its descent over the Pacific and the colors were their usual shades of spectacular. Peacock placed a finger on James' thigh, then slowly, lightly, traced it round and round, inching ever higher. "How about we pull over and watch the sunset? There's no reason to hurry back," her voice husky, full of sex. The feeling in his groin rendered him incapable of protest and so he braked, turning into a lot on the ocean side of the road.

She sighed, a deep, breathy sigh, "It's beautiful, isn't it? Like God's painting a picture just for us."

The colors in the sky, the waves crashing upon the shore, the ocean beyond, and the girl in the bucket seat, her fingers now atop his manhood, all of it made him think that maybe life didn't get better than this. He looked at Peacock and wondered: Could she be the one? Having fully abandoned himself to her touch, he didn't much care.

As the sun slipped below the horizon and the sky glowed a hazy shade of orange, they began to kiss, and to kiss deeply. "Let's get in back," she purred. James, still heady from the day, was more at ease than usual and he eagerly followed her lead, tumbling into the backseat. After a bit of their usual virginity-sustaining moves, Peacock began slowly, rhythmically to move her hand up and down the front of his pants. It was almost dark when she unbuttoned her shirt, then opened wide her dress. In spite of himself, he moaned. Feeling the warmth of her bare flesh against his, he struggled for control because, to him, control was everything, but he couldn't help himself, not with her persistence and the will of his body.

"Peacock. Stop, please…," he pleaded, his breath coming in gasps, shorter, faster, more urgent. It was odd how desperate ly he tried to hold onto his virtue, unlike every other boy she'd been with, religious or not.

"It's okay, James. For me, it's only ever been you." She unzipped his pants, and let her tongue roam freely below his waist, slowly moving down to his member. "I love you, I hope you realize. Besides, no one will know."

He could scarcely speak, so great was his want, but his vow of chastity was strong and he tried to push her off. "Peacock, we can't. Not until we're married."

Continuing to grind atop him, she popped upright. "Is that a proposal, James Alger? Because if it is, the answer is yes! Yes, yes, yes!" With deliberation, she dove underneath and turned over onto her stomach, raising her naked buttocks high. With words soft and low she urged, "Come in the back door, if you know what I mean. It's what everyone does. It's not real sex and has nothing to do with virginity. It's for you, James. For us. In fact, it's God's will." His resistance evaporated and, with their strangely virginal mating, he was bound to her forever.

For the next three years, James and Peacock spent their summers in California. They found work at The Creation Institute and continued their stunted sexual encounters. Immersed year-round in the biblical world, his ties to his grandmother's beliefs deepened. It felt as if he had joined God's fraternity, and indeed he had. With the Lord on his side, he was certain that one day he would gain his rightful place, and that that place would be one of authority.

On the last day of April, the sun smiled down on Pepperdine's Class of 2008, with only James' mother there to see her son graduate.

One week later, James Alger, III and Peacock Allyson Tremont joined together with God, Pastor Hillcox performing the Covenant Marriage at Male Headship Church of God, James II's displeasure evident.

That night, when James entered Peacock frontally, they lost their virginity together, or so James thought. Even if what they had wasn't true love, Peacock was more than content. She had gained the Alger surname, certain that together, they would scale whatever heights James desired.

8

May 2012

JAMES AND PEACOCK settled in the wealthy Northern Virginia suburb of Great Falls. Through Grandfather's ties, James gained immediate entrée into conservative circles and, after a short time, he secured a job with Virginia's senior senator, Leroy Cuthbert, known to most people simply as Roy. Four years later, Republicans were bandying about James' name as a possible replacement for Virginia Congressman Filmore Widdicomb, who had recently announced his retirement. When the party asked Alger to step in, he readily accepted, seeing it as a solid first step.

That evening he said to Peacock, "It has begun. The Governor appointed me to stand in Widdicomb's stead until November and then to run for his office. With Grandfather's name and your help, it should be an easy win. Keep on with your women's groups. In fact, increase your presence, especially at church. I'll make sure your efforts get publicity, particularly in the Christian press. These are voters I might not otherwise reach, ladies who'll get to know me through you."

Having been largely sidelined since their move back east, she was thrilled.

"James, if you'd let me, I'd love to come along with you when you campaign. I wouldn't have to talk or anything, just be there so that people see you as a family man."

Her hands rested on her still flat belly, their three-month fetus growing its fingers and toes inside of her.

"I think voters will like it, especially once I start to show."

Her first trimester fatigue had passed and, aside from his frequent demands for sex, there remained little else between them. He'd grown sharper, more dismissive. She couldn't remember the last time he'd asked her for advice. Maybe this could be a way back in.

"That's not a bad idea. It'd be good to be seen as a family man."

Early on, when Peacock asked James if he wanted to learn the baby's sex, he'd looked at her with incredulity.

"You must be kidding. As long as there's a heartbeat and the fetus is developing as it should, the rest is God's mystery."

But in late October, when she delivered a healthy baby girl, James made his disappointment clear.

"Maybe next time you'll do as you should and give me a son."

Stung by his intended cruelty, she fell silent.

Come November, as expected, James won by a comfortable margin. He was elected because of his name, his religious leanings, and a singularity of mind that might not have surfaced had he stayed in the South near to his parents.

The times that James read the Bible, he was particularly drawn to passages that spoke of absolute authority. One from Matthew, in particular, was emblazoned in his mind; *The kingdom of heaven suffers violence, and violent men take it by force.* It excited him more than it probably should, so he kept the thought to himself.

The day James put hand to Bible, he was twenty-six years old, one of the youngest persons ever to serve in the United States Congress. A man of keen intelligence and indefatigable drive, he would remain there for ten years, building a national profile as a strong and principled Conservative, all the while biding his time until bigger things came his way.

9

October 10, 2028

"GOOD EVENING. Coming to you live from Xavier University's Cintas Center in Cincinnati, Ohio, it is my great pleasure to welcome you to the second and final 2028 presidential debate. My name is Adam White and I am your moderator.

"Tonight's panel of esteemed journalists are, from left to right: Liz Boorman of Truth Be Told, Ron Glesser with SHOX News, Geraldine Bost of Public News Daily, and finally, Barron Thompson from the well-known vlog, *Truth, Not Consequence.*"

White turned to face the stage and the two podiums set far apart from each other, the distance between them a metaphor for the nation's profound division, and began: "It is a privilege and an honor to introduce the candidates for the 2028 presidential election: For the Democrats, the two-term senator from Pennsylvania, Paul Greenfield, and for the Republicans, from the great Commonwealth of Virginia, Congressman James Alger." Greenfield supporters clapped politely, while Alger's supporters stomped their feet and cheered loudly, White breaking in to ask that audience members reserve all outward expressions until the end of the debate so that they would have time to get to the important issue.

The questions elicited answers so predictable that there was little chance any minds would change. Alger was the more practiced of the two, his debate skills serving him well. Not only that, but the audience was heavily weighted on his side, forcing White to request after every question that the crowd "remain silent until after the debate."

The Republican candidate held sway when he said he'd severely reduce funding within the bloated government. But seventy minutes in, instant polls favored Greenfield after he pointedly noted Alger's campaign promise to eliminate Social Security and Medicare once and for all.

"Congressman, the second to last question goes to you. As president, would you give equal rights to all religions, races, and sexual orientations?"

Alger looked squarely into the camera. "The Constitution made it clear that we are all of us equals, the three Abrahamic religions derive from the same source, making all of us equals. As to race and sexuality, the same thing goes; we are each of us the same in the eyes of our Creator."

So far, the senator had forced himself to remain inside the bounds of decency, but he couldn't stay silent a moment longer and he lurched for the microphone. "First of all, if you want to be president, know your history! What you just said is from the Declaration of Independence, not the Constitution, though facts are hardly your strong point."

"Mr. Greenfield, you are out of turn!," White snapped. "Not only was that last remark unnecessary, but the congressman was not finished."

"I was about to correct myself when he so rudely interrupted," Alger sneered, sputtering in anger. Audience members were on their feet, shrieking at Greenfield.

White, his voice now that of a toady's, jumped in. "Please accept my apology, Congressman. The senator was given the rules, rules he just now broke.

"*Now*, Mr. Greenfield, you may take your turn."

The senator smirked, his contempt for Alger out in the open. "Thank you. Congressman, I expect you aren't aware that it was the Jewish sages who taught that every man, woman, and child is worthy of the same dignity. As a Jewish man with a gay son, while I should be relieved with what you just said, I've known you for too long to accept your words as truth. Since we live in a 'don't believe your eyes and ears time,' particularly when it comes to this, I'd like to direct the audience toward Fact Flash, our certified truth-checker. Approved by both parties, I might add." Greenfield pointed to the screen that stood mid-stage, and an unsettled buzz swept through the auditorium. "There are too many examples of my opponent speaking... 'untruths,' I will call them, to be polite. It seems that every time he speaks, Fact Flash reads 'False.' Why should anyone take him at his word, especially when we've seen how he votes?"

"Adam, I will not tolerate his calling me a liar because that's what he just did. I should hope you'll put an end to this debate right now as I will not stand by while that Socialist sullies my good name before the entire country."

The sounds from the audience turned threatening, his sup-porters on their feet chanting, "Al-ger! Al-ger! Al-ger!" After a few moments, White banged the ceremonial gavel on the dais, "Ahem. From this point on, interruptions and unnecessary insults will be cause to end the debate."

Around the auditorium, officers made their presences felt, hands atop holstered guns speaking for them. Greenfield seized the opportunity to verbally attack.

"Congressman, I'd like to remind everyone that, in all your years in Congress, not once did you support equality. To the contrary, you have consistently been one of the strongest advocates for White Supremacy on The Hill. There, I said it. Just as I'll also say that I am sick to death of your lies, and yes, I dare call them that! For you, sir, are a liar!"

The crowd lost control, stopped from going up on stage and after Greenfield only when officers stepped up to create a human barricade.

Alger thought for a second and, inelegant as it was, he realized it would work to his advantage if he pretended to want a fight. He removed his coat and tie and rolled up his sleeves, stepped from behind the podium, and moved toward his opponent. The cameras zoomed in. It was all so primitive, so male, so satisfying.

In a supremely out-of-character moment, Greenfield went towards him, the veneer of civility gone. Here, in America, four weeks before the presidential election, the two candidates stood poised for battle. The journalists whispered into their headsets as tens of millions watched the unfolding drama from their homes. What was happening here bested any reality show ever aired.

White pretended alarm but, inwardly, he saw dollar signs, aware that this unprecedented political drama would make him an overnight celebrity.

The moment held its breath, and until after what seemed a lifetime, Secret Service agents stepped from both sides of the stage to restrain their charges. That was when White got between the two men, playing the hero.

"I'll thank you gentlemen to return to your places and remain there," White ordered, his voice firm, his mind celebrating tomorrow's headlines. Greenfield was first to back down.

"Ms. Boorman of TBT will ask the final question."

The attractive thirty-two-year-old leaned forward. Her chestnut-brown hair fell over her face as she covered the mic and whispered into her headset. Taking her hand away, she spoke, "In the press, we all too often depict our politicians as one-dimensional and in doing so, we don't give citizens a full and fair picture. Once again, we find the country at the edge of civil war, even as we just saw in microcosm," and she gestured towards the candidates. "Congressman Alger, tonight, here in Ohio, I want to take this opportunity to ask you: As president, how would you unite our fragmented nation?"

"Interesting that you of all people should ask, Miss Boorman. We are not nearly as fractured as you say. For a long time it has been you people in the media who continually stoke our differences. If you reported the news accurately, as the name of your network implies, you wouldn't have to ask this question. You create false narratives in order to call them divisions, all to drive up your ratings. It's reprehensible and you should be ashamed."

The other panelists showed varying shades of discomfort except for SHOX News' Ron Glesser. Boorman didn't take the bait, instead turning her eyes to Alger's opponent.

"Senator Greenfield, the same question."

"For the first time this evening, the congressman has spoken the truth. Aside from a certain network known for its non-stop dissembling," and he looked defiantly at Glesser, "even the so-called 'liberal' networks kowtow to ratings. In the end, we are all the losers." His voice settled. "Listen closely because I am about to say the most important thing I have ever said. If this man," he said, thrusting a trembling finger towards Alger. "If this man becomes our next president, I guarantee you that a free, unfettered press will be a relic of the past."

"Congressman Alger, your rebuttal?"

"I will not dignify the senator's slanderous accusations with a response. What he just said is the biggest lie of the night!"

Drawing on Alger's many past statements, Fact Flash blinked "False."

10

October 12, 2028

AT 12:33 A.M. Eastern Standard Time, a dozen explosions targeting bridges, hospitals, and shopping malls rocked the nation. In cities large and small, bombs ripped through commercial districts, in New York's Penn Station, BART's 16th Street station in San Francisco's Mission District, and the Fifth and Wabash stop in Chicago's Loop, to name but three. Within minutes, public transportation and commerce ground to a halt and the Dow fell seventeen thousand points.

The networks cued up their quickly prepared visuals, each one accompanied by somber, pre-recorded soundtracks—the music kept at the ready for the next inevitable shooting or other crisis to come along. Before long, the words "Assault on America" became the nation's watchwords.

"This is Jessie Stabenow of SWBN reporting live near Chicago's Fifth and Wabash Station, where, minutes ago, a massive bomb detonated. There is no word yet on casualties, but the number of body bags I am seeing coming down from the elevated platform is alarming. ISIS, Al-Qaeda, and other known terrorist groups have independently claimed responsibility," the lens zooming in on a stretcher, its sheet darkened with blood. "All we can say at this time is that these were highly coordinated bombings suggesting that a great deal of money and planning went into them."

People gathered their loved ones close. Few ventured out, as eyes remained glued to screens where, without facts, pundits heaped blame on the Arab world. The 'Nation's Pastor,' John Christian Hillcox, broadcasting live from his pulpit in San Antonio, gripped his Bible as he stood before SWBN's cameras and those congregants brave enough to have made their way to the church on this chilling day.

As after 9/11, Christian dispensed with the need for evidence before he spoke. He looked into the cameras, his eyes on fire, and without pause, he roared, "Fellow Americans. Today, as hate-filled Arabs from Islamabad to Kabul celebrate the slaughter of innocents, they are laughin' with joy as they dance in the streets." A fake video of Arabs rejoicing somewhere in Saudi Arabia ran on a loop on the big screen behind. He gave viewers time to digest the images, then continued, this time calmer, more pensive.

"Father God deserves our trust, perhaps t'day most of all. Yea, scores of innocents were sent to their deaths, in ways too gruesome to imagine. As to those who died today, them what believed in the Lord, they are with Him now. I ask, should we despair?"

He clasped his hands together, a hint of excitement lightening his voice.

"Maybe it's better that we celebrate instead."

Whispers ricocheted across the sacred space..

"I know. I know what y'all are thinkin.' How dare we feel gladness when the blood ain't even near dry? Well, I'll tell you how. An' I'll tell you why. Our bless-ed End came a fair shot closer today, an' as it hurtles toward us faster an' faster, when it finally gets here, will we welcome it?"

Slowly but surely, comprehension began to dawn.

"I say, will we welcome it?"

"We will."

"We will WHAT?"

"We will welcome it."

"You don't sound so sure a yourselves."

"WE WILL WELCOME IT!"

"That's right. An', when it arrives, do you think—no, do you *know* – who will be victorious? Will it be Allah?"

That is when millions of voices thundered from Headship to sofas and armchairs across the nation, his followers calling out Christian's oft used slogan, "Not on our watch!"

"Or will it be our Lord an' Savior?"

From the church and beyond, believers cried out, "Jee-zus! Jee-zus! Jee-zus!"

"Guh-lory to the Lamb of God!" he bellowed. "Just as Jeez-zus died for our sins, there is reason in today's murderous aftermath to bow the head an' bend the knee." And he did. "To the curs-ed A-rabs listenin' now, we affirm, YOU WILL NOT WIN, for the Lord is on our side!"

"Father God," and he looked skyward, "unfetter our eyes so that, as one people, we see what happened as glo-ri-ous proof of what is to come. That we see it as testament that our Final

War has begun, a war that, together, we welcome." He made a dramatic turn. "Of this, we can be certain.

"*You are my war-club, My weapon of war, and with you I shatter nations. And with you I destroy kingdoms.*"

Carefully, meticulously, intentionally, Christian's voice rose, hovering above the frenzied audience and those watching from home, "They used our Christian generosity, lived in our country, all the while they plotted an' planned."

From his home in Great Falls, Candidate Alger watched from the start, as spellbound as he was on that September day, twenty-seven years ago. A young teen then, Grandmother Eunice had taken ill and James had accompanied his mother to San Antonio to spend a few days by her side. It was there at her sickbed that the three of them watched the tragedy of September 11 unfold. The elderly woman urged Little Jimmy, as she called him (although by then he was six-foot-four) to use her driver and go to Pastor Christian's church where she was certain he would find solace. The sermon he heard that day was the first time he had ever found expression for the combination of his inner rage and the sense of white, male, Christian superiority he'd always owned.

Today, as Christian preached and raged and laid the blame squarely at the feet of the Arab world once again, as he ranted to those physically present, but more so to his vast televangelical audience, Christian had no way of knowing he was speaking to an audience of one. His call to remake America was everything Alger had envisioned. It was then that James knew what one of his first acts as president would be.

Christian continued, "On November 7, we will set aside our fears, place our trust in the Lord, an' with Father God on our side, we will march to the polls to cast our votes like a stone for the one He hath anointed — the one who will bring us to our final guh-lory, the only man who will lead us to the mountain-top. That man, my friends, is the great an' godly James D. Alger."

Christian stepped down from the dais, seeming to reflect, as he paced back and forth, and back and forth, across the stage. With the well-timed intentionality of his every sermon, he lifted the Bible and, ratcheting up the tone and pace, swiped his trademark black hankie across his brow.

"Believe you me, our boys learned the Truth with a capital T when they were forced to stand by in Iraq as they watched their friends bein' blown to smithereens by them what hate us for our freedom." He was on a roll, scarcely stopping for breath. "An' look where it got us. It got our malls an' trains blown up, an' hunnerds of civilians murdered in our homeland, that's where. There'll be a new sheriff in town once Alger's in charge.

"Lord knows, we love our God an', by God, as the only real Christians in America, we're more than ready to take 'em on because we will not live in a world ruled by Allah. It's that simple. Truth is, it is God's will."

Cries of whipped-up excitement melded with canned whoops and hollers as citizen warriors watching on screens across the land joined in.

"Do not think that we have come to bring peace to the earth. We have not come to bring peace, but a sword!"

He lowered his eyes, picked up his Bible, bowed his head, and walked off, glad to be back in the business of hate. As for Alger, he returned to his grandmother's side forever changed.

11

Eight p.m.

SENATOR GREENFIELD went on air that evening to plead the case that the United States could ill afford to engage in another stateless war. He welcomed the many international offers to root out those responsible for the attacks and warned against condemning an entire religion or people.

Greenfield's poll numbers went into free-fall, Alger's conversely taking to the stratosphere when he pronounced, live from SWBN's Washington studio, "Liberals and their tolerance will be the death of us." When Alger promised a final war against Islam, a terrified citizenry listened. America hungered for vengeance.

What the American public would never know was that it was not the Arabs who had executed the bombings. The plans originated with The Patriots, a small and dedicated group deep inside the secretive National Home Special Protection Agency, known to a very few as TCT, or The Christian Takeover.

The Patriots had equipped twelve bombers with matériel and a promise of one million dollars apiece. What Alger's proxies had neglected to tell them was that none of them would survive. No one would be caught, no one held accountable. To Alger, who had initiated the actions, the death of others mattered little in the furtherance of his anointment.

Four days before the election, three more bombs went off: in an Iowa strip mall, an Ohio bakery, and a Pennsylvania farmers' market. Seventy-six more lives were lost.

When it came to Greenfield asking a terrified electorate for its vote, the majority leaned into fear and willfully chose to indict an entire religion. Support for Alger crossed party lines and America seemed as one for the first time in decades. On November 7, 2028, middle-of-the-road Americans joined hands with Liberals, Progressives, Conservatives, and Far-Right ideologues to put their stake in the ground with that of Christian Dominion. James Alger swept into office with the largest mandate in the nation's history, carrying with him both houses of Congress.

12

November 7, 2028

IN A GRAND HOTEL ballroom, hands reached toward the ceiling, fists clenched, as the sounds of bliss-filled swayers and babblers ruled the room in their ecstasy, some in English, most in tongues. A woman, her eyes glazed, shrieked "Bshalmanga-remanoosa," while others joined her in their own unintelligible cries. Shrill delirious joy filled the air.

And He shall reign forever and ehhhhhh-ver.

King of Kings. And Lord of Lords.

The kingdom of this world and of His Christ. And of His Christ.

Hallelujah!

At 11:00 p.m., Senator Greenfield appeared on the jumbotron to concede defeat, and a Jesus-fed adrenaline rush surged through the crowd as they awaited the entrance of their earthly savior. A chord rang out from the organ keyboard and eight shapely, gingham-clad dancers swirled onto their marks.

The handsome and wildly popular television star, Dale Fortenberry, joined them, his face transforming from unspeakable joy to holy sincerity in an instant.

Fortenberry bowed his head and waited for the cries to subside before intoning, "Oh Father God, what glory you have bestowed upon us. Forced to dwell too long in Sodom, we, the people have spoken. Praise be, He hath prevailed!" Looking out over the excited crowd, he invited them, "Sing with me." And from the Washington Hilton to victory parties from the East to the West, from the North to the South, the voices of the young and old rang out:

To God be the glory
For these things He hath done . . .

Tears flowed freely as the celebrants joined together and wept for the glory of His Coming.

A phalanx of uniformed agents fanned out across the ballroom and a hush fell over the crowd. A marching band announced itself and slowly, the rear curtain rose. The brass section issued a brief blast, then gave way to one lone soldier who, marching centerstage, stopped on his mark to stand in place beneath a spotlight where steadily, he beat the fife drum strapped across his chest.

Famed country singer Lee Hodges, clad in crisply pressed blue jeans and a red, white, and blue tee-shirt, strutted onstage. Behind him, the newly commissioned American flag, handsewn by a Christian dressmaker in Philadelphia, was unveiled. At first, it seemed just a brighter version of the Stars and Stripes, that is, to those who didn't take the time to stop and look at the symbol of today's Christianity, a gleaming silver sword, superimposed atop the fifty stars. A spotlight swept from the flag to Hodges, his cue to begin. His deep, sonorous voice and the words of the newly official American anthem brought the faithful to tears as he sang,

Mine eyes have seen the glory of the coming of the Lord
He is trampling out the vintage where the grapes of wrath are stored
He hath loosed the fateful lightning of His terrible swift sword
His truth is marching on.

Full were the hearts that rejoiced.

Enter President-Elect James D. Alger, the resplendent Peacock at his side.

13

RYAN GRAY, the thirty-four year old son of William Gray, the CEO of the privately held company PAX Aeronautical and Security based in Spokane, had recently been named Chief Operating Officer of his father's company. At eighteen, he had tried college, but after a year he had been far too restless to continue, not when he had the whole of PAX open to him. During his twenties, he had earned obscene amounts of money, partied hard, never once thinking about the death and destruction his father's company facilitated.

Then one night he met Libby Dunham. Not only did she sweep him off his feet, but she was as gentle and peace-loving as his father and PAX were not. They married in a small civil ceremony and, two years later, by the time their first child was born, Ryan was a changed man. He could no longer justify the source of their privileged lifestyle. With Libby's urging though, rather than leave the company, he stayed on to keep watch, all the while concealing his thoughts and fears.

PAX was the second largest weapons manufacturer in the world. Through the company's lobbying arm, Bill Gray and James Alger became friends, so much so that their families vacationed together, giving Ryan a front row seat to the congressman's casual cruelty. When Alger won the primary, Ryan's decision to remain at PAX , or as he and Libby had come to call it, the "Merchant of Death" proved prescient. He would continue in his role in the event that the day came when he could use his position to fight back.

Then, when Alger won and nightmare became reality, Ryan and Libby attached themselves to the blossoming resistance. By this time, Bill was no longer involved in PAX's day to day operations, giving Ryan the freedom to siphon off the latest weapons and technology in preparation for whatever might lie ahead.

14

Late November, 2028

THE NEWLY FORMED Neo-Christian Party established a Religious Police Force. From then on, free-roaming thugs ruled the streets, no one stopping them. These religious sentries made a public show of force whenever they caught an 'Undesirable,' reporters somehow already there, at the scene, camera-ready to broadcast the new reality.

"There was a roundup of Undesirables once again this morning. Police arrived at the scene of a violent protest directed at the incoming administration." Stock footage of a police clash flashed across the screen. "In the end, several Christian Americans were injured, two of them critically. As dangerous as the situation looked to be, thankfully, the dissidents were arrested and taken away. This is Charles Korteen reporting live outside Lafayette Park."

While the reigning military retained the power and responsibility to arrest this shadow police force, the reality was that for decades, a slow and silent indoctrination by Christian

Nationalists of those in the military had been taking place, to little media or public notice. The power structure necessary to maintain discipline within the armed forces made them an easy mission field, enabling the Christian Nationalists to weed out 'unbelievers' and make devoted Christians of most of the rest. The majority of those serving when Alger won the election swapped their old uniforms for new and began taking their orders from the incoming regime. The others, those who remained loyal to the Constitution, followed the lead of their profoundly cowed lame-duck Commander in Chief and did nothing. In the end, their late-term inaction would prove the fatal last blow.

Democrats, and middle-of-the-road Republicans who had voted for Alger, regretted their choice, as they quickly realized the gravity of their mistake.

15

January 20, 2029

AT NOON, James Dorritt Alger, III was sworn in as the forty-eighth President of The United States. He shook hands with the former president, then turned and walked off. There were no inaugural balls, only a brief luncheon at which the president raised a glass to Jesus. The toast was as dry as it was brief. There was work to be done.

16

Three p.m.

PRESIDENT ALGER made his way to the Oval Office. It had been a protracted yet well-thought out journey, and at long last he had arrived. After years of unrelenting drive, he entered the sacred space, the most powerful piece of real estate on Earth.

A short stack of blue folders sat on the Resolute Desk, each containing a document awaiting his signature. He settled into the stiff leather chair and picked up one of the many embossed, gold Cross pens.

Alger's first Executive Order abolished State's Rights, ensuring that no state, or group of states, would have the power to keep the president from changing or adding constitutional amendments, while at the same time preventing any single state from imposing its own laws.

The second Order gave full and complete authority to the president. While somewhat repetitive of the first, Alger wanted it on the books. He signed the third Order, deeming it a punishable offense to plan or participate in any form of protest.

The fourth Executive Order added two words, 'Moral Deficiency' to Article II of the Constitution. It now read, "All Civil Officers shall be removed from Office by Impeachment for Commitment of Treason, Bribery, or Moral Deficiency."

The House would vote to impeach the remaining liberal Supreme Court justices for perceived Moral Deficiencies. Their Senate convictions inevitable, the judges would resign without a fight. Alger would also dismiss any Democrat-appointed lower court judges, as well as those elected who identified as Democrats. Going forward, only men of biblical principles would serve in the judiciary.

The fifth Order did away with Freedom of the Press, revoking all broadcast licenses but for three: SHOX News, Pastor Christian Hillcox's Save the World Broadcast Network, and Truth Be Told. Promoted as an independent outlet, TBT's content would be closely monitored and controlled by the Administration. *The Daily Christian Times* was the sole sanctioned print publication, and radio licenses were limited to stations with Christian music and content.

The sixth and penultimate Order, once signed, would gut the machinery of government, satisfying the long-term conservative goal to do so. The president would reduce the number of Cabinet departments to four: State, Treasury, Justice, and Defense—and add a fifth, The Department of Faith.

Last in the pile was an amendment to the Constitution, the document that backed up the action Alger had taken on his first day in office. Going forward, the county would legally be known as The United Christian States of America.

The signing complete, Alger ordered his Chief of Staff to hand-carry the papers to the Office of the Federal Register.

Alone for the first time that day, James moved to the sofa, then made the call that would assure the complete takeover of the former United States.

"Christian, is that you?"

"Mr. President! What a thrill your callin' me an' on today of all days! Why, it's the greatest honor of my life!"

"Hillcox, please. To some degree, you're one of the reasons I'm here. I'm calling today to ask you to serve as the nation's first Secretary of Faith."

Genuinely flabbergasted, Christian said nothing, not at first, his mind tracking unbidden to his long-dead father.

"There is no one more suited than you to put an end to the nation's moral decline."

Christian physically shook himself, then re-engaged. "I hardly know what to say other than that I'm honored before God. An' yes, I accept your callin'. I pray I live up to the confidence you place in me."

"I'll announce tomorrow. Get on a plane tonight."

The call concluded, Christian started to stand, when all of a sudden he went all a-wobble, his muscles turned to jelly. The chair from which he had risen pulled him down with a jerk, his father's voice hiss-whispering inside his head.

"Chrissss-tee-een," it sang. "You go on 'head with it darlin' girl, git yoreself ta Washinton. Jest r'member, 's'a dangerous game yore playin' at. Like a pig inna poke, yore president'll larn that which you are. A loser what's a faggot, an' that's all you'll ever be, fancy title or not. You an' I, we know the truth."

Christian took a deep breath and, with great effort, pulled himself out once more from his personal Hell, choosing instead to savor the moment. The president of the greatest country on earth had chosen him, John Christian Hillcox, to be the nation's first ever Secretary of Faith. From the bowels of Hell, Mason could think 'n' say all he wanted. Up here, this was the stuff of dreams, not nightmares.

He summoned Dwight Sessions, his second-in-command and, within an hour, he'd arranged for him to take over the business. In position to do anything he wished, Christian would ready his countrymen for the glory that lay ahead.

17

January 25, 7:45 p.m.

FROM THE RESOLUTE Desk, Alger squared his chair to the makeup artist who went straight to work concealing the small wrinkles at the corners of his eyes and dusting the shine from his high forehead with a powder blended to his skin tone.

Just before the clock struck 8:00, the director signaled, "Three, two, one."

"Good evening fellow Americans. When I won the election last November, it was with the largest mandate in history. I've used the time since to act upon many of my campaign promises. Thanks to a fully functioning Congress, we have passed more legislation in the shortest time of any American transfer of power.

"Tonight, I want to share with you several Orders I have signed. These will not only keep the country safe, but equally important, give us the moral standing deserving of the greatest nation on Earth.

"To begin, so as to best shepherd your tax dollars, I have eliminated all but four Cabinet departments."

For Secretary of Defense, he had brought on Thad Riggins, CEO of Lackaman Morton, the nation's largest defense contractor and a friend in Jesus, Alger having brought him to Christ two years earlier. Justice Horton Huffmeier, once Chief Justice of Mississippi's Supreme Court, a devout man wrongfully indicted in the early aughts for distributing Bibles to citizens as they entered the state courthouse, would head up the Department of Justice. Nehemiah Jones, renowned political anchor at SWBN, would take the helm at State, and billionaire Maxwell Patience become Secretary of the Treasury. Patience had built his fortune on Family Forward, a national Christian bookstore chain, and Sit On Our Porch, the highly successful roadside restaurants that blanketed America's highways and byways.

"Lastly and perhaps most consequentially, I signed the Twenty-Eighth Amendment to our God-breathed Constitution into law. I have renamed our great and holy nation The United Christian States of America.

"Because citizens have for so long been permitted, dare I say, encouraged to attack Christianity itself, it is eminently clear that this is not a trend that will disappear on its own. Even now, as the Christian Republic we are, there remain too many in need of spiritual intervention. For that reason, I have added a fifth and brand new Cabinet-level department, The Department of Faith. I am proud to announce that the 'Nation's Pastor,' John Christian Hillcox, a man whose *bona fides* are without rival, has agreed to serve as the first ever Secretary of Faith.

"I am certain you will come to see the wisdom in my decisions. I pray that God continues to watch over and bless these United Christian States of America. Good night."

Alger stood and patted down his trousers, smoothing his suit for the photographer's historic shot.

Once the crew disbanded, and the office was left to him, one of the secretaries announced, "Your father is on the line."

"Tell him I'm busy," he answered coldly.

He retook his seat at the desk and looked around in wonder. Directly across from him hung the iconic painting of George Washington on one knee, praying at Valley Forge. Portraits of American heroes such as John Winthrop, Robert E. Lee, and Francis Schaeffer hung prominently on other walls. Photographs of Alger with modern-day religious heroes and foreign leaders joined a single family portrait on the bookshelves. He pondered the plaque Peacock had given him on their wedding day: "We Are One In Jesus" and thought how right he was to have married her. She had developed into the perfect helpmate. Leaning back in his chair, he savored his position as the leader of the most powerful kingdom on earth.

18

January 23

SERVERS BUSTLED about the center court of the Washington, D.C. Waldorf Astoria, filling water goblets and setting salads onto the festive red, white, and blue tablecloths. Christian mingled with the media, drinking in the attention that came with being a Cabinet member. SWBN's cameras, closest to the dais, captured the most intimate record of the goings-on. SHOX was also well-positioned, something about which niggled at Christian, unable to stop himself from seeing them as competition for advertising dollars. He had more money than he could spend in a hundred lifetimes, so did it really matter? Furthest back was TBT. Due to the secular nature of their reporting, Christian continued to distrust them. He hadn't thought they deserved to keep their license, but it wasn't his decision. Alger told him it is well-documented that autocracies in which citizens believe they enjoy an independent press are more likely to be compliant.

The president made his way to the small stage at the front and clinked his water glass.

He held up a document for the cameras to capture.

"What I have here is the Identification Decree my transition team drew up." SWBN's lens zoomed in as Alger put the paper down and signed it. "This edict authorizes UCSA agents to visit the households of those who, for ethnic, religious, or political reasons stand to do us harm."

An unmistakable chill filled the expanse. This couldn't mean what it sounded like, could it? Still, those there today were Alger's most prosperous supporters, men confident that the president would do whatever necessary to ensure their safety, while also looking out for their prosperity.

"You will learn more about this process as it ramps up. Now, may God bless and keep The United Christian States of America."

Sizzling steaks were set down at each place, Christian tucking into the bloody meat even before the president had time to take his seat.

During the lame-duck period, The Patriots made use of the substantial amount of leftover campaign funds to hire a team of computer and AI experts who located and categorized Americans according to race, ethnicity, religion, and politics. At the same time, well-heeled backers funded the production of armbands for each of the different groups. Door-to-door "interviews" by the military would be visited upon those of Arab ethnicity, and all others with brown or black skin, no matter how light or dark. Also Jews, Atheists, Buddhists, Native Americans, Latinos, Asians, Catholics and other Christians of the wrong kind, political dissidents, and so-called sexual deviants.

That evening, at 5:00 p.m., a time when youngsters sat in front of their televisions tuned to the popular SWBN cartoon, *Rascal Timken, the Godly Tweep,* Secretary Hillcox broke in, "Fellow Christians," the lens capturing his round face in full frame, "in order to protect you, starting tomorrow, government representatives will visit designated households, to distribute identifying bands."

Few adults saw the Secretary's intentionally timed announcement, though rumors began to circulate. The next morning, squadrons of conscripts fanned out from the Americans Only headquarters in Lanham, Maryland, beginning with cities, towns, and rural communities along the East Coast. Many who received a knock on the door were alarmed to see men in military dress on their doorsteps.

Armbands with the crescent moon, a five pointed star within, went to people of Arab descent. Latinos were given bands of green, white, and red of the Mexican flag, while Native Americans, while naturally identifiable, were made to wear bands with tomahawks on their upper arms. Rainbows, a thick black line drawn through them, made gay the biceps of queers and other sexual deviants, while Democrats, Socialists, Reformists, Libertarians, Constitutionalists, and members of the Green Party would sport a red and yellow hammer and sickle. Catholics, whores of Babylon that they were, along with Americans who worshipped the many other unacceptable branches of Christianity, were issued bands with a black on white silhouette of Satan. Finally, the Confederate Flag topped the arms of African Americans, there solely for the purpose of humiliation. Should an Undesirable appear in public without his or her identifier, the consequences would be grievous.

Alger's proxies pushed North and South and then inland in something of a well-choreographed ballet. The operation was an organizational marvel. UCSA drones showed, like God's eye, phalanxes of agents pushing westward. It would have been a beautiful sight, a work of performance art, were it not for its evil intent.

Ignorance was no excuse for nonadherence. Signs detailing the ruling were ubiquitous: on billboards, storefronts, inside trains and buses, at workplaces and churches. No one could credibly say they hadn't known.

Alger had thought most about how to handle the Jews, the trickiest subset of all. From a biblical perspective, Christians needed more Israelites to make Aliyah, or move back to the homeland, so as to claim the lands that, from the beginning of time, God had bequeathed them. With centuries-long memories of persecution and annihilation branded into their communal DNA, foisting armbands upon Jewish citizens required delicacy. Necessity was the reason they were the last to receive visits, and comforting ones at that.

"Good morning, Mrs. Goldberg," the government agent said in the most decent voice he could muster. "My name is Lieutenant Vince Spaeckerle, and I'm from the Special Protection Unit. Is Dr. Goldberg at home? I'm here as a representative of the president to offer your family the government's protection."

No matter the woman's beauty and grace, both of which were considerable, Spaeckerle could not help but envision this

Jewess drinking the blood of Christian babies from a bejeweled cup. He shuddered.

"Robert," she called with a dignity belying her fear. "Someone from the military is here."

She led Spaeckerle into the living room, his boots tracking mud onto the rare Aubusson. While they waited, he looked around the room at the finery, the furniture and art, all of it incensing him as he compared it to the dingy apartment where he and his family lived.

A distinguished-looking man entered and held out his hand, "Dr. Goldberg. May I help you?"

The agent held his arm stiffly at his side.

"Sir, as I told your wife," whom he no longer regarded, "I'm with Special Protection." He pointed to his badge. "I'm sure you've heard by now that we passed out armbands to individuals likely to harm people like you and me. Because of the Jew's unfortunate history — and this comes from the president — we want to relieve you of any fears you might harbor. The UCSA has a holy commitment to the Hebrews and to the State of Israel, and as such, we've devised a plan to keep Jewish Americans safe. He handed two blue and white Star of David armbands to Goldberg, who was careful not to touch him. That these brutes were so simple-minded as to think that Jews would be duped by their charade could hardly have been more insulting.

Like a robot, Spaeckerle continued with the script he had recited many times that morning. "These identifiers," he pointed to the bands the doctor had set aside, "give your group the unique status of being 'Untouchable.' They tell the authorities that your government stands with you and always will."

Before the inauguration, when it was easier to travel, a number of Jewish people contemplated what the future might hold under Alger and they had fled West. Canada closed its borders to Americans on January 10; Mexico followed suit on the 19th. The Goldbergs had considered a plan to escape before Alger was sworn in, but like so many, they hadn't. It was now painfully obvious how wrong they had been not to leave.

19

January 30

IT TOOK LESS than a day for Congress to ratify and the president to sign the Christian Bill of Rights into law. *The Daily Christian Times published* the changes the next morning.

"To expedite the work of our courts, the Faith-Based Bill of Rights printed below is now the law of the land. Praised Be He." – James D. Alger, III

The Christian Bill of Rights
Amendment 1: Congress shall recognize America as a Christian nation, thereby prohibiting the free exercise of all other religions. Freedom of speech, or of the press; or the right of the people peaceably to assemble, and to petition the Government for a redress of grievances is unlawful. The consequence of insubordination is execution without trial.

Amendment II: Unchanged.

Amendment III: Soldiers shall, in times of war and peace appropriate or quarter in any house, without consent of the Owner.

Amendment IV: The Government reserves the right to search and seize persons, houses, papers, and effects, supported by Oath or affirmation.

Amendment V: No Government official nor private citizen shall be held to answer for a capital, or otherwise infamous crime against a suspected traitor; traitors may be deprived of life, liberty, or property, without due process of law; private property may be taken for public use, without compensation.

Amendment VI: In all criminal prosecutions, the un-churched shall have no right to a trial, neither must they be informed of the nature and cause of the accusation nor be confronted with the witnesses against him. Assistance of Counsel for defense is prohibited.

Amendments VII, VIII, and IX have been struck, the Tenth Amendment is to stand as is.

20

January 31

AS THE CLOCK struck eight, President Alger stood at the lectern across from the Oval Office, state media there to broadcast the important address.

"Fellow Christians, today I delegated full responsibility for training up our children to The Department of Faith."

The director cut to a two-shot of the president and Christian.

"To that end, I have charged Secretary Hillcox with heading up one of the most critical new agencies, 'Truth In Education.' Going forward, the secretary will ensure that our children learn God's truth alone. He comes to the position with vast experience, his church—Male Headship—having run a successful Christian school, kindergarten through twelfth grade, for more than thirty years."

"Secretary Hillcox kick-started the complex process today when he shut down all existing government schools. We will continue to use their buildings, but not their curriculum. No longer will students' heads be filled with the sinister lies of the past. The secretary is in the process of replacing school administrators and teachers with teams of qualified educators, some of whom began work this very morning. Until schools are fully staffed, we have arranged for government-accredited facilitators to stand in the breach. If your student's school is closed, check with the agency and they will redirect you. With no time to lose and the future to gain, the critical work of reprogramming has already begun."

The camera panned to Christian who, unaccustomed to a teleprompter, read awkwardly from it. "For the first time since nineteen-sixty-two, erm, students will greet the day with prayer. Courses without scriptural relevance have been discontinued. Faculty . . . uh, will source lessons directly from the Bible, and submit their curricula to the agency's supervisor for approval.

"The priority for female students will be Homemakin', as teachers guide our young ladies towards traditional marriages. Qualified males will do their studies in Av-van-ced Leadership Trainin', while those who measure up go on to university level. Others will be directed towards vocations or to the military. Additionally, we are in the process of federalizin' the university system. This will happen quickly."

Alger eliminated the smaller departments and agencies, the same as he had done with the Cabinet. Along with putting Christian in charge of Education, he decided the Secretary was best placed to run the nation's former disaster agency.

Calling Christian to the Oval the next morning, he informed him, "Christian, for obvious reasons, I have abolished FEMA, creating its replacement, The Almighty Crisis Administration, or ACA," chuckling aloud at the irony of the acronym, "belongs at Faith. As of this moment, Disaster is yours."

Christian was taken aback, but maintained an outer composure he did not own.

"Makes sense. Long past time we stop throwin' money at disasters we both know to be God-sent." He swallowed hard.

"Precisely. When something happens, do the minimum, no more. I will never second-guess you."

Christian began to sweat. Disaster management? As a preacher, he knew grift, he knew false hope, and he'd always and only depended on empty promises and charm to get by. But this? Whether born of desperation or an idea come from God on High, a plan brilliant in its simplicity came to him.

"Here's a think. How 'bout we gather together a squadron a fine Christian men, train 'em up an' call 'em the 'Pastor Brigade?' Uniformed men what'll answer the call to save souls when catastrophe strikes. I can't think of anything more worthwhile when you got people staring death in the eye."

"Not bad, Christian. Not bad at all," Alger mused. "It will give the impression that we care." He clapped Christian on the back. "Go ahead with it."

He turned to the papers on his desk, the signal for Christian to leave.

Whether or not they continued to support the president, Americans lived in a heightened state of fear. The administration had successfully transferred the blame for the frequent bombings that had continued from the Arabs to fellow Americans, the Undesirables to be precise. Every altercation, large or small, sent the military into the streets, free to act however they wished. Soon, citizens were given permission to assault anyone who wasn't white and obviously straight, turning violence into a form of recreation, a way for the masses to release their tension.

The constant drumbeat of fear must be maintained, no matter the cost.

21

February 14, 2029

VICE PRESIDENT Bickle's stiff stance was reflected in the gleaming mahogany table in the overly large Cabinet room. "Father God," he prayed aloud, "we humble ourselves before You, free at last to do Your will. More than sixty years ago, when a certain Negro proclaimed, 'We shall overcome,' we sat up and took notice. We may not have liked the color of his skin, but we saw his ability to communicate. Liberals listened, and we paid the price for nigh on sixty years.

"So taken were the hippies with their drugs and sex orgies, their violence against the nation that had served and sheltered them, that they paid no attention to us. Didn't see that we were many and that not only were we watching, we were also making long-term plans, even beginning to build a network of our own, a network that has finally come to fruition. Today, after all we have suffered, it is our turn to say, 'Praise Jesus, our day has come. We, the Long-Suffering Majority, Have Overcome.'"

As if sent by God, a ray of sun broke through the clouds, piercing the room's bullet-proof windows, bathing the tabletop with shades of gold.

Bickle checked his tablet, "Hallelujah! President Alger just signed an Order that eliminates the Hate Crimes Act, the law that criminalized free expression, the one we referred to as the 'Hate Christians Act.'" His screen lit up again, "Add to that, Congress just passed a bill that legalizes warrantless seizures of electronic and telephone records. No more warrants needed! Men, this is how governance is meant to work.

"One last thing: later today, Congress will enact the passage of the 34th Amendment to the Constitution, a document establishing The Ten Commandments as the law of the land. This is the most consequential amendment in our history, one over which you can be sure the Founders are rejoicing in Heaven."

He looked around the room, his eyes resting on each man, the communal excitement palpable.

Christian piped up, "With the Ten Commandments as law, we now have the legal authority to prosecute religious offenders an' other some-such traitors for anything. To which I say, Guh-lory to the lamb of God!"

The usually staid Vice President grinned. "Though Satan will most certainly try to bring us, the mighty, down, no one in this room need fear. Whatever you do, there will always be cut-outs for those of us in high places." The men salivated as each began to understand the full extent of their patriarchal rights. The Shining City on The Hill had truly assumed its God-given place.

22

March

CITIZENS CONTINUED their attempts to escape West to the areas the government now referred to as 'The Territories.' They left behind jobs, savings, family, and friends. It wasn't easy, nor was safe passage guaranteed, but those who survived the journey found a warm welcome among the growing community of Resisters centered in Portland. The UCSA had every intention of taking the region once their dominionist machine was fully functioning.

Those who chose to stay behind and fight from within were courageous in different and equally inspiring ways. To be surrounded by the enemy, to serve as the movement's eyes and ears, its spies and seers, was in many ways, America's last hope.

23

April 1
Easter Sunday

HE IS RISEN.

24

The Ides of April

WHITE CHRISTIAN upper-class men fared better than ever. Businesses formerly owned by 'Others' were seized and transferred to deserving citizens. The Jews remained untouched for now. Change was never simple and in this case if it meant allowing the Yids their last hurrah, well then, that was a temporary price that must be paid, no matter how it angered the majority.

The infinitely expendable middle and lower classes worked longer, harder and more, never mind that childcare, healthcare, and life-saving medications were out of reach. All that mattered to those at the top was the muscular, authoritative Jesus they worshiped and adored, the white guy with a six pack and an automatic, the dude who showed himself in all aspects of daily life, always a verse or two to justify whatever the earthly Alger did.

Consumed by official duties, Christian relaxed more and thought less about Darlene, as late meetings and parties filled his nights. This was the life he was born to lead, the mantle he deserved, and even if it would have been better with a helpmate by his side, he finally felt born to the lot.

For now, life on Earth was good.

25

May 6

AS FASCIST economies tend to do, Alger's continued to trend upward. Seeing his business statement this month made Christian want to visit San Antonio and Headship. To walk among his people and confer with Dwight in person. Which is why, in the predawn hours on Sunday, Christian boarded the company jet bound for Texas, arriving at his church in time to preach. His marketing instincts strong as ever, a televised sermon from his home church offered an unparalleled opportunity to share his accomplishments with a devoted audience. Arriving to a warm, even awed welcome, he drank in the love. He had missed this . . . the simplicity, the ease, the adulation. At the same time, he knew he'd remain in Washington for as long as Alger would have him. Yet while this return to Headship massaged his ego, it also brought home how alone he was in the real halls of power.

The congregation quieted and Christian dabbed his eyes with the familiar black hankie. "I tell you, the love I'm feelin' here today is unlike any I remember." He chuckled, "Maybe I ought stay away another coupla-two months."

Members of the congregation stamped their feet, at the same time shouting "No!," a lone voice called out, "We're nothin' without you Pastor C!"

"B'lieve you me, the moment I cain't accomplish what matters, I'll hightail it back here faster than a rattler at dusk. But like yesterday, I was sittin' in the Oval Office, jawin' with the president 'bout our new Christian Bill of Rights an' I thought to myself, what we're doin' here, ya cain't beat it with a stick. I'm here ta say: Alger, he's one a us, a president what's got real biblical commitment. With President Alger in charge an' me at Faith, we got it sewn up. The days of Sodom an' Gomorrah, of queers an' baby-killers, of men what are women, an' so on an' so forth, they're no more. The president an' I, we done this country an about face we can be proud of."

The roar inside Headship rivaled that for a winning team in any sports arena across America.

"The tolerant, all those years they preyed on us an' our young uns. Oh, how we suffered. We saw the results of their secular ways, hecky-do, we lived 'em. Even though the Foundin' Fathers declared us a Christian nation, we never were. Because we, the faithful, we never took the ungodly to task. Till now, that is. T'day, them what sin, I promise you —they'll go through Hell on this earth."

He cued the choir and, from the risers, a gospel, foot-stomping version of "He Is My Rock" excited the already ramped-up crowd. Dancers ponied their way onstage, every one of them convinced that their God-given pulchritude would grease the way to Heaven. The hymn and dance concluded and, after telling his flock he'd be back, Christian brought the acting pastor back on. With a signal to Dwight, he walked off, to thunderous applause.

Seated in his office, Christian shook his head in wonder. "What a mornin', praise the Lord! How I've yearned for a dose a this! As goes to you Dwight. All good?"

His more prosperous looking second replied, "Couldn't want for more, Pastor. I mean, Mr. Secretary."

"Dad gum it, call me Christian. Gotta be myself somewheres."

"Sure thing. I'll try, not that it'll be easy, you bein' so high up an' all. As ta business, things are goin' great guns. The flock has grown somethin' fierce. What with you bein' secretary, SWBN's been coinin' money. Even Straight On's fit ta bust outta its space thanks to the final war on faggots you got goin'. Which brings me to my question: it be okay if I use summa the funds to buy us another facility or three for reprogrammin'? Demand's there for sure."

"Dwight, you don't gotta ask. You're in charge so do as you see fit. But how 'bout the staffin'? New instructors, they gotta be tough, an' straight as an arrow themselves. Can't have queens teachin' queens," and the two men slapped their thighs and hooted.

"Amen to that. By the by, you remember that fellow Joss Dedham? The one that, shall we say, gradiated with honors?"

The blood drained from Christian's face. He'd never known Joss' last name, just as he'd never forgotten his first.

Joss, the one who made him fall. Satan had sent the younger man his way all those years ago, adding to Christian's life battle, bringing to mind his growing up years. How Mason made him question his sexuality as a boy, even as he abused Christian in ways that would cast a shadow over his entire life. In Christian's waking hours, he could mostly forget his Luciferian dance with Joss, but nights were different. And why, oh why, on this day of homecoming was Joss's name on Dwight's lips?

Joss Dedham. He who'd waltzed Christian down the pansy-strewn, sodomitic path, introducing the good pastor to that most unbiblical of pleasures. Joss, who'd lit the spark that, over time, grew into a flame, or more accurately, an inferno. Joss, the man who'd made his father's words come true.

Unaware of Christian's inner turmoil, Dwight went on. "Yessiree. Joss turned out to be one a our finest. Sure, he use ta be a pansy, but not no more. Straight as an arrow that one. Even got hisself a woman. I've yet to see better proof conversion works. Big an' brawny as all get out, he keeps the girls in line. I put him in charge a trainin', an' the fellows he's hired have, to a man, been A-Number One. Not a nancy among 'em, these boys can whup the gay outta any fruit."

Christian struggled for a semblance of composure. He had to get out of there. If Joss saw and recognized him, all bets were off. Aside from him, no one else knew of their coupling. More than ever, it had to stay that way.

"Dwight, do what you think best," he said with forced composure. He pulled out his phone. "Duty calls. Time for me to go. We'll talk soon."

The morning's joy vanished along with the feeling of genuine authority Christian had pretended since becoming Secretary. On the plane back to D.C., his thoughts continued to unspool, but when the wheels hit the ground, an outwardly disciplined man emerged from the jet.

26

May 17

AT 11:47 A.M. Pacific Standard Time, the most powerful earthquake ever recorded in the continental United States struck the Oregon coast, the epicenter a half mile off Cannon Beach, eighty miles southwest of Portland. To Christian and the rest of the administration, the disaster was nothing less than prophetic, even welcome, in large part because God had struck at the heart of the Resistance.

Alarms blared. Sirens went off from the Canadian border to Northern California. Within minutes citizen journalists documented the ravaged highways and buildings turned rubble in a city that had flourished moments before.

Because geologists had long warned that an earthquake of this magnitude was likely to occur at some point over the next hundred years, the Oregon Office of Emergency Management had drilled citizens for such a moment. Residents followed protocol, "Drop, Cover, and Hold On. Wait for the shaking to stop before moving, lock your wheels and remain in your car until the tremors cease."

Some 2,800 miles to the east, President Alger stood in the sunshine on the White House lawn, observing a photo session with the First Lady, their daughter Esther, and the twins, Adam and Joshua. The occasion was to introduce Peacock's fledgling organization, "Celebrate Life," and with the kickoff, to mandate that every woman over the age of fourteen become a paid member within thirty days.

At 2:49 p.m. Eastern Standard Time, the president's phone pinged. His press secretary Grant Wallace, the man tasked with screening his calls and texts, saw the word "Emergency" and jogged across the lawn. Alger looked at the screen, nodded, then excused himself from the small crowd surrounding him. From the lawn's outer edge, he listened, "At 11:47, PST, an earthquake of magnitude 8.2 on the Richter scale struck a mile off the Oregon coast, 78 miles southwest of Portland, epicenter at longitude 45.9932°N, latitude 123.9266°W." He pocketed the phone and went back to the shoot, his expression unchanged. Five minutes later, his cell buzzed again and he saw that it was Christian. Exasperated, he stepped away for the second time.

"God has visited the West Coast."

Alger sighed with frustration. Why did these people come to him, particularly Christian, with everything? Couldn't they deal with anything without hand holding? A president could only do so much. It was the reason he'd delegated ACA to him.

"I'll see you in my office in twenty minutes," he huffed.

He scurried to the White House. Seated across from the president, Alger ignored him, concentrated as he was on the images coming from the UCSA drones. Fortunately, nothing had gotten out to the public yet, but it was only a matter of time.

"I already seen this," Christian said. Curiously unaware that his day of reckoning had come, he asked, "What're you gonna do?"

Alger looked at him, a combination of rage and astonishment shooting from his eyes. Just then, the intercom buzzed and a secretary announced, "West Coast Adjunct, Stan Chisolm on the line."

"Put him through," Alger snapped.

He picked up and Chisholm's terrified voice jumped through the receiver, "All hell's broken loose."

"Hillcox is with me," Alger replied expressionlessly. "He'll get back to you with a plan."

That's when it hit Christian.

"Don't hang up! "Chisholm panicked. "A huge crack is opening up in my office! I don't know what . . . " The line went dead.

Alger glared at Christian, "You ask what I'm going to do? This one's on your buddy." Alger looked out the window and saw the press gathering. "They'll expect a statement and I can only put them off for so long." With that, he stormed out, leaving Christian, his mouth agape.

Earthquakes, unlike hurricanes, aren't given names but are known by where they occur. San Francisco, Fukushima, Haiti. Christian saw value in naming this one, and so he dubbed her Delilah.

The reality was that it was a Megathrust Cascadian Subduction Earthquake, the largest one in known history to strike the continental US. During the first minutes, an unknowable number of people died outright or were trapped beneath mammoth chunks of concrete and steel. Survivors poured into the streets to escape structures threatening to collapse. Roads buckled and cars spun out, some into newly formed canyons. As luck would have it, April and May had been rainier than usual, even for Spring, and Portland's sandy soil had turned into something that resembled jelly. This phenomenon was called liquefaction, and it caused houses to slide from their hillside perches. Homes, office buildings, and towers built before 1974 that had not been retrofitted, collapsed. Chemical storage tanks ruptured, releasing hazardous substances into the air and water, their toxic fumes instantly injuring or killing those nearby.

Bridges over the Willamette and Columbia Rivers collapsed, some hanging precariously over the rushing waters. Buckled runways shut down Portland International Airport. The one hospital and smaller medical facilities that survived were quickly overwhelmed. Local police and fire departments operated at skeleton capacity, and when state troopers helicoptered in from east of Portland, they were relegated to crowd control. More than anything, Portland resembled a war zone.

Tremors were felt to varying degrees for hundreds of miles, the greatest destruction extending from the Siuslaw National Forest, a hundred miles southeast of Portland, to ten miles from the mouth of the Columbia River.

Then there were the low-lying areas that made up the magnificent Pacific Northwest coast. The summer season had begun and the population had swelled. Permanent residents who knew enough to escape to higher ground, did so, aware that they had fifteen to twenty minutes to reach safety.

The sudden disappearance of friends and neighbors resembled the very Rapture in the Book of Revelation that Christian had prayed on for so long.

27

That Same Day

ON THE DAY Alger took office, twenty-six-year-old Ned Burroughs was a G-13 employee at FEMA, where he had served as assistant to Jefferson Dixon, the agency's second in charge. Career employees like Ned, who swore an Oath of Loyalty to the new administration, retained their jobs. When Alger named Dixon as Christian's top man at ACA, Dixon brought Ned with him. The son of an evangelical preacher, he was convinced the Lord Himself had chosen President Alger and that thanks to His glory, he, Ned Burroughs, had been blessed to work at Faith. Tasked with destroying all evidence of FEMA's past, Ned worked tirelessly, often into the night. Dixon, a savvy manager of people, sensed Ned could use a break.

Dixon and his siblings owned a cottage on Oregon's Cannon Beach. A long-time political insider, he once ran the Pine Society, a conservative think tank that for decades had quietly injected its Christian views into the national conversation. Jefferson saw a lot of himself in the younger man, and since his house would be empty all of May, he thought that Ned and his wife Brenda might enjoy a family vacation there. So, he offered it to Ned for a week and Brenda, knowing her husband would be around to help with their seven children, jumped at the idea.

On the morning of June 2, Brenda suggested they take a picnic across the road to the beach and spend the afternoon there, rather than stay in the cottage until after the young ones' naps. The children, who had never been on vacation before, much less to a beach, liked nothing better than to build sand castles and chase one another to the water's edge. This being the fifth day of vacation, Ned found himself more worn out than he ever was after a normal work week. When he told Brenda he needed time to himself, her face fell. "I think a hike will do me good. How about you put together a sack lunch for me? You and the kids'll do fine on your own."

With their youngest on her hip, Brenda heaved a sigh of resignation and, while inwardly steaming, she put on a cheerful face and threw together his provisions. For her, it was to be another day of servitude, her dream of help from Ned exactly that—a dream.

Ambling over to the counter where Brenda spread mayonnaise onto four pieces of crustless white bread, Ned whispered in her ear, the throaty catch in his voice foreshadowing his manly desire, "As God is my witness, I promise you the ride of your life tonight." To God-fearing Ned, married sex beat all other kinds, hands down. Why, he owned this woman, owned her by divine right. He could make her do anything he wanted, including bearing and birthing seven new Christian lives before she turned twenty-five.

Grabbing a handful of the soft flesh that had accumulated at her waist, he reproached, "Don't you think it's time we put you on a diet? Wouldn't want you to lose your girlish figure before you hit thirty, now, would we?" While sex with his wife remained all he had hoped for, he did worry that the day might come when he'd wake up and no longer desire the woman he'd married. Far too often he heard about husbands who ping-ponged their way between marital sex and adultery, each time clawing their way back to forgiveness.

"You're right," she answered dully. "I'll try to lay off the kids' meals and snacks. It's tough when that's what I eat most days." How dare he demand nightly, unprotected sex from her, then seven children later, complain she'd put on weight? Her life had not turned out as she had thought it would. Where was her pleasure, her satisfaction? Other than doing her part in Christian population growth, it didn't seem she contributed much of anything. Yet it was the life she'd signed up for and the only one she knew. Her daily responsibilities usually left her so depleted that by day's end, she had nothing left to give. But come nighttime, give she did.

With a gleeful farewell, Ned picked up his thermos and lunch bag and pushed them deep inside his daypack. He chose a walking stick from the back porch and started up the trail.

An hour later, Ned stood atop Bailey Point and looked west at the Pacific, thinking he might be able to pick out the spot where his family had settled on the beach the day before. Pulling out his binoculars, he scanned the shoreline and, although he did not actually see them, he could imagine his brood running, playing, dipping their toes in the water. He thought of Brenda, dear Brenda, on a blanket below, their youngest at her breast.

His heart swelled with pride at all he had created, and he almost regretted not being with them. In that moment of sentimental reverie, he felt the ground beneath him judder, jerking him hard. He was thrown back, falling to the ground. The response to a person's first earthquake is often one of confusion. Had he lost his balance? Was something wrong with him, something like the brain tumor that had taken his friend Joseph Milhouse last year, remembering that it was a seizure and subsequent fall that first announced his illness?

Splayed on the stones, he was alarmed by the amount of blood that gushed from a deep laceration in his leg. In a state of shock, he was so focused on his injury that, unaware of the downed trees and boulders surrounding him, he forgot about Joseph's brain tumor. He pulled off his backpack and retrieved the first aid kit from inside. Gently swabbing his wound with alcohol, he winced at the sting. He applied pressure with a large bandage but, distressed to see so much blood bloom through the gauze, he realized how frightened he was to be alone, so far from help. Sitting there, he wondered again why he'd taken such a bad fall.

Then he looked around, and what he saw alarmed him. It came to him that it hadn't been his brain at all: he had just experienced his first earthquake and it must have been a doozy. Picking himself up, he began to move. Slowed by pain but more by the large crevasses and tangled vegetation, he advanced slowly and with care. Paying close attention, he skirted the obstacles in his way, stopping when he reached a clearing that offered a view of the beach. What he saw below completely disoriented him. Through the unbroken lens of his binoculars, he made out a landscape so altered as to be unrecognizable.

Instead of the flat, sandy beach that had been there, he found himself looking upon massive fissures in the sand, a landscape of hills and valleys. He spotted a lone group of people huddled together atop a rise, and knew with certainty that it was his family. So relieved was he to see they were alive, he spoke aloud, "Praise Jesus, You have saved them." From where he stood, the dull sound of a freight train sent additional confusion to his already dazed mind. Fully concentrated on the beach, he failed to see the ocean rise up high as a skyscraper and head towards the shore. Until it hit.

His binoculars dropped from his hands and the larger picture unfolded. He stood helplessly on high as what looked to be a hundred-foot wall of water ripped across the land. Frozen in place, he watched in disbelief when shortly after, gravity pulled the water back to sea, taking everyone and everything with it. Buildings vanished, as did the two-lane road that ran in front of where Dixon's cottage had stood. As for his family, they were gone, gone forever.

Too dazed to digest what he had seen, Ned's first inclination was to pray. But then, he thought, pray to whom? For what? To a God who, in the blink of an eye, had allowed the only people he loved to vanish? What good could prayer do now? He looked to the skies and instead, howled, "This is your plan? Then fuck you. Fuck you and your everlasting pile of lies." Keening with a wail so primal, the sounds that came from him seemed to represent the agony and grief of the whole of humanity, for all eternity. He collapsed onto the broken ground, and sobbed.

Brenda, Elias, Luke, Bethany, Zachary, Martha, Talitha, and baby Timmy. Gone. All of them. Swept away—not in the

Rapture he had so eagerly awaited, but dragged away, drowned like Noah's venal neighbors. If this was a test sent him by God, he would have no more to do with any of it. Second Coming? A thousand years of Peace? Where was he, Ned Burroughs, to find peace again?

As sand slips through the fingers in one's hand, newly formed cracks in his faith opened, but these were huge and fractured, like the land below. There was no holding on. It was then that he knew, truly knew for the first time in his life, that no one was up there. God was a lie, a myth, make believe, nothing more and he'd always been so, with Ned the fool. From this moment on, the threat of Eternity in Hell would mean nothing. Not when, in the blink of an eye, it had arrived.

What will my father say should we ever meet again, he wondered?

Will he preach to me about the righteousness of a God who swept his seven grandchildren and daughter-in-law out to sea? Tell me they are in a better place? If Ned knew anything, he knew that what he had just witnessed was not the Beginning of The End about which his father preached, but instead, a random act of nature.

Normally a resourceful man, Ned wasn't sure he had it in him to continue. Or that he wanted to. But hours later, as the sun began its descent, he fell into survival mode. Pushing aside the pain in his leg, he dug out a rough shelter using broken sticks, lined it with brush, pine needles, and leaves, and lay down, covering himself with the same. Grief washed over him, his only "prayer" being that he never awaken. At last, exhaustion won the day and unconsciousness rushed up to meet him.

28

The Death of Faith

BUT THE SUN did rise, and with it something of Ned's will to live returned. After sizing up what remained of his food and water, he knew that if he wanted to survive, he'd better find help. Setting out, the going was difficult and his leg throbbed, but in a very real way he welcomed the pain and difficulty as the punishment he wanted. Like an automaton he ascended, only to cut back down in order to navigate around a fallen tree or gouge in the earth. As the day passed, aftershocks, some bigger than others, rocked the ground, increasing his growing sense of despair.

When the sun began to set, he stopped and finished what remained of his provisions. If he was going to die from lack of food and water, so be it. The will to live was gone and so he prepared mentally to meet his end. He would build no shelter nor seek out food or water. He was through. At this moment when he cared the least, he heard voices call out, not far from him, "Hey . . . Over here!" Peering through the brush, he spotted a band of people huddled over a small fire. Ned was surprised to feel anything, much less relief. He might not perish tonight after all. Exercising great caution, he made his way over to the group of eight individuals. As he explained what he had seen, the word tsunami entered his mind when it exited his lips.

"Christ!" a voice said. "Why didn't I think of that? Of course there'd be a tsunami with a quake that size."

"This nightmare keeps getting worse," said a man with cuts and scrapes that crisscrossed his face and body. "I was on a hike like all of you when all at once I was thrown to the ground. Brian and Tom here," pointing to two others, "were on a ledge. They barely made it to safety before it broke off."

"It's hard for me to say this, but things are much worse than you know," Ned began. "You see, I am—well, I was—an employee at the Department of Faith." There was a collective gasp. "An assistant to the Crisis Administration's Director." The group seemed to recoil physically.

"My family and I came here on vacation. Yesterday, I wanted some time to myself so I had my wife pack me a lunch, and I started up the mountain. Imagine when, as a lifelong believer in the Almighty, I witnessed," and he held up his battered binoculars, "my wife and seven children swept out to sea, while I stood watching, safe. My Brenda, a woman as steeped in the Lord as I was, stayed on the beach atop a hill of sand, keeping our children close, even after the earthquake remade the landscape around her. She didn't run like everyone else, so certain was she that everything that happens is according to God's will, a will she never questioned, not even then. There can be no other explanation for why she stayed.

"As for me, what I saw was not the final reckoning I'm ashamed to say I spent my life praying for. No, what I saw had nothing to do with God. It was a random act of nature, that's all. One that took everyone I loved away from me, in front of my eyes. In that instant, I rejected everything I'd spent a lifetime believing. I've been such a fool," he said, lowering his face between bent knees.

A man put his hand on Ned's shoulder. Ned lifted his head, his eyes haunted, unable to meet anyone's else's.

"As profound as it is for me to reject my faith, in the grand scheme of things it amounts to nothing. What matters is the role I played in destroying this country. Had I been in Washington, my job would have been to deal with this disaster. Per my superiors, I'd have done nothing to help, even felt virtuous about it."

The group was still, all of them thinking about what Ned said. That if they were lucky enough to make it home, the problems they'd face would be insurmountable. Not one of them could have imagined that any administration, even one as sinister as Alger's, wouldn't already be on the ground helping. To think there'd be no aid forthcoming defined their doom in a way nothing else had.

Ned looked up, his face awash in shame. "If you think for a minute that anyone cares, think again. When Alger abolished FEMA, Hillcox turned it into a ministry. The only thing he did was to put together a group of thugs, spiritual warriors he named The Pastor Brigade. They'll come, sure enough, in fact they're probably already there. Not with food or water, medicine or tents. They'll have come to offer Salvation to those at their most desperate, thinking that in times of disaster human beings grasp at anything.

"The fact that God struck here, in this place of people they so deeply revile, will have fueled their fervor. To Alger and his administration, the people in The Territories are either a mission field, or they're nothing. I've spoken those same words myself, in fact received 'Hallelujahs' when I said them in churches filled with believers. But if the scales ever fell from a man's eyes, they did from mine. A lifetime of belief turned sour in seconds."

He collapsed inward, his sobs so wrenching that, despite what he'd revealed, the ragtag group gathered around in sympathy, offering the broken man the only thing they could—compassion. No one spoke, until with forced determination Ned looked up to say, "I'll never go back." It seemed so obvious, but to voice it gave him something of a relief, and release. Although everything in his life was turned upside down—he had lost his family, his faith, his work, and his future—this brought him an unexpected glimmer of peace.

Josh was the first to speak. "Alternatively, Ned, as difficult as it would be, you could turn your loss into something mean-ingful. If we get to Portland, and that's still a big if, you could work with us from the inside."

That was when Ned understood that the "community" with whom he had fallen in, that these kind and decent strangers were part of the enemy he had, as recently as two days ago, been committed to destroying.

How was a man to deal with the loss of his wife and seven children all at once? Dear Brenda, a woman whom only now did he realize he had used as his handmaid. A beautiful girl whose soul he had broken and whose body he'd plundered for his pleasure, gone in an instant. And his children for whom he had rarely spared the rod. A memory that forced him to look with shame at his hands, hands that had so readily struck their small bodies and disappointed their trusting faces. He'd shown them so little warmth, speechifying and preaching at them instead. Rather than nurture each one, or encourage their budding curiosities, he'd quoted Scripture. He'd never played or explored nature together with them, or read to them, other than from the Bible, exactly like his father before him. His heartache was unrelenting, yet the thought of not confronting the evil inherent in the Alger administration was equally powerful.

Setting the harshness of self-recrimination aside, Ned plumbed his mind for the only biblical passage that mattered. Call it cherry-picking. Call it morality. Whatever it was, it was the force he needed:

Remember this when you are at the crossroads in life. Stand in the ways and see, And ask for the old paths, wherein is the good way, and walk therein.

"I'm in," he told the group.

29

Almighty Crisis

THE SUN PEEKED over the horizon when Christian's limo pulled to a stop in front of the ACA offices on C Street. Dixon greeted him at the entrance, looked into the iris scanner, and the door clicked open. Upstairs in his office, his desktop monitor displayed live, military drone feed as it switched between Portland and the coast. A television screen, set on mute, played on the wall. Simultaneously, as officers at a nearby Oregon base shouted updates into a squawk box, Chisholm patched in from his newly relocated headquarters in the only hospital still functioning.

Dixon pointed at the monitor. "Ned Burroughs and his family were staying at my place. Right there, below that hill," and he pointed to an approximation of where he thought his house used to be. "It was in my family for decades. I've tried to reach him many times, to no avail."

"Best accept he's gone to God then," Christian replied, devoid of emotion.

"I've arranged for a transport to fly 280 of your Pastors to a base near Portland, as you asked. It leaves Andrews at 1100 hours today. There's a serviceable runway at Fort Skarlatos where they can land, and a fleet of vehicles able to handle the new terrain."

"I got the Pastors' street sermons at the ready. Had an assistant to do it."

Ignoring the man, Dixon continued, "The base has fifteen thousand gallons of fuel. Some of the vehicles are electric. They can use generators and recharge them for short trips."

"Yeah. Them what preach local to the base can use them hippie machines."

Dixon wondered, not for the first time, why the president held this incompetent man in such high esteem

Christian glanced up at the television, set on TBT. As he watched, a small office building fell to the ground, bricks, concrete, and glass raining down, while those nearby fled in terror. "Turn it up! I gotta hear what these Judases are sayin'. Dixon took it off mute in time for the correspondent's wrap, "This is Liz Boorman, reporting on what yesterday was the thriving city of Portland."

"What the . . . ?" Christian stammered.

Dixon exclaimed, "That's not what Alger said last night."

The prior evening, Alger had gone on air. "It has come to my attention," he had said, "that there's been a lot of disinformation showing up on the Shadow Web. Hand in hand with Hollywood, the Resisters have put together video showing a devastated Portland, imagery that, without proper scrutiny, can appear convincing. Our people on the ground in Oregon have assured us beyond a shadow of a doubt that the earthquake in

Portland was minor, registering in at 1.0 on the Richter scale. Aside from an elderly woman who fell and broke her collarbone, the damage was mostly to kitchen crockery.

"This is to say that unless a report emanates from my office, or from that of the Department of Faith, consider it propaganda. We are living in an increasingly deceptive world, one in which we can no longer believe our eyes and ears. Remember, there's great danger in relying on lies. My promise to you is that you will never hear anything but the truth from me."

What Christian and Jefferson just saw on State TV belied what the president said. Christian would deal with TBT, but for now he decided to remain silent, in the hope that no one in the administration had noticed the brief flash of reality.

30

Ten a.m.

AS CHRISTIAN'S limo approached Faith's headquarters, the now-familiar pressure in his chest asserted itself, a pressure which he just as quickly disregarded. Placing a nitroglycerine tablet underneath his tongue, the pain abated, making way for the pride he experienced every time he approached the building.

Originally designed as The National Museum of Afro-American History and Culture, Christian could scarcely believe how quickly the edifice had become synonymous with his name. An important building architecturally, the fact that it was under his command did much to squelch the feelings of inadequacy that had dogged him since his arrival in the Capital. It surprised him when he realized how much he had come to appreciate its aesthetics: the play of light on and through the metallic webbing that enrobed the exterior, and perhaps most of all how, throughout the day, the lighting altered the building's aspect, whether inside or out. From his top floor aerie, the only story that was all glass, he loved to watch the weather come in, the crowds below, the shadows which the Washington Monument threw across his office late in the day. No matter that the museum was originally designed by a Negro for Negroes: Faith employed Whites only and would do so for as long as Christian was in charge. Oh, he used to pussyfoot about, feigning racial inclusivity, but he'd never meant a word of it, even towards the ones in his church. Growing up, he had learned to look down on the darkies and Chicanos, not just because it was the Texas way, but more because it made him feel better about his own lowly origins. When the world went fuzzy on the subject, he never did. He might be a far cry from his redneck roots, but to admit equality would put him at their level, something that emotionally he couldn't afford.

The car pulled to a stop. Hauling himself up out and out of his seat, Christian rued his expanding girth, simultaneously musing about Manna, his favorite Washington restaurant, where he would lunch today on veal in cream sauce with Tim Gleason, CEO of the National Bible Museum. When it came to earthly pleasures, what did health matter, knowing that when his time came, he was headed to a better place?

Early on, Christian saw that Faith's headquarters were too large for his department, so, in the spirit of synergy, he offered the three subterranean Lower Concourse levels, the main exhibition areas, to Gleason. Gleason, hungry for the space, jumped at the idea.

It was only 8:15 a.m. but already a line of ticketed visitors snaked its way across the plaza, museum-goers eager to get a first look at The Genesis Adventure, an exhibit of recently unearthed relics from Earth's first days. Christian, surrounded by Security, disembarked from the limo and when the sea of people parted, he passed through to the lobby.

Before heading to his office, he went into the space formerly known as The Contemplative Court, thinking that the thirty foot wall of gently falling waters might calm his nerves. It hadn't gone well with Dixon, and Christian knew it. Everyone expected too much of him these days, much more than he could accomplish.

He exited the hall as agitated as he had gone in. Neither fountains nor any other kinds of hocus-pocus could help him. Only God could do that. When the elevator opened on the fifth floor, he was met by his frantic secretary, Lurleen. In her hand she held a stack of messages, messages that echoed the urgency of those left on his digital voicemail. He set his briefcase down, listened to the first, and phoned Dwight Sessions.

31

Eleven-Fifteen a.m.

First Lieutenant Brent Jameson of the Marine Corps, a tithing member of Christian's Male Headship Church of God, was home in San Antonio on leave. Taking his M27 Infantry Automatic Rifle out of its case, he drove to the Islamic Center of Southeast Texas, the area's last remaining mosque. He stole inside and, began to shoot, his finger pressed to the trigger as he methodically gunned down the sixty-three men who had come to pray.

On leave from his fourth tour of duty in the Middle East, he had seen and done too much for any man to reconcile.

Buzzed hair, body like a rock, and eyes so dark they appeared black, the sum of his parts contributed to the ferocity of his appearance. In between stints, Brent spent his time in his childhood home in San Antonio, cosseted, pampered, and idolized by his parents. His father was an oil executive who sat on Headship's board, and his mother a lady of Texas society. What set the family apart was their standing with the Secretary of Faith.

Before Alger took office, nothing would have stopped the media from the twenty-four hour story of the mosque shooting. Networks would have started each segment with a unique-to-the-tragedy theme as anchors faded in and out of their coverage. Neighbors would offer, "He was a quiet guy . . . kept to himself . . . a military hero." The gun-rights folks would proclaim, "Only way to stop a bad guy with a gun is a good guy with a gun." Politicians would offer thoughts and prayers, and gun sales would soar. The difference this time was that, in the administration's eyes, Brent was the good guy.

The good guy in the right place with an assault rifle. A guy who had spent most of his twenties fighting over there to keep us safe here. Innocent until proven guilty, Jameson was as blameless as a man could be. All he had done was to take out sixty-three of the enemy, this time in the homeland. Who could say how many acts of terror he had prevented?

The Justice Department swooped in, whisking Brent to D.C. to babysit him until things died down. Mass shootings retained a capacity to frighten people and had to be handled with care. Secretary Hillcox did not doubt that the tale could be massaged into a Stand Your Ground defense if necessary, but for now, spin was critical, time of the essence, and citizens would be kept in the dark.

Surveillance videos of the mosque and the area around it mysteriously disappeared, and with no survivors to identify the shooter, the case was closed.

Clive Tenderly's phone picked up on the first ring, "It's Clive. I'm either out huntin' or fishin' so leave a message. If it's a good day, I'll hit you up. If I come home empty-handed, maybe not. Leave your name, your digits and I promise, we'll talk sooner . . . or later. Beeeeeeep."

Clive was a pain in the ass, a prima donna of a lawyer if ever there was one. But when it came to trouble, he was worth every penny of the twenty-seven hundred dollars per hour that Christian paid him. He had saved Christian's skin more times than he could count, so he put up with the man's ego and astronomical fees.

Christian left a message for Clive, then called Brent's father and advised him not to speak to anyone. When all was said and done, Fred Jameson, President of AmeriCash Oil, remained on Headship's board with no one the wiser. First Lieutenant Brent Jameson tithed his tithe and headed back to the Middle East for his fifth tour.

Other than transferring $275,000 from church funds to Tenderly's bank account, the day that sixty-three American Muslims died and San Antonio's last mosque was shuttered was a good one.

In fact, it was a great day for a godly nation.

32

Three-Twenty p.m., Eastern Daylight Time

DELILAH WAS NOW Christian's bad girl as well as his first governmental nightmare; and, as with Samson, she was a whopper. Christian appreciated the hand of God in the destruction He'd unleashed, but beyond dispatching his Brigade to Portland, he hadn't a clue what else to do. Even as the plane carrying the pastors landed, Christian knew all too well that the clock on his political life was ticking.

He switched on SWBN to see Charles Korteen welcome the Brigade. Korteen had been in Portland producing the documentary, *Jesus Rejectors: Eternity's Losers*, when he too experienced the quake. Yet there he stood today, alive and unharmed, in front of a quickly rigged green screen. Behind him, the intact Portland downtown stood against a sky so clear, it appeared that you could see the snow atop Mt. Hood.

Korteen stood on his mark as the first pastor headed his way, the anchor pointing the way across the debris, "With me now is Pastor Storm Vorderseit, the Brigade's head pastor.

Good to see you, Chaplain. Tell us, would you, what brings you here?"

The decorated army captain leaned toward the mic, "We've come to help in the only way that matters, to save souls. In dispatching us, Secretary Hillcox has blessed each and every one of you."

"On behalf of everyone here as well as those watching on T.V., we give thanks to the Department of Faith for caring enough to minister to the people of Portland."

"And thank you Charles for supporting and spreading the word that it's never too late to welcome our Savior." Vorderseit clapped the anchor on the back.

"Back to you Rob with tomorrow's schedule for the National Revival Meet-Up. This is Charles Korteen, reporting live from Portland."

Christian switched over to SHOX, heartened that there was no mention of Delilah. Lastly, he scrolled to TBT, where with equal measure shock and fury he saw the crushed and bloodied bodies of toddlers lying motionless inside a room in what had been a daycare center. For whatever reason, no one had said anything to him about the earlier Boorman reportage, but now, here it was two days in and suddenly this? As the visuals became increasingly graphic, he lunged for the phone, every image feeling as intentional as it did threatening. Waiting for Mansour to pick up, Christian raged, "Son of a bitch! He won't get away with this! Thinks I'm a fool, does he?"

Eric heard the tail end of Christian's rant, and answered calmly, "Mansour here."

"You got dead kids on your feed! Shut it down. Now!"

Mansour tried to break in,, "Wai . . ."

"Else I'll rip that license out from under you an' whisk you off to a place you don't wanna know 'bout."

Another ill-fated child filled the screen and Mansour made the cut sign to the engineer.

Eric Mansour was head of TBT's programming, and aside from Liz's slip-up, the station had followed the rules.

Scripture might be filled with tales of plagues and storms that equaled or surpassed Delilah, but scenes of unattended death and devastation had the power to evoke a kind of compassion that could be lethal to the Administration's survival.

"I sent the Pastor Brigade to Portland. You got the release. I'd think that'd be the story you tell."

"Mr. Secretary…."

"Other stations open with the lead that we're savin' souls, givin' folks the chance to get right with the Lord. Not you. You go for the heartstrings, thinkin' to ramp up your ratings with dead babies an' such. When will you learn it ain't food nor drink what the Heathens need. It's Salvation, plain an' simple. T'ain't no fluke Delilah struck where she did."

Eric caved, "No sir, it's not."

"From here on out, if you report the quake as anything but minor, you'll find me a-toppa you like white on rice. Y'hear?"

Prior threats to shut down the network had been subtler. Eric had no choice but to agree, no matter that it went against every atom of his being.

Back in his office, Eric summoned Liz. Three screens lined the wall opposite his desk, none of them reporting on the worst natural disaster ever to take place in America. The first was set on SHOX, where a panel bantered over a woman's duty to freshen up at day's end in order to welcome her man back to his castle after a hard day's work.

Choosing his words with care, a male commentator alluded to a man's needs, grinning lasciviously, "Once the children are settled in for the night, the only word you ladies need remember is Submission, and yes, that's with a capital S."

SWBN's screen showed a pre-recorded interview between Korteen and mega-pastor Jay Breedlove discussing Breedlove's newly released self-help book, *Giving Hope to the World In The End of Days*, a blockbuster in its third printing in as many weeks.

Finally, the center monitor was set on TBT. On it, the pretty blonde reporter, Doreen Newberger, finely minced root vegetables for a mirepoix, "the base," she explained, "for so many delectable recipes guaranteed to please the menfolk."

Liz exploded into the room, "What the friggin' fuck? We're not reporting on Delilah?"

"Hillcox called. He said follow their rules or we're finished. Actually, it was worse. He threatened me."

"Jesus. Thousands dead that we know of and god knows how many more injured, yet the country can't come together because people aren't allowed to know how bad it is?"

"I'd like to say I stood up to him, but I won't lie. So there you have it," he pointed to the cooking demo, "they've turned the country's worst disaster into a mirepoix. Their plan is to lie because they don't give a rat's ass about human suffering, especially in The Territories."

Liz understood that submitting to Hillcox allowed them to maintain their license, and with that came access and mobility, both of which were key in order to continue their work.

"Eric, people are terrified." She paused, deciding she needed to warn him, at least in a limited way, of her plans. "I've thought about whether I should say anything, but I think you should at least know that I'm about to dive into something and need to keep you out of the loop."

"O-kay," Eric ventured, holding back at the same time. It came to her that the office might be bugged. So she suddenly walked to the door with a quick "See you later."

Outside, on the street corner, she wondered how things had deteriorated so quickly, when in fact the changes had been years in the making. Much of the nation's passivity towards the politics that really mattered had brought the country to its present state. That, and fear. All she could do now was turn her anguish into action. She pulled a burner from her pocket and texted the members of her cell: "Dinner tomorrow night, 6:30. My place. Bring the family." She removed the chip and smashed it before tossing it in a nearby trash can.

33

May 20

"FATHER," ESTHER said with wonder. "I saw dead children on my screen this morning."

Peacock flashed a look of concern at her husband.

Alger stooped to eye level with his ten-year old and replied, "Esther, what you saw was made up by people who want to hurt us. Now, give me your phone. She pulled it from a pocket in her dress and Alger handed it to Peacock. "The rest of you, give your phones to your mother. Everyone hurry up. You've a busy morning ahead."

With her eyes, Peacock implored her husband to add something comforting, anything.

"It's Pentecost today, which means that this evening you will witness God's glory manifest in the skies over Washington."

He looked at Peacock, "Make sure the teacher plays up the fireworks at your Women's Bible Study."

Though it was Sunday, Alger had called for the Cabinet to convene before church. A busy man, he turned and exited the residence.

❖

Bickle was the first to arrive, his many years in government having trained him to be readily available. Huffmeier and Jones followed, then Riggins and Patience. Christian seated himself only after Alger had taken his place at the head of the table. Outside, the sky was overcast, its gray light in stark contrast to the brightly lit room.

"I called this meeting to share with you the pernicious reports appearing on the Shadow Web coming from The Territories." Alger pushed a button and the monitor along the back wall descended. "The Governor ordered Oregon State Militia to conduct a Search and Rescue, the Feds haven't lifted a finger, not even to help carry off the deceased."

The video cut to a second reporter in a different location, "What you're seeing used to be one of Portland's busiest highways. Now, it's a sea of flattened vehicles."

The screen went black.

Alger turned to Hillcox, "I want every cell tower in Oregon shut down and that means today!" slamming his fist on the table.

Riggins agreed, "This cannot stand!"

The president kept his eyes on Christian. "As head of Almighty Crisis, it was *your* responsibility that nothing like this happen. Handle it!"

The pressure in his chest asserted itself and Christian swallowed hard before squawking meekly, "Yes, sir."

Alger pressed a button that sent the screen back into its recess. "Maxwell, give Christian what he needs. The same goes for you, Thad."

"Mr. President," Riggins nodded, bristling. Over the past several months, he'd become increasingly put off by Christian and his country boy act. The way he spoke might work when it came to barn-burning sermons, but not here in Washington. Besides, what had he accomplished other than a revamp of Education, while in the same amount of time Riggins had used his expertise to remake six branches of the military?

Alger looked at Jones. "Nehemiah, get me language that gives me cover to take over a hostile part of the country. Make something up, need be."

"That won't be necessary. It's just like we did in the 1800s. Same thing."

"Good. Then everyone is up to speed. Hillcox, I expect you to deal with this today. This meeting is adjourned," he scowled, no longer waiting for a second. "I'll see each of you at the fireworks tonight."

Christian lagged behind, hoping for a private word with the president, but Alger brushed right past. Christian's mind was a twisted web of worry when, suddenly, Riggins emerged from behind, his face so close, Christian felt his hot breath on the back of his neck.

"Phony," Riggins hissed at him. "A phony and a charlatan, that's what you are," then he stalked off.

Shaken by the meeting but more by Riggins' words, Christian scuttled outside and into his car. "The Watergate," he snapped. "An' fast." He replayed the scene with Riggins, knowing well that the man was right. The latest responsibility tasked him didn't help, and he felt himself veering off into dangerous places.

During a rough patch years ago, pills had all but destroyed him. Even knowing that, the amount of stress he was under now made it impossible for him to resist the escape that drugs offered.

Outside the Watergate, he told the driver, "Wait here." Then, moving as quickly as his bulk allowed, he went inside and rode the elevator to the twelfth floor, nodding at the agents who followed. "Wait here," he said, opening the door to his unit. "I'll only be a minute," trying hard to keep his anxiety from showing. Inside, safe from prying eyes, he reached behind the clutter of his bedroom closet and pulled out a bag that contained his ancient stockpile: a store of Ativan he'd held onto just in case. Long expired, he hoped they would do the job until he secured a new prescription. He swallowed one, then another, and returned the bag to its hiding place.

Back in the limo, he phoned his office. "Lurleen, line up my plane for t'morrow mornin'. I gotta get to Portland early. Then let Tenderly know that our plans for coyote huntin'll have to wait."

Contrary to pharmacological lore, the pills retained enough of a punch that, by the time he was back at his desk, the familiar relief had taken hold, a wave of calm washing over him. Yes, this was the answer for now.

He punched in Stan's number. "Chisholm, Hillcox here."

The panicked official exploded, "Praise Jesus you called. Things are out of control! I need help!"

"Not about you, bub. There's a more important sitch-e-ation you gotta handle. You got video comin' outta there what's gotta stop. Shut down yer cell towers. That's an order from the president."

Chisholm calmed. "That shouldn't be a problem. George Stephens, CEO of the area's only cell provider'll be at outdoor church this morning. I'll relay the command."

"See that you do. I'll be there in the mornin' an' this better be sorted by then."

34

Nine-Thirty p.m.

BRUCE BAUMAN, Matt Henefield, and Jessica Stapleton completed Liz's four-person cell. For safety's sake, they traveled separately to that evening's meet-up. On his way in from Arlington, Bruce watched the fireworks and drone paintings fill the skies, as did Matt, who had just left his apartment on the Hill. Driving south from Georgetown, Jessica looked high above Key Bridge as the red, white, and blue UCSA flag exploded over the Potomac. The three young people continued to glance upward, each sparkling image disappearing after its brief show of grandeur. These designs of Christian iconography reminded them of how much had so rapidly and easily been lost.

Bruce worked as a videographer at SHOX News, where he had intentionally cultivated a friendship with one of the station's top news anchors, Byron Stepford. Three years apart in age, they had coincidentally grown up in the same Chicago suburb, so they had much in common. From the get-go, the

TV-handsome Stepford welcomed the relationship. By design, Bruce became Byron's wingman, spending several nights a week with the star at his watering hole du jour. It took but a couple of scotches to loosen Byron's lips and, on most outings, Stepford shared invaluable information about the kinds of things his superiors could and would not air.

Both men were single, and most nights Byron left first, a leggy blonde or shiny brunette on his arm. Bruce would return home and write up what he'd learned, delivering his notes to Liz the next morning.

Jessica and Matt worked at the Department of Faith, where they enjoyed top security clearance. The daughter of prominent Evangelicals from Des Moines, Jessica had soared through the department's vetting. Unbeknownst to her parents, at the age of fourteen she'd rejected their beliefs even though, while she was still at home, she played the role expected of her. After she graduated from Simpson College, a small, local Christian school, she moved to Washington. A like-minded friend connected her with Liz at the time she was putting her cell together. They clicked and, after a background check, Liz welcomed her in, then pointed her to the job at Faith. That Jessica worked for the Secretary went a long way towards assuaging her parents' concerns about her move to the big city. In truth, they couldn't have been prouder, telling everyone they knew about her position.

The State Department recruited Matt out of Wheaton College, where he majored in Computer Science. A practicing Christian, Matt shunned the Evangelical Right. In early February, he put in for a transfer to Faith feeling the need to learn what went on inside this newly formed department.

From the outset, Matt was given access to everything that came across Faith's server. When a trusted colleague told Liz about him, she approached him as she had the others.

Aside from her own cell, Liz was one of three national leaders who had come together after the October bombings to establish the Resistance.

As the world turned into a showdown between Good and Evil, the Resistance grew. It only took Delilah to expose more broadly the administration's emptiness, the miserliness of their souls.

Anticipation shimmered in the night air. Lights danced merrily in the breezy night, the expectant crowd's excitement growing by the minute. Bickle took his place on stage, a backdrop of tiny red, white, and blue crosses flickering about, surrounding him. His hair gleamed silver and his blue jeans and red and white striped polo succeeded in making him seem more like a man of the people.

"Praise Be To God!" he shouted, simple words of devotion that were met with ecstatic acclamations, some in English, others in tongues. "Think how far we've come these few short months!" Members of the Cabinet lifted their faces to the heavens. On cue, Bickle called out, "Let the show begin!"

The pyrotechnic and drone displays were the grandest display American taxpayers had ever funded. Upbeat Christian pop pulsed from loudspeakers spaced all along the Mall and Ellipse. Forty minutes in, when the finale arrived, it was something viewers would never forget. Drones painted the sky with a two-hundred foot likeness of the president, an image so real in its artistry that it drove home the all-seeing eye of the government in a way that nothing before had done. While having an authoritarian figure as the nation's ruler was comforting to the masses, the majority, thrust into a far different reality than they had ever imagined, turned silent and obedient.

Upwards of two hundred thousand energized but weary celebrants gathered their blankets and belongings and began their journeys home, many with tired but happy children in tow.

At 9:55 p.m., Alger stepped down from the podium. Cozying up to Riggins, he remarked, "Nothing like bread and circuses for the masses, eh?"

Riggins chuckled. "Indeed. The divine glory of distraction."

35

THE SUN WAS below the horizon when the president's ringtone startled Christian awake. Groggily, he picked up.

"Right now, at this very moment, I am looking at a black site where Governor Lee is leading survivors out of an area that looks as if it was wiped off the map. You said you'd taken care of this!"

Shirley Lee, Oregon's beloved governor, had been on the ground since the very beginning. Though depleted and disheartened, she kept on.

Christian stammered, "What the f . . . fudge? Stan tole me they'd gone offline!"

"You fool. Cell communications aren't the whole of it!"

Black sites? That he was charged with shutting those down too? He didn't even know what Alger was talking about.

Feeling like he was tied down in the center of a five-way intersection with cars careening towards him at breakneck speed from every direction, warning lights flashing red, Christian knew that if he didn't find a way to stop the leaks for good, he didn't want to think about what would happen to him.

"I'm headed to Portland shortly."

"You get it done this time," Alger snarled. The line went dead and Christian reached for his pills.

Many years ago, when he and Darlene started Male Headship, they did it on a wing and a prayer. Knowing they were in way over their heads, they pushed on, Darlene the brains, and he the charm. As a duo, it had worked spectacularly. But he was alone now in the world of realpolitik. Scripture and empty promises got a man nowhere. Should he be exposed as a failure, the world would see him as the man behind the curtain, a Texas huckster whose game was up, the ineffectual faggot his father always said he was.

36

One-Thirty p.m., PST

ON AN AIRSTRIP two miles south of the Hood River, sixty-two miles east of Portland, agents hustled Christian from Faith's jet onto a Navy Seahawk. The UCSA pilot navigated the helicopter to a place near the center of town that was flat enough to land upon. As they looked down at the designated spot, the airman spoke into his headset. "It's a much smaller opportunity than anticipated." Christian paled as he took in the ruined landscape, afraid of a crash landing, but even more of his likely failure.

They touched down and the rotors quieted. Korteen and his crew picked their way around the fissures until they stood beside Christian.

"Mr. Secretary, thank you for taking time out of your busy schedule to come here. Please, tell our viewers why you are here and what you hope to accomplish."

Christian smiled, warming to the deception in which he was about to take part. Looking beyond Korteen at the hellscape surrounding him, he answered, "I've come today out of love for the American people." Passers-by slowed. Unable to resist the thrill of a live audience Christian turned toward the growing crowd, calling out in his finest preacher voice, "May I say how much it gladdens me to see y'all doin' so fine!"

A woman upfront heard the words, not meant for them but for television audiences everywhere, and shouted, "Liar!"

"Look around you!" another chimed in. "You call this fine?"

Cameras filmed from behind. Korteen raised his hand, and the crew cut its audio feed. In the studio, hallelujahs would replace jeers .

"Chuck," the secretary continued, oblivious to the escalating anger, "I don't see natural disasters as unexpected. Truth is, they're inevitable. God's warnin' ta sinners, best get right with Him before it's too late. It's why I named this little hiccup Delilah . . .ta give y'all a biblical jolt. Believe you me, this here minor shake-up is but a first shot to them what dwell in this present-day Sodom." Christian trained his steely blue eyes on the lens. "Only through Jehovah God can you be saved."

For two days after the quake, Korteen was housed and fed by some of the same people standing before him now. Yet rather than feel gratitude, he looked at them with contempt. Despite the kindness they'd shown him, it only took being in Christian's presence to return him to the slavering sycophant that he was.

The crowd grew restless, their intent clear. Christian's security detail signaled him to leave at the same time Korteen whispered, "Time to get out of here. Let's wrap."

"Thanks Charles, and to all of you for comin' out today!"

"And there we have it. The word of our Lord coming to us today in the body of Secretary Christian Hillcox. I'm Charles Korteen reporting live from Portland, the New City of Faith."

The crowd surged forward as Hillcox was pushed into the waiting tactical vehicle. Starting off, the tank bumped and jostled its way over and around great slabs of broken asphalt, more off-road than on. A drive that normally took twenty minutes lasted the better part an hour. Christian was safe inside the armored car despite chunks of pavement and other projectiles periodically hurled their way. Mid-journey, he looked through the periscope to see a crane operator direct a girder off the road. He knew that Governor Lee had ordered state workers to clean up, but It was unsettling to see so much undamaged equipment, because where had it come from? He shrugged it off. What else could he do?

At last, the tank reached the UCSA's temporary headquarters, now housed in the basement of the only functioning hospital. Christian peered out to see a long line of the walking wounded waiting their turn to see a doctor. When he climbed out of the vehicle, his eyes lit upon a towering billboard straight ahead. On it was the image of Jesus ministering to the people, underscored by the words "Get Right With God" in bright red script, the only hint of color in the otherwise bleak landscape. That and the life-sized color portrait of Christian's beaming visage in the lower right-hand corner, the attribution reading, "Brought to You by The Department of Faith." It was downright heartwarming and he couldn't keep himself from grinning.

Suddenly, a man burst through the barricades. Security officers pushed Christian back, shielding him with their bodies.

Never a brave man, he was terrified but, in effort to appear unafraid, he stepped atop a makeshift platform, picked up the megaphone and called out, "Let us pray!"

"Fuck you!" a woman yelled. "We don't want your phony-ass prayers! Prayers won't give us food or water. We've lost everything and you want us to pray?"

Christian continued over her, "Oh Lord, give us the words to banish the disbelief from our brothers an' sisters, and we will use them. Help us to . . .."

No one saw who tossed the device but it caught the eye of one of his agents as it arced through the air. The soldier leapt to cover his charge, and with his face to the crowd, he spread his arms wide, the grenade finding its home in the man's sternum, where it exploded. The impact threw Christian backwards and to the ground, his detail instantly surrounding him.

Blood surged from a wound on Christian's scalp, and he was propelled inside. Down the corridor in Emergency, a nurse examined him, exhibiting a coldness he had not experienced in his adult life. He felt woozy, not good at all. She told him his wounds were superficial, denying him one of the few remaining beds, and then she hurried off.

His fury rising, not once did he give a thought to the agent who had died so that he might live.

Finally a doctor headed his way. Christian was relieved until he noticed the color of the woman's skin and heard her speak.

"Good afternoon, Secretary Hillcox. I'm Dr. Khouri. Let's take a look."

Christian bristled at the immigrant's touch, visibly shrinking back.

Ignoring the affront, Dr. Khouri continued, "Let's see what we have here." Gently, she felt around the wound, his anxiety growing.

"Please, sir," the doctor urged, "you can relax. It's only a surface wound. There are an awful lot of vessels in our scalps, which is why there is so much blood. There's some debris I need to remove, and I'd like to put a few stitches in so the wound mends properly." Just then, a tech hurried over and whispered in her ear.

"If you could hang on a bit?" she said. "I left an amputation mid-surgery and must return there until the patient is out of danger. I'll be back to finish with you shortly. I'm sure you understand. For now, keep this towel pressed against your head." She began to move off.

"I certainly do not understand an' no, I will not hang on. Do you *know* who I am? I've an entire nation what depends on me an' you speak of one person? You'll disappear an' I won't see you for hours, an' that, '*Doctor*,' if you even have a medical degree, is time I do not have. You'll see to me now so's I can get on with my work."

He gave her no choice but to tend to him. She cleaned the wound in silence, extracting bits of shrapnel from Christian's scalp, and soon she began to stitch him up.

"Yeoww! That hurts, you, you, you … curry muncher!" When it came to ethnic slurs, Christian could tangle with the best. He checked her arm, further outraged to see her without an armband. Come to think of it, he hadn't seen a single one since his arrival. A military sweep of The Territories couldn't come soon enough.

Dr. Khouri spoke abruptly, "I'm sorry but I cannot use a numbing agent for something so minor. Our situation is dire. We have to keep what little we have for serious procedures."

Christian held back but not for long. As soon as Dr. Khouri finished stitching and bandaging him, he ordered the officers standing by, "Take Swami here away. She set out to hurt me an' she damn well succeeded." No sooner had he spoken than the men hauled the doctor off.

Pulsing with pain and indignation, Christian wove his way down the hall and onto an elevator to Basement Level Two. Once inside the newly designated Area Six, Stan Chisholm's secretary, Bonnie Heflund, saw him, and exclaimed, "What in God's name happened?" His bloody clothing combined with the swath of gauze wrapped around his head made the injury appear more serious than it was.

"Someone damn well tried to assassinate me, that's what happened!"

Chisholm emerged from his makeshift office, certain the blame was about to fall on him, "Mr. Secretary …."

Christian surprised him. "Chisholm, you got computer whizzes out here what spend their days an' nights sendin' out the kinds of stories an' visuals we cain't have. All the sudden it's my job to shut these leaks down. We can handle our own networks, but you seem to have some kinda Resistance TV goin' an' that's on you ta take care of. Shut 'em down. Full stop."

"Mr. Secretary, sir, you asked me to pull the plug on cell service and I did. As for satellite communications, we don't have the wherewithal to handle it. It has to be you people at the federal level. No threat or amount of pressure can change that. Right now, it's enough for each of us just to live to see another day."

Christian looked around at this fragment of a basement in a city that was all but destroyed and took his leave, his head near to exploding. He had only just climbed back inside the tank when a violent aftershock roiled the ground below. His heart juddering, he looked through the periscope to see the hospital fall, a mere two hundred yards behind him, its remains now a shell surrounding a massive pile of rubble. If Dr. Khouri was still on the premises, she was dead. So too was Stan Chisholm.

At the same time that Christian skirted death in Portland, three explosions at the Country Club Plaza Mall in Kansas City claimed twenty-four innocent lives with countless others injured. Simultaneously, a suicide bomber self-detonated in New York's Union Square, taking fifteen with him. Islamic terrorists rushed to claim responsibility but Christian feared that the explosions lay not at the feet of Jihadis, but that they had been planned and executed by members of the Resistance.

Only Alger and a select few knew the truth.

The president declared Martial Law. To many, it was a relief. To the Administration, it was natural progression.

37

May 22, Two p.m., PDT

CHRISTIAN TOSSED and turned on the flight back. It wasn't the seat that kept him from dozing off, medicated though he was, but the fact that he couldn't erase the vision of Stan Chisholm's body lying crushed beneath the weight of the five story structure. However, Chisholm's death only bothered him because, in losing the Portland office, he would no longer have anyone there to help, or to blame.

Christian had always and only supported politicians whose votes positively affected issues concerning Israel. Since November, membership in his organization, Christian Zionists of America, topped fifty million and continued to grow by the day. CZOA had raised upwards of one hundred million dollars, monies dedicated to taking back the lands Jehovah God had deeded the Hebrews 3,500 years ago. For over three decades, the organization had used these funds to resettle Russian and Ethiopian Jews in what little land still remained in the so-called

Palestinian Territories. These Hebrew emigres, along with the homegrown and American-born Israeli settlers, were hard-right Zionists, armed and eager to defend what they knew to be their land, land decreed in the Bible as their birthright. Like the UCSA, Israel had alienated itself from most countries, making Christo-American financial and military support more crucial than ever.

As restless as could be, Christian reached for his phone and scrolled to the G's. Lighting on the name, Gideon Goldfein, the Prime Minister of Israel, he punched 'Call.' It was midnight in Jerusalem and, asleep or not, the leader of the party, Jewish Strength, would not complain.

"Shalom Gideon. Christian here."

"Erev Tov, Mr. Secretary. What is happening in your country? I just turned on the TV and, lo and behold, I see that there was an attempt on your life! After so much death and destruction in your beautiful state of Oregon, that they should try to kill you? Of course, as you know Israel holds out her hand to you. Whatever you need."

It struck Christian that even as he was tasked to control what reached the American people, the administration had no such power over what the Resistance sent out to the rest of the world .

"Very kind of you, but we got it," Christian replied brusquely, as Goldfein watched the unaddressed human disaster on KAN 11. He was sickened by the Alger administration's flagrant disregard for life, no matter that he himself championed Israel's own racist and religious ways and wars. The prime minister, afraid to look in history's mirror, needed to believe that what was happening in America was far worse.

"I'm calling to ask when you plan to declare your sovereignty over ev'ry inch of the land God gave you? You been too passive for too long."

"I have to disagree with you on that. It's not a matter of being passive, but of being political. You and I talked about this not long ago and you agreed. It's a delicate game we play. You know that better than most. This is not the right time to stir the pot."

"Tsk, tsk, an' too bad. I'm callin' in the debt, Goldfein. It's on you to take back the lands you promised, no matter the blowback. An' I ain't askin'."

The prime minister had no choice, "I'll do my best."

"Make sure you do."

<h1 style="text-align:center">38</h1>

May 22, Ten a.m.

MATT HENEFIELD took his daily stroll to Faith's break room where he greeted the two coworkers with whom he pretended an office friendship. He readied his coffee, then leaned against the counter, sipping on the steaming mug.

The conversation became animated. "Son of a gun!, the blonde one said, "They nearly caught the Kansas City bomber. When they do, they'd better go a lot farther than throwing him in the big house, if you get my drift." He winked conspiratorially at Matt.

The second, shorter man drew close. "Between us," he began, then lowered his voice, "I'm thinking yesterday's explosions might have been an internal operation. False flag, you know? Scare the bejeezus outta the volk. Keep the fear-fires stoked."

"Freakin' A!" exclaimed the first. "Hadn't thought about that, but you could be right."

Volk, Matt thought, thoroughly chilled.

A cluster of employees was watching the television, tuned to the current episode of *Lost To God, Soul Harvest* when it was interrupted by the now familiar BEEP-BEEP-BEEP. "This Is a Breaking News Alert." The picture cut to Alger.

"Based on the increasing number of Resistance terrorist attacks, I hereby declare a National State of Emergency. Beginning tonight, a curfew will be in effect from 6:00 p.m. until 7:00 a.m., seven days a week, until further notice. The curfew applies to all citizens, excluding those with security passes. During the daytime hours, it is essential that all citizens remain vigilant. Keep your eyes and ears open, and report any suspicious activity or conversation. Remember, information can come from anywhere — from coworkers, friends, family, on subways, buses, in stores, restaurants, even in church. Remember, it is better to report than to regret."

The chyron "Contact 202-BELIEVE 202–235–4383" crawled across the bottom of the screen. The general consensus among the employees was one of relief.

Fortunately, Matt had driven in today. He made certain his peers heard him as he excused himself. "Golly, I just re-membered. I left my notes for today's Challenge meeting in my car." He made a quick exit and headed to the garage a few blocks away and texted Liz, "Poker tonight. My place. 5:30. BYOB. Due to curfew, plan on staying over." He pressed Send, removed the chip, then tossed it into a dumpster on his way back.

❖

Christian strode into Faith that afternoon, wearing his bandages like a crown of thorns. He drank in the sympathy as he moved about, graciously accepting the remarks about his bravery. After submitting to Lurleen's cluck-clucking, he shut his office door and was settling in when his phone lit up with a text from the president: *I need everything you have on Operation Raptor. ASAP.*

Desperate to prove his competence, Christian pulled together the papers and called for a courier. Within minutes, an attractive young woman appeared. It struck him that he'd never noticed her before and that underneath her modest skirt and sweater set, he liked what he imagined. In her twenties, she was comely, nubile, reminiscent of a young Darlene. The kind of body that used to turn him on.

She felt his eyes undress her and, as repulsed as she was, she put on a sympathetic voice, "Are you all right, sir, after what happened to you?"

"I tell you, dear, my near brush with death, it only strenthened my faith. Made it clear as day the Lord has more for me to do on this earth."

"He certainly does," she replied as evenly as she could.

Christian moved in to read her badge. "Jessica, is it? My, my, but you're a pretty one," relieved to think he might still have it for a woman.

She stammered, "Oh, I don't know, sir."

"Oh, I do, my dear. What say we break bread together? Let's plan on t'night."

Her cheeks went scarlet from equal parts fear and revulsion, her perceived shyness making her all the more attractive to Christian.

"I would like that very much," she lied, hoping her true feelings weren't on show.

"D'you like a good southern meal?"

"Yes, sir, I do," trying to quell the quiver in her voice.

"Good. Then that's what we'll do. I know just the place. Dinin' with you'll get my mind off what I went through. I'll get your address and call for you at seven o'clock." He handed her a folder marked 'Top Secret—Eyes Only. "Get this to the president quick as a rattlesnake at high noon. Now run like the wind, chile."

He watched her walk away, enjoying the fullness of her buttocks, the sway in her step. Maybe youth and purity were all the medicine he needed to cure him of the lurid fantasies that had been showing up more and more often.

Shaken by the secretary's lechery, and frightened about the evening ahead, Jessica stopped by Matt's desk. Dismayed he was nowhere to be seen, she left a hemp bracelet, their agreed-upon signal that all was not right, prominently on his desk.

As she headed towards the elevator, she peeked inside the folder, staggered when she saw the words "Containment Camps." As if on automatic pilot, she changed her path and headed straight for the stairs. She raced down to the sub-basement and when she reached the bottom she used the flashlight on her phone to help find her way along the dim hallway on Concourse Three, an area closed to visitors. A storage room, there was nothing sinister about where she was. Opening door after door, she was about to give up when she turned one last handle, and found what she was looking for. The silence surrounding her gave her the impetus to continue. Slipping inside, she closed the door. She located an old scanner and plugged it in. As the machine whirred to life, its sounds nearly made her shut it down and leave, the danger of it all suddenly overwhelming her. Yet she continued, even though every click and buzz sent her heart plunging. After what seemed an hour but was only a minute, the start-up finished. As quickly as her shaking hands allowed, she scanned the pages and saved them to a thumb drive she kept secreted on a chain inside her sweater.

One floor above, Faith's Security Supervisor, Elvin Snodgrass, swiveled in his chair, glancing from monitor to monitor with his usual sense of boredom when, from the corner of his eye, he spotted movement in a seldom visited room. Excitedly, he texted Joe Squire. "Meet me outside the stairwell near C3-103. STAT."

Jessica's task complete, she shut down the machine and switched off the light. Her hand on the doorknob, she jerked it back when she heard voices in the hallway. With barely enough time to squeeze behind the scanner, the door swung open and two men stepped inside. Elvin threw the light, illuminating the room.

"Here, in this corner, I saw something move." They glanced around. "Don't see nothin'," he shrugged.

"Yeah, sometimes there's rats," Joe offered.

They started to head out. "By the by, did you hear 'bout Sue Anne in Accounting? Word is she's doin' Bill Freytag somethin' fierce. What I wouldn't give for a piece a that." As he spoke, his hand rested atop the warm scanner. "Hot damn. This thing was just used!"

It was then that a rodent of some kind brushed against Jessica's ankle. Despite the danger, she couldn't keep from making the slightest movement, the smallest sound. Elvin looked at Joe, raised an eyebrow, then together, they dragged the scanner from the wall.

"Well look-ee here! Dang girlie, whatcha hidin' from?" Joe saw her slip something beneath the machine. "Git up!" he snarled, and she stood. He reached down and grabbed the folder she had tried to hide. A quick look at its intended destination and confidential status told him all he needed, and the thought of what such a discovery might do for his career sent his voice up an octave. "Hands behind your back!" he squealed.

"For your information, I have clearance to be here!" she pointed to her badge, her voice filled with an authority she did not feel.

Flicking up her nametag, Elvin left his hand on her breast and slowly, deliberately, fondled her. "Yet here you are, hiding behind a machine," he sniggered.

Joe picked up a loose metal tray and hurled it at the ceiling, aiming for what he knew to be in the corner. Smirking when the tray hit its mark, the small camera shattered, its pieces falling to the ground.

A pair of rough hands grabbed her, then forced her up against the machine.

"What do you think you're doing?" she screeched.

"I'll hold her, "Joe said, relieved to hear his voice return to normal.

Elvin's breath coming hard and fast was his only answer. He grabbed her hem and yanked her skirt up in one move.

"Get off me!" she screamed, flailing helplessly. "Help! Someone. Help!" Elvin shoved his hand over her mouth to silence her and she bit down hard.

"Bitch!" he snarled. "Hold her Joe!" and, wiping the blood from his hand on her skirt, he ripped a length of tape from the roll looped on his belt and sealed her mouth shut.

"Now, where were we?," slamming back into her with a ferocity born of lust. He came quickly.

It was Joe's turn. He slapped her in the face, her breath now short and tortured. "What're you moanin' about whore? You know you love it. B'sides, you gave up your rights when you copied secret information. Ain't a soul alive gonna care what we do to you."

Two minutes later Joe, heaving from exertion and excitement, zipped up his pants and Elvin said, "Let's get the tramp down to Interrogation." They muscled Jessica into the corridor, yanked her down the hall and into a black box of a room. Elvin shoved her onto a metal chair and bound her to it. Once he was certain she was secured, he stepped back and switched on his walkie-talkie. "Do me a favor an' let Secretary Hillcox know we got us a predicament down in Interrogation. Somethin' he'll wanna deal with hisself."

Once upon a time, Jessica could not have imagined worse than what she had just been through, but the knowledge that Christian was about to learn of her treachery filled her with a whole new kind of terror. When minutes later, the quiet click of an unseen, outer door opened, she thought about her cell, and determined she'd cede nothing.

Ellison Mann's parents had divorced when he was young. His father was a Catholic and his mother, Protestant. He grew up with little supervision and plenty of money, the result being that he fell in with the wrong crowd. He turned to religion after nearly losing a battle with opioids. There being no bigger zealot than the 'saved,' he joined the Alger bandwagon early on. Through his mother's connections, Ellison got the job as Alger's Midwest Campaign Chair. When Alger offered him the position as Christian's Under-Secretary at Faith, Ellison jumped at the opportunity.

Mann stood behind a one-way mirror in the observation room. Looking in, he was surprised and sorry to see the formerly polished young woman he had hired four months earlier, now so disheveled: her hair tangled and her clothes torn and bloodied. A harsh light shone onto her tightly shut eyes.

He entered the interrogation room, his affect non-threatening. "Jessica? Stapleton? They tell me you were found copying classified documents." She looked straight ahead, the tape on her mouth preventing a response. Referencing her appearance, he added, "I apologize if you feel you've been treated poorly." He reached out and gently removed the tape.

Poorly, she thought. If being gang-raped meant being treated poorly, then she supposed she had been. Yet she remained silent, knowing well that these were the sort of men whose disdain for women was part of their identity. Her eyes, filled with pain and terror, bored through him. He nodded to Elvin, "Untie her and leave us."

Alone with her, Ellison was forced to play a game for which he no longer had the stomach. He held up the folder, "So this is what you've been up to."

Jessica cleared her throat, surprised to have a voice. "Whatever you suspect me of, I beg you to help," she pleaded, all pretense gone. She spoke with dignity. "If you have a mother or daughter —" she stopped, reminding herself he wouldn't care.

She had been absent for less than forty minutes and she shivered for what the next few hours would bring.

"You, a trusted employee of Faith, a woman with the highest level of clearance, you were caught red-handed copying Top Secret documents. Normally, someone with evidence as damning as this wouldn't get an opportunity to work things out, but because Secretary Hillcox seems to have taken a shine to you, he asked me to convey this one-time deal."

Mann continued with carefully chosen words. "If you show your regret by sharing what you know, in particular for whom you work, the Secretary will release you to a facility where you'll have the opportunity to repent." He paused. The sooner she gave in, the faster he would be done with his role in this sordid business. "This is an extraordinary offer, I hope you realize. Take a minute and think it over."

Her silence came back at him.

The inner door opened again and this time, a grizzled older man dressed in a tuxedo and white gloves entered. He placed a prison-issue uniform and a pitcher of water on a long table in the back corner. Mann untied her then excused himself to give Jessica time to change from her bloodied clothes, the attendant following behind. Fear, but more so determination, kept her seated.

Mann left the room and retook his place behind the mirror. Hillcox stepped in the anteroom, joining him. "Whadda ya got for me?"

"Nothing so far. She hasn't said anything."

Christian seethed. "The treasonous she-devil. We'll git what we need no matter what we gotta do." This was not what Ellison had signed up for.

The white-gloved man returned, this time wheeling a table spread with white linen. On it was a dinner plate laid with a thick slab of prime rib, potatoes gratin and grilled asparagus. A small bowl cradled a generous portion of cream-drizzled fruit cobbler. The server poured a liberal amount of wine into a tumbler. Jessica, cognizant of the Evangelicals' disdain for spirits, knew it was there to weaken her resolve. Aware that Mann was watching from the other side of the glass, she didn't consider that Christian might be as well. She raised her glass, took a small sip, then stood and limped about the room, softly whimpering.

Hearing her, Mann winced.

Hillcox nodded to Ellison and they went in.

"Miss Stapleton, I believe you know the Secretary of Faith."

She stared blankly while Christian scrutinized her. The lack of respect she exhibited, particularly in her current circumstances, fired his anger up another notch. Nonetheless, he kept a tight rein on his tongue, gesturing for Mann to continue.

"While the secretary's presence underscores the seriousness of the charges against you, you seem a reasonable young woman. And so, for your sake and ours, we ask you to share the names of your colleagues, beginning with who you copied the documents for."

She thought fast. "Mr. Secretary sir, I didn't want to chance losing your important papers. With all that's been going on, I was worried that someone would grab the folder before I got to the White House, so I decided to back them up, just in case. You of all people know how many evil individuals are out there, people who'll do anything to stop your glorious work. "

Christian stepped forward. "Clever as you think you are, I'm no one's fool. Iffen you thought I'd buy that yarn, you're a bigger ninny than you seem. I trusted you, was even gonna take you out." Mann's eyebrows rose at the revelation. "Then you go off an' copy Top Secret information. Well, I aint buyin'. You tell me who you did this for," his spittle flying. "This ain't no game."

Thoughts of Matt and the others stiffened her resolve. "I have nothing to say." Looking at Mann, she detected a sliver of concern cross his face. Not so with Christian. She knew well the peril she was in.

Christian handed Mann a pair of handcuffs. "Fasten her to that table there, then give us some time alone, no cameras, y'hear? An' curtain off the mirror. I want privacy." Loyal lieutenant that he was, Mann did as told. Christian followed him to the door, then threw the lock.

Hillcox watched Jessica struggle beneath the straps and found himself oddly turned on. Whether it was the girl or the bindings that titillated, he didn't know or care.

He approached, his fleshy round face drawing near, his odiferous gut-breath assaulting her. She tried to shrink away but was stopped by the steel table. His wrath near to exploding, he roared, "To think I was gonna take you out an' treat you nice." He smacked her hard across the face, the sound reverberating throughout the room. "Tell me who's runnin' you. I ain't askin'."

"I don't know what you're talking about."

"You—lyin'—tramp." His face purpled with rage. "Girlie, this is your last chance. Who're you doin' this for?"

"I did it as a backup for you. In case the papers were stolen."

Christian's rage escalated when he thought about what would happen if Alger learned that Jessica had had the opportunity to expose the camps. If it got out, it was doubtful that even Father God could save him. A man with scant capacity for control in the best of times, reason departed as the Devil's blood rushed in. Without further thought, he wrapped his hands tightly around her neck and squeezed. Kicking and bucking, her movements grew increasingly weaker. At the last second, he let go.

Gasping for air, she coughed and spluttered, her desperate wheeze leaving him unmoved. "You answer me or I'll finish you!"

Fear and pain opened her lips. "I'm in a cell!"

Christian was flabbergasted, turned upside-down. A cell, like with Jihadis? She's workin' for the A-rabs, he wondered in astonishment.

"Cain't say I'm surprised," he lied. "I always suspected camel-jockeys were runnin' you people, an' now I got proof. But I still want names!"

He struck her again. Other than a low moan, she offered no more.

"Still not talkin'?" His brief moment of self-control gone. "How's 'bout I shut that lyin' trap a yours forever!" The madness within took over. He pressed his hands hard on her windpipe, but there was no more fight. She was no longer of this earth. Unbinding the shackles, he turned her limp body over so that her buttocks faced him. Tearing at the zipper on his pants, he entered her from behind, slamming into her again and again. In those moments, he genuinely believed he was showing the world, and his dead father, the man he really was. A lifetime of betrayal urged him on, taunting him, mocking him. For now, in this time and place, it wasn't Jessica he savaged. It was Mason, Darlene, Joss. In truth, it was his life.

Sensing that the scene required a witness, Mann had ignored Christian's orders and was watching through a slit in the curtains, sickened as much by his own complicity as he was by what this so-called man of God had done.

When it was all over, Christian spoke into the monitor and called him in. With no choice but to obey, he went. Ellison looked at the young woman with whom he had spoken only minutes ago and, seeing the condition of her body up close, he knew his days at Faith were numbered. Christian leaned against the table, breathing hard. As difficult as it was for Mann to look the crazed secretary in the eye, he needed time to think, so look him in the eye he did.

In a deep and sinister voice, Christian intoned, not to Mann but to some unseen presence, *"Judge not, that ye be not judged. For with what judgment ye judge, ye shall be judged: and with what measure ye mete, it shall be measured to you again."* Then he stormed from the room, slamming the door behind.

Mann turned Jessica over onto her back. He straightened her sweater and covered the lower half of her body with the unused uniform. This was not the time for horror and revulsion, nor could he allow entry to thoughts of grief and shame. He would keep the Secretary's terrible secret for now. He picked up the folder, with plans to deliver it to the president, buying himself time to think. He buzzed for Maintenance, and while he waited he tried to shut down the physical sense of shame that nearly drowned him.

The door opened. "Daryl," he said to the custodian. "Please remove the body and clean the room." Disposing of a corpse from Faith's basement, while not common, would cause no uproar, trigger no investigation.

What Mann had seen a person of faith do to another human being would be his cross to bear for all time.

39

Five p.m.

LIZ PUSHED open the door of Matt's fourth floor apartment to find him seated in front of his computer, pulling at his hair with one hand—a childhood habit to which he returned when stressed—while continuously refreshing the screen with the other.

"What's going on?"

He pressed PLAY on his phone. She listened to the conversation between two of Matt's co-workers that he'd surreptitiously recorded that afternoon. The sound was muffled but for the part when one said, clear as day, "Cameras caught her copying classified documents."

"I wouldn't wanna be in those shoes," another voice said.

Matt shut it off. "It's Jessie they're talking about. I know it is. She left a bracelet on my desk early this afternoon, the signal we set up to warn one another if something's off. And then I didn't see her for the rest of the day. Please tell me you've heard from her."

"I haven't, but let's not assume anything. I'm sure she'll be here any minute," he said, although neither of them believed it. Jessica was never late. An incipient migraine sent its familiar signals to Liz, the last thing for which she had time, not if they were to find their way through this.

Bruce hadn't arrived, but late was normal for him. By now, Jessica was forty-five minutes overdue. "Okay, Matt, I'm calling it," she said as dispassionately as she could. "I'm afraid you might be right. Did she text you this afternoon?"

"She did. Around two, asking if I wanted to grab a pre-curfew beer."

The viselike pain in her head worsened. "Shit. That means she had something important. Okay, here's what we do. Grab everything we can't afford for them to get their hands on. If they have her, they may well already know about you. We've gotta move." Her head felt like it was about to explode, so in order to function, she downed one of her few remaining migraine pills. Fishing her phone from her bag, she removed the SIM card, broke it into pieces, then extracted the hard drive from her computer, indicating for Matt to do the same. They put both drives and their remaining few burners into a small bag, locked the door, and took the back stairs down.

Matt drove. On the way, Liz texted Bruce, burner to burner: "Aunt Charlotte not well. Asking for you." The text reached him as he left The Hot Zone, a trendy, passes-only bar in Georgetown. Liz had never before invoked Aunt Charlotte. Following protocol, he moved his car to a public garage and tossed his phone in the nearest garbage receptacle. He quickly made his way to the bus stop and, two transfers later, arrived at the safe house, certain he hadn't been followed.

The moment he arrived, Liz stated. "They have Jessica," because from the onset, she'd had no real doubt.

He set his bag down. "Who?"

"Hillcox's people."

"My god."

Liz handed Matt a burner. "Call in sick tomorrow. Tell them you were just diagnosed with a highly contagious stomach virus so you're turning your phone off and going to bed."

Matt leaned over, head in hands. "I can't believe this is happening."

"Matt, the length of Jessica's silence means that if she emerges, we can't engage. If she's alive and tries to contact you, it'll be because they're using her as bait. While we know she'd never willingly expose you, or any of us, what we can't know is how she'll hold up under torture."

Matt felt numb, like he wasn't there and none of this was real. Even so, he couldn't keep from imagining what she was going through if, as Liz said, she was even still alive.

40

May 23

THE BLACKOUT drapes were so effective that when Christian awoke the room was pitch black, even though it was well past eight. The bed linens were tangled around his feet, the rest of his body cold and damp, all signs of a night spent thrashing about. Navigating the soupy wilds of his unconscious, he fought his way to the surface. The fog of too many pills and a feeling of soreness in his manhood jolted him upright, and as he focused, he was flooded with relief to see he was home, in his own room, and not in a strange bed with some strange man.

He stood and stumbled around until he found the light switch and flipped it on. His phone buzzed and the display showed it to be the president. That was when he remembered the previous day.

Anticipating the worst, he was surprised to hear Alger in such a cordial mood. "Christian, I'm calling to say how pleased I am with how you handled the documents yesterday. Most wise."

What in God's name?, he wondered, totally confused.

"Mann brought the folder to me this morning and I'm pleased to say it's secure in my safe. I'm heartened by the caution you are taking to keep this particular, shall we say, 'subject,' off record. From now on, continue to hand-write anything that pertains to our little project, if you know what I mean."

Christian pulled himself together and summoned his best preacher voice, "All I do is in His guh-lory." While he spoke, he fingered the thumb drive that had hung from Jessica's neck just yesterday. Clearly, Alger didn't know about Jessica, and Christian intended to keep it that way.

"I knew I was right to bring you on."

"Why, thank you, sir."

They disconnected, and Christian headed through the kitchen for the service door, crossed to the utility room, opened the trash chute, and tossed in the drive.

Even with Martial Law in force, sporadic incidents of unrest began to increase. So far, they were easily controlled, but there was a growing awareness within the administration that the continued leaks on the Shadow Web posed an existential threat to Alger's government. Then there were the rebellions inside the Containment Camps that took but a spray of bullets to quell. If word were to get out that they existed, everything they'd accomplished so far could come crashing down.

It took less than three months for the existing camps to exceed capacity, automatically triggering an order to build more. While not an easy undertaking, the level of compensation made it well worth the builders' while. Every camp required guard towers, water and sewage systems, high-wattage security fencing, barracks, and a commissary. Each was to accommodate three thousand offenders, and builders were given thirty days from first shovel to completion.

❖

With Jessica's disappearance, Liz's apprehension increased by the minute. Early that afternoon, she messaged Eric, "Do you have time to talk about the tournament?" With no escape valve, she gave in to something she'd vowed to never do, and that was to bring Eric in.

"Sure. My office in ten."

Christo-Fascism had been on the rise her entire life. Beginning in the sixties, committed right-wing leaders and their deep-pocketed funders began a stealth game, one they played exceptionally well. By the beginning of the twenty-first century, the signs were everywhere but, as in the days of Weimar Germany, most everyone looked away. Life was good and wildly fun, at least for the fortunate. This was America, after all, so why worry?

She had begun working for TBT ten years ago. Back then, feeling as if she were shouting into the wind, she called out the growing Christian Nationalism at every turn, but with so many distractions and so few paying attention, religious extremism marched steadily forward. Biblical politicians backed by deep-pocketed believers filled the ranks at state, local and federal levels: inside school boards, in lower courts and state legislatures. Over the decades, they'd burrowed into key departments within the federal government where they'd stayed, growing in number and influence, waiting for a man like Alger to take the reins.

❖

Liz was all business when she burst into Eric's office. Aware she looked as terrible as she felt, she picked up a notepad from his desk, and scribbled, "A friend has disappeared," then passed pen and paper to him.

"What does it have to do with you?"

"Everything."

Their eyes met. He tore off the page, crumpled it up, and put it in his pocket. With false cheer he asked, "You up for a walk? It's a nice day and I could use the air." He opened his desk drawer and put his phone inside, indicating that Liz should do the same.

Minutes later, they were headed north on Connecticut Avenue in the direction of DuPont Circle. "There's something I haven't told you," Liz said.

"Mmmm?"

"I head a cell. Here in D.C.. The friend who disappeared was one of mine."

"I see."

"She worked as a runner at Faith, with top-level security clearance. There's every reason to believe she was caught copying confidential documents. We haven't heard from her or been able to reach her for two days."

Eric pointed to a coffee shop. "Want something?"

She looked around. "You think we're being watched?"

He shrugged. "Can't be too careful."

Crossing L Street, cups in hand, they found a bench and sat. "How can I help?" he finally asked.

"For starters, I need equipment."

"Such as?"

"A couple of hard drives installed into our computers. Also, I'm nearly out of burners."

"Consider it done. Anything else?"

She was encouraged by his lack of commentary. Normally, he worried far too much about her. "There's one more thing. I'm also the Coordinator for the Eastern Resistance."

While genuinely scared for her, he wasn't surprised, for he'd always admired her more than he could say. Now he implored, "If you'd consider it, I'd very much like to join your cell."

She hesitated. She had come intending to ask for his help but had found she couldn't shake her original concerns. "Eric, so far I've drawn the line at people with families. Besides, the movement needs the access you can provide through your position. It is as important as anything you could do."

"Important? How? With a mirepoix? I lost my country too, you know."

"I'll be honest with you. I came to you today to ask if you'd join. Jessica is gone and I'm about to lose another. But I hate the idea of putting you at risk. Damn, I'm all over the place, aren't I?"

"Liz, I've already talked to Manny about this, so whether I'm with you or him, it's what I'm going to do. I must if I'm to live with myself."

"Eric, despite my all waffling around, I do want you with me. I need your help."

Not daring to embrace, lest someone recognize and report them for inappropriate intimacy, he simply said, "Thank you," the warmth in his voice giving her new energy .

"As for computers and phones, remember Manny? Manny's Sporting Goods in Bethesda?" She nodded. "He'll take care of what you need. Bring them to me and I'll get them to Manny right away. Would you be able to pick them up this afternoon?"

"Are you kidding? Of course I can."

He stopped to quickly scribble the address on the coffee receipt and handed it to her."

They returned to the office. Liz brought down the hardware, retrieved her phone, and Eric gave her a key to his car. While there, he shot off an email to TBT's Softball teams: *"Greetings players. The schedule is up. Thanks to an anonymous donor, new bats, tees, and tournament caps are coming our way. You can pick them up in the second-floor supply closet after 10:00 tomorrow morning."*

41

Three-thirty p.m.

TRAFFIC WAS slow on Mass Ave until Liz crossed the District line. If she was stopped, Eric's note on TBT letterhead should suffice: *"Liz–Pick up the tournament equipment today at Manny's Sporting Goods on Wisconsin in Bethesda. Leave it in the supply closet by 10 tomorrow morning. They're open till 5:30. Thanks, Eric."*

The suburban D.C. store was the flagship of thirty-three others spread across the country. Manny worked out of the original shop. A product of the '60s, after becoming a father, he resigned himself to the fact that he could no longer devote his life to political protest, not if he wanted to feed a family. Divorced for many years, he was no longer responsible for his adult children, both of whom lived in Northern California and had careers and families of their own. On Inauguration Day, Manny was free to return to his political activism. With nothing to lose but his life, there was everything to gain for his children and their futures.

Manny and Eric, friends since grade school, shared a deep and abiding love for one another, which is why Eric felt safe asking for his help.

When Liz pulled up, Manny greeted her as he would an old customer. They chatted a bit and then he helped her transfer the duffels into Eric's trunk. He had thrown in some sweats for padding, dividing and burying the equipment beneath the bats and other apparel.

A big guy with graying curly hair and a warm smile, he grinned. "Best of luck with the tournament. I'll try to drop by. What could be better than watching Eric strike out?"

"Thanks, Manny," she said, returning the smile.

For Liz, computers and phones in hand, knowing Matt was safe for the moment, and now, Eric on board—it was as good as it could get these days.

If only she could stop thinking about Jessica.

42

May 24, Eleven a.m., PDT

A TWENTY-FOUR-YEAR-OLD father cradled his newborn, as tears streamed down his face. His name was John. A few minutes earlier, five days after Delilah destroyed much of Portland, his wife had taken her last breath. She had had a complicated birth, and although she and the baby had survived, the streets made for an impossible convalescence. John was seated on the sidewalk next to her body, keeping watch over it when he heard a voice, "Mister, you look like you've lost your faith."

John's head snapped upward in disbelief. "Who the fuck are you?"

"Call me Pastor Phil. It looks to me like you could use a bit of cheer. I've come to share the Good News and offer you His blessings."

He put a hand on John's shoulder. Instantly recoiling, John shoved him off. That this charlatan dared speak to him, much less push his contorted religion as a salve for his wife's death. "Get the fuck outta my sight and take your mythical god with you, you fucking tool. If any of you had wanted to help, my wife would still be alive."

"All the more reason for me to ask: Have you found Jesus?"

John's grief mingled with fury. He pushed his free arm against the pavement to stand, and gave the interloper a one-handed shove.

Pastor Phil responded with a gut-punch, sending the now wailing newborn onto the concrete, where her crying abruptly ceased. John fell to the ground, grabbing the child, his fingers traced with blood, whereupon God's Representative slammed into him with the metallic toe of his boot. John's head struck the concrete, the baby still in his arms. A former wrestler, Pastor Phil was 275 pounds of muscle and it didn't take him long to know that both father and infant were dead—yet still he kicked. Over and over and over.

Phil dusted himself off, looked around and, almost mugging for the crowd, he regained his godly expression, then melted away.

Unbeknownst to him, ten cameras had videoed the murders, each from a different angle.

Twenty minutes later, Wim Stiffel, Alger's Chief of Staff, rushed a tablet into the president's office, showing him the scene already racing across the Shadow Web. Alger took one look and snapped, "Get me Christian."

43

Two-Twenty p.m., EST

STIFFEL FOLLOWED Alger to the Oval Office, passing the president's phone to him, Christian on the other end. The chief of staff rotated a digital screen towards his boss, mouthing the words, "Shadow Web."

"Half the world must have seen this by now!," Alger shouted as he watched the same scene playing out on BBC. Stiffel touched the screen, and there it was on France 24. Then Germany's lead network, Spain's, Australia's, the Philippines', each with a chyron spelling out the murder in their own language, "Alger's Executioner," "Alger Unfit to Govern," most in words that took no fluency to understand.

Alger grabbed the tablet and shooed Stiffel out. He waited until the aide shut the door, then shouted into the phone, "How could you let this happen?"

Christian had no idea what the president was talking about. "Huh?"

"This thing in Oregon! Your pastor! He killed a man and his infant and there's video! It's gone viral!"

Christian gasped, then opened his computer. Struck by the animosity in Alger's voice, he focused on the citizen-anchors' words and he understood.

"Do you hear what they're saying about me? They're calling me a monster!"

"James, James. I'll look into it."

"You'll do a darn sight more than that! You'll make this disappear, fully and completely. Whatever you have to do. Alger clicked off, ending the call, each man in his own emotional tunnel, Alger's one of fury and Christian's one of fear.

On cue, the mental demons who inhabited Christian's mind stepped up. They whirled about, the hellish specters that they were, sending their fiery flames of energy through him. Phantom whispers of death, of rage, murder, exposure. Visions churned, haunting the realm where the unconscious, not Jesus, rules. From hellfire to depths unknown, Christian, the First Lord of Morality, battled an irrepressible pull downward. Down, down, down to unfathomable depths where, struggle as he might, the urge to succumb was irresistible. To give in, to submit, to welcome the darkness.

He stumbled from his office past a gape-mouthed Lurleen, disregarding the passersby, some real, others not. Finally outdoors and free of the building and its ever-present eyes, he lurched past limo and driver as, impelled by a world of psychic ghosts, he continued onward, half inside his head, the other half in the world of streets and sidewalks and human beings.

On the opposite coast, the sun gave off its last bit of light. The streets buzzed with desperate activity as citizens did a final search for that day's food and shelter. Adding to their trauma came the word-of-mouth report that a government pastor had murdered a man and his newborn child. At the same time, the now familiar sound of Vorderseit's preaching droned on nearby.

Storm's phone buzzed, interrupting his scriptural jeremiad. "Mr. Secretary?"

"One a your pastors murdered a father an' his newborn. There's video!"

Vorderseit stepped away. "It's bad out here! People are about to explode. I tell you, it's about to get violent."

"Now you listen up an' you listen good. I jest tole you that video of an execution by one a your pastor's has gone worldwide. I don't give a hot dog 'bout yer problems. Create me a whole 'nother narrative an' I want it by mornin', y'hear?"

Christian hung up and walked on, each step of the seemingly never-ending journey bringing him closer to the Watergate. Very nearly on his last breath, he fell into the door of the infamous complex. A blessedly empty elevator took him to the eleventh floor and his unit.

He mumbled to the guards standing watch, "I'm-a stay in t'night." Bang! slamming the door so hard, it nearly flew off its hinges. The men in his detail looked at one another and shrugged.

Hours later, when night turned to the small hours of morning, most of Washington was asleep, but not Christian. Desperately alone, the Devil came calling and need overtook reason. With darkness his cape, he crept out through the service door and around the corner. Hat slanted over his eyes, eyes further shielded by the darkest of shades. Down the back elevator, a stumble down New Hampshire Ave to the garage.

Ford Focus unlocked, keys over the visor. His secret chariot, in wait.

"To the speakeasy for faggots!" he yelped. His favorite songs thumped rhythmically on the sound system. Loud, primal, exciting.

Private entrance, money, and threats more than enough to ensure silence all 'round.

44

May 25

CHRISTIAN'S ALARM sounded at its usual time, the religious chorus rousing him to the most un-Christian of thoughts. Rather than induce shame, the pleasure he'd experienced in the wee hours of the morning came at him in a rush and, sinking back, he replayed the night in streaming technicolor, all the while pleasuring himself. Blast all, as hard as Satan worked to take him down, it was his right to do as he pleased. Try as he might, Lucifer had no chance against a living God, one whose powers of forgiveness would always prevail. What Christian had done a few hours ago might be the flip side of Straight On, but like Christ, he would rise again.

As if in validation, his smartwatch buzzed and there it was, a short video from Storm. He watched it once, and then again. What Vorderseit accomplished was masterful, relieving Christian for another day. He took a sip of coffee, then switched on SWBN in time to hear Charles Korteen announce, "This just in. The truth of what really happened in Portland yesterday." Vorderseit's video played while Korteen narrated the scene, laser-pointer in hand. "As you can see, the father clearly attacked the pastor, not the other way around, as the enemy would have you believe. Chaplain Brickell remains in serious condition, lucky to be alive. All to remind us how critical it is that we remain alert to fraudulent videos. Last night, these terrorists transmitted false information, purposefully meant to deceive and incite." Ominous music rushed in, then out. "Theirs wasn't even a good fake, seeing that their "video'"— and here his fingers denoted air quotes— "was not even set in Portland." "Instead of the burnt out metropolis they portray, this is how the city actually looks today," and a week-old clip filled the screen. "These Agents of Evil would have you believe the entire area was destroyed when in reality things go on as always.

"We must all be on high alert. If you suspect something is a fraud, report it immediately," the call-in number running across the screen. "Your information may, in the end, prove vital to the nation's security.

"This is Charles Korteen, reporting live from Portland."

Christian knew it was a matter of time before other such videos surfaced, images that might not be so skillfully altered and contained. If he wanted to remain in Alger's graces, and in his position as Secretary, he would have to do something substantive about it. But what? And how?

If he was good at anything besides pastoring, it was his uncanny ability to portray himself as other than he was. Whether pretending to be an astute administrator when Darlene was the one running the business side, or coming to Washington to take on a position far beyond his capabilities, he had always been able to stay a step ahead. For Christian operated on razzle-dazzle, and razzle-dazzle alone. Even the Pastor Brigade was a con, knowing full well that Alger's expectations were real and what these pastors could accomplish was not. Dispatching them to Portland had bought time, but not much. Which is why, when an idea of a different kind of deception struck him, he decided to follow his instincts and make a different kind of visit to The Territories.

He would leave this morning and begin the job of rooting out those responsible. No one in the Administration would know of his plan. That way, they could neither judge his success, nor the lack thereof.

He dressed and made a quick stop at Faith to finish up a piece of necessary business. Then he called for Lurleen. The red-headed receptionist appeared, a rhinestone-studded fish resting atop her cleavage.

"I need-a get to San Antone. Get Andrews on the horn an' tell 'em I'll want my plane within the hour. There are issues at Headship what only I can handle. Should anyone come lookin' for me, tell 'em where I'm at."

"Yes, sir."

The first leg of his journey would be known to those who asked.

45

One-Forty p.m., CST

FAITH'S PILOT brought the ten tons of screaming metal to a halt at San Antonio's International Airport. Deplaning, Christian spotted the two agents who awaited him.

"Mornin' boys. I'm aimin' for home, but first take me ta Headship."

"Will do, sir."

His church spoke to him of better times. It brought to mind the simple art of manipulating congregants and the adoration that went with it. Throw a little Jesus at 'em, an' suddenly, no problem was too big, not like the tightrope he walked in Washington, where a pride of hungry lions, their teeth bared, sat in wait for him to fall.

Inside, he found Dwight at his desk leafing through a stack of papers. Christian walked in and crossed over to him, pulling him close in a warm embrace.

"Woo-ee! Pastor C! I mean, Mr. Secretary. Heckuva surprise to see you back so soon. Y'here for more 'n a day this time?"

"Jest the night."

"Dagnammit, seems I hardly ever get a piece a you these days, but hey, I ain't complainin'. Anyhows, you're here, so how 'bout we take care a business? T'wont take but a minute or two. I find I could use a little help with Straight On."

Discussing the gay conversion program was the last thing Christian wanted to do, particularly in light of last night's cut and bob with the Dark One.

"Despite Joss' fine management," Christian winced at the mention of his name, "I noticed the squad's gotten a tetch squishy with the boys, treating 'em like they're normal 'stead of bent like that oak over yon'.

"Maybe you might could spend a few minutes with the trainers? I'm thinking', you bein' Secretary a Faith, you could surely set 'em straight."

"Would that I could Dwight, but I'm done in." He held up his phone and added, "An' I got work to do. Seems it never ends. But say, how's 'bout you an' I catch up tonight? Six a'clock at Bubba's? I'm fixin' to make an early night of it. Plum tuckered out, I am."

"Bubba's it is," Dwight said, clapping his boss on the back. "Leastaways we'll have ourselves some time."

"Indeed. Jes' you an' me, y'hear?"

"Sure thing, boss. Jest us. See ya then."

Christian grabbed the keys to Headship's van and hustled out the back door.

Arriving home at Second Coming, he called out, "Afternoon Cora! How-dee-do?"

"No one tole me you were comin'! I'd a prepared somethin' had I known. An' here I am, with nothin' in the Frigidaire!"

"Don't you worry your purdy little head," he mugged. "I'm here for a short bitta church business is all. Truth be told, I've a hankerin' for Bubba's. I'm-a meet Dwight there for what you might could call the earlybird special. Sure as heck wouldn't say no to a plate a your biscuits an' gravy t'morrow. I'm talkin' early. I'll be gone afore the rooster crows."

"Anythin' you want, Pastor C." Cora was more surprised by her boss's demeanor than his sudden presence. She couldn't remember when she last saw him this relaxed, what with J.J.'s disappearance and Darlene's passing. Thinking back on the old Christian, it gladdened her to see him this way.

She finished her busywork and departed. Left to himself, Christian roamed from room to room, stopping momentarily outside Darlene's door, willing her to be inside but, being no one's fool, he did not so much as jiggle the handle. Had she not taken her life, even though they weren't on friendly terms, her position as wife woulda dictated she'd-a have to have helped him through the current crisis. An' she woulda figgered it out too.

He walked the house to assure himself no one was around and, once he was sure, he climbed the stairs to the third floor and the attic. Advancing through cobwebs, he pushed past the stacks of dust-covered boxes, drawing ragged breaths in the hot, musty air.

There it was, just as he remembered: a small trunk that held all that was left of his mama. He wrestled open the rusty hasps to find her old housedress and wig, both of which he'd held onto. Combined with a faded sepia photograph of her as a young woman, they were his sole inheritance.

After removing his travel clothes, Christian put on the ample shift and messy blonde hair. He pulled the sheeting from a nearby full-length mirror and admired himself. Indeed, he might look like a Christine, the girly-girl sobriquet Mason used to taunt him with, but no sirree bob, he was Christian, a man of consequence.

Chosen and Forgiven. He'd survived back then, as he would again.

❖

SHORTLY BEFORE six, clad in full Texas garb, Christian swung wide the doors at Bubba's.

"Dang if it ain't Pastor C!," a man called out.

"Mr. Secretary! You still my preacher?," another ribbed.

"Always, Jim-Bob. Yours an' everyone else's," he winked.

"A-men. What you're doin' out there, enforcing' the Word, makin' us the Christian nation we was meant to be, why you're a blessin' to us all."

"Much appreciated."

Glorying in the praise, Christian took a seat on one of the wooden benches, setting his hat beside him. Running fingers through his heavily pomaded hair, he raised an arm and Jaylin, the pretty little server, appeared at his side. Having not seen her for many a moon, it spooked him to see how much she favored Jessica. He shuddered and drove the thought away.

"Hows 'bout you bring me a sody-pop an' a plate of loaded fries? Heavy on the bacon. Dwight's on his way, so might as well make it a two-fer all 'round."

169

By the time the food and drinks arrived, Dwight was seated on the splintered bench across from him.

"You're lookin' mighty prosperous, Dwight. All good?"

"Mr. Secretary, I'm right as rain, an' all the better now you're here. Worried you'd gotten too big for yer britches when you didn't have time for me back to the church. Okay we talk a little business now?"

Christian clutched, but only for a moment. "Sure thing. Go on right ahead." Even if it was about Straight On, leastaways he wouldn't be face to face with Joss. Learning the boy remained in the ministry's employ and that Dwight thought him so fine had shaken him. Made him wonder why Joss hadn't exposed him, what with his fame an' his face showin' up everywheres, 'specially here where he was the pride an' joy. Then too, it had happened so long ago an' the boy musta been so off his head with drink an' drugs, likely t'was he didn't remember a thing. Still and all, there oughtn't ever be a face-to-face twixt the two.

"SWBN's been pullin' in more money than I know what to do with. Makes Headship's tithes look a pittance. Wanna say upfront, I used summat to buy me a spread near rivals Second Comin'."

Relieved it wasn't Straight On that Dwight wanted to discuss, Christian's nerves settled.

"You know I said 'fore I left you oughtta get yourself a place. One that befits your station. As to cash flow issue, I'll run it by my accountants."

"Aw thanks. Still, makes me feel better ta know all's good by you. I been raisin' my own herd out to my place, like you. Which brings ta mind—Tibbs get anywhere with your heifer?" Exeter Tibbs, the Book of Revelation-driven bovine expert whom Christian had engaged when he and Darlene bought Second Coming, was still trying to breed the biblically perfect Red Heifer, another prerequisite for End Times.

"He's close.'" A flash of suspicion crossed Christian's mind and he leaned in. "Say, you ain't tryin' to birth one-a my reds over to your place?"

"Pastor, it'd be a cold day in Hell I double-cross you like that. My herd's strictly for eatin'."

Christian stood, and raising his soda-pop, loudly proclaimed. "To Red! The gal what's gonna signal our journey home!" From around the diner, raucous cheers erupted from the knowing crowd.

46

May 26

EARLY THE NEXT morning, Christian's personal plane, The Messiah, lifted off at dawn from the runway at Second Coming, bound for Hood River. Referencing the recent attempt on his life, Christian secured a vow of silence from Digger Tuttle, his well-recompensed pilot, a man who had been with him since the early years. Digger would tell no tales.

"Wait here Tuttle. Should be but a coupla two hours. Might could be less." Digger nodded and as soon as the secretary walked away, he pulled out his stash of rumpled girlie magazines.

Hesitantly, Christian stepped into the waiting helicopter. Prior to leaving D.C., he'd found a retired pilot to ferry him to and from Portland. The airman, a strong believer, lived in one of the area's rural Christian communities. Aside from a none-too-subtle threat should the fly-boy talk, not another word passed between them, not even when Christian changed into his mother's clothes.

One dowdy, overweight woman clambered down from the helicopter, near the city's downtown. According to his research he knew that Resistance members gathered on the plaza outside their destroyed former meeting place, The Grotto Bar and Cafe. Having landed fairly close by, it didn't take long for the tattered woman to navigate there.

Delilah was a leveling experience for the entire city. Six days had passed and, while some had fared better than others, none went unscathed. As with most tragedies, people felt the need to come together. Some of the survivors looked like they had lived on the street before the quake. Others gave the impression of having recently been prosperous, well dressed but as grimy and grim as the rest.

A jumble of chairs and tables salvaged from the square's former restaurants and bars, each of which had been busy with commerce a week earlier, filled the plaza. All that remained of The Grotto was its wooden floor, the rest of it having spilled out onto the leveled common space. People had cleared enough of the area so as to be able to congregate.

The rotund woman moved confidently among the mixed groups. She wouldn't have been the least bit surprised if, like her, some of the women she saw were men, and vice versa. Wending her way through the crowd, she stopped to listen at each gathering just long enough to hear the subject at hand. Passing several teens, one said in a voice so numb it chilled even Christian, "My dad died, and my mom can't get medicine for my dying sister."

Christian moved on.

Happening upon a larger group , she lingered at the edge. A bespectacled young man looked over and seeing Christian, greeted her with a welcoming smile, "Hey." Christian raised a hand to her throat to indicate she was mute, an idea come to her in the moment. A breeze kicked up and, hanging onto her wig for dear life, she was struck by the pungent odor coming from her armpits. No matter, she thought. In this group, it would serve as a mark of belonging. Christian felt an unexpected exhilaration from the sense of freedom which the disguise gave him.

The day was unusually damp and cool for June. The shabby woman pulled a thermos of coffee from her bag and moving closer, unscrewed the top and took a pull of the lukewarm brew, then passed the vessel on to the worn-looking young man next to her. Hand after dirty hand, the strangers passed the liquid around until it was gone. To each grateful thank you, she patted her throat, reemphasizing her condition. After the offering, no one questioned the large woman's presence.

At first all Christian caught were scattered phrases, none of which meant anything. About to move on, she stopped short when she overheard the words "hidden server."

"At least we figured out how to get around the tech block. This time." A young woman countered. "This is the federal government we're up against. They'll come up with something we won't be able to bypass and you'd better believe that'll happen soon. We have to let Lucy know what's going on and fast."

Sheeeee-it! Lucy! As in LucyInTheSky. Lord-a-mercy, if he wasn't Johnny-On-the Spot, then who the fuck was?

What to do? He could call in the troops and take out the lot of them, but instinct told him to wait until he had more. This was the time to exercise patience.

It began to rain. Those who had them pulled out umbrellas, ponchos, plasticized tarps. The wind picked up and Christian shivered in the thin dress. A ghostly-looking teen rushed up and laid a poncho over her shoulders. Taken aback by the gesture, Christian indicated her gratitude.

It struck him that all he had seen from these people was kindness. In that instant, when he felt a hint of doubt about them, he shut the feeling down. After all, they had rejected the Lord, or at least the Lord he and Alger worshipped. They deserved what they had coming, and he was there to ensure they'd get it.

That was when he overheard someone say, "As long as we stay a step ahead of them, we'll be okay." Unbeknownst to Christian, the voice belonged to Josh Rubens, the head of Western Resistance. He scoffed to himself, "A step ahead? Hah! Not with Christine Hillcox, Girl Detective!" With that thought, he decided it was time to head back to Washington, but he would return.

Leaving the plaza, his eyes lit upon a woman slumped against the remnants of a wall, her breathing shallow. A laceration running the length of her arm oozed green and she looked to be near death. As her lids fluttered, she caught his eye. Perhaps it was the moment of doubt he had just experienced, but all at once, he found himself back at the Tex-Mex border when he was eighteen years old, running drugs and, unknowingly, humans. Here, on this chilly Portland afternoon, he could almost feel the stifling heat of the semi's interior when, on that long ago day, he watched one barely-alive illegal beg for her life with her eyes, seemingly the exact same eyes with which this woman looked at him now. Thrust back to the split-second decision when he made the choice to smother the migrant rather than risk future identification, Christian forced himself to look away .

After all, his role in that long-ago death was what had brought him to God, proving there is a reason for everything.

Today, as he watched the woman on the sidewalk take her last breath, her death stare locked on him, he shook himself and quickly took his leave. These people were godless traitors who, given half the chance, would willfully destroy him and the greater mission. They had already tried once.

"I am John Christian Hillcox, Secretary of Faith to the United Christian States of America. Not a man to be trifled with," a voice inside his head intoned. "I'll be back." The large woman climbed inside the helicopter and suited up, morphing back into the man of stature he was. As the chopper rose, Christian looked down on the ruined city, struck by the thought that, dressed as the mother he had lost at four years of age, today she had cloaked him, from on high, in her protection.

Although the return trip took the remainder of the day, it was time well spent. As he neared the Capital, Christian's thoughts returned to the Resisters. Most incredible to him was that these people didn't see the good that he and Alger offered. If they didn't come around soon, there would be Hell to pay.

Liz kept up to the minute with the activity in Portland. For the fourth time that day, she logged on under the moniker, #Lucy-InTheSky, to see what was happening.

The most important thing was that Liz be ready for the inevitable. There was a system in place for when a cell was discovered; after a short time of inactivity, another would continue their work. Before Delilah, Josh Rubens in the West, Bill Tyson in the Midwest, and Liz in the East represented the three regions. The fact that fear kept so many silent was no indication of what the majority of citizens felt. It was Liz's belief that, except for the hard-core religionists, Americans wanted their country back.

Pacem in Terris

Ryan Gray and Josh Rubens had maintained their relationship over the years, seeking out opportunities to spend time together whenever they could. They'd sailed together as children and talked about girls as teens. Come 2015, their conversations turned almost exclusively to politics.

On the morning of November 8, the day after Alger had won, Ryan immediately set to work secretly siphoning off PAX's most sophisticated weapons, storing them in shipping containers on a piece of property he had bought for this purpose. He and Josh made a point to rendezvous monthly on a little-traveled road outside of Yakima, a city roughly halfway between Spokane and Portland.

On the morning of June 3, the old friends sat in Josh's car, on a cutout that looked out over a lake, their windows open to the scent of pine. They marveled at nature's ability to retain so much beauty in a world turned ugly and menacing.

Josh updated Ryan on the Resistance and in return, Ryan told him about the weapons cache he'd amassed.

"You're kidding me, right?"

"I already have four containers packed with drones, hand-held missiles, and rocket launchers and can get much, much more. I can start sending them your way as soon as you have somewhere to store them."

"For real? Because we literally stumbled on the perfect place last week. A deep cave hollowed out of a mountain on the western side of the Cascades. We figure it was there from the war. Probably used for the same purpose—weapons storage."

"Now you're blowing me away. Were there any signs there of recent activity?"

"Not a one. We were scouting out a place in case we have to retreat. It's in the middle of nowhere and clearly abandoned. It's perfect."

"It sounds too good to be true but, on your word, let's move on it. Do whatever it takes to make it operational ASAP. I'd like to begin sending transports there to free up space at my end and keep the pipeline moving. Oh, and we'll need an airstrip."

"I'll get right on it as soon as I get back."

Josh rested his head on the seatback. "Who could have guessed that one day the two of us would stand together at the forefront of the fight against evil?"

They sat together a while longer, each one daring to feel hope for the first time in months.

47

May 27

FLANKED BY SECRET Service, the First Family made its customary Sunday morning promenade down the center aisle of Living Word Fellowship, the official church of the United Christian States of America. Located inside the former Air and Space Museum, several galleries had been joined together to make up the mega-worship space, one that was filled every Sunday. Row after row of congregants rose in homage to the president and his mission. Membership was mandatory for all of those who worked in government, no matter their position, and attendance was scrupulously taken at the doors. A meeting spot for the Washington elite, underlings looking to scrabble up the socio-political ladder benefited as well, the weekly gatherings being the place to see and be seen. Instead of former entitlement deductions, twenty percent was automatically subtracted from government employee paychecks, at all levels below Agency Heads, indicated as 'Required Tithe,' swelling Faith's bank account as well as that of the good and godly Pastor Roland Culpepper.

Christian had led four services in as many months. While marginally more subdued than the holy-roller sermons he preached in San Antonio, each time he addressed the congregation, the worshippers left excited and inspired to meet the week ahead. Scheduled to deliver today's homily, 'Dare to Discipline,' Christian was weary from travel and lack of sleep, so he begged off, promising a raincheck. Instead, he sat as usual with the Cabinet and their families in the rows directly behind the president. Flushed with excitement from his progress, he determined to keep what he knew to himself until he had more. He could hardly wait for his next trip to Portland.

48

SEATED AT THE bar in the Old Ebbitt Grill, Bruce Bauman awaited Byron, hoping for a short night. The odds were in his favor, what with all the good-looking women there, looking to score.

Byron greeted him with cheer, "Hey buddy, how goes it? Good day off?"

"Decent. I got some things done I'd been putting off. And you? How was work?"

"Quiet." He waved the waiter over, flashed his Select Pass, and ordered a round of drinks. "I did hear that Alger, Patience, and Hillcox had a big pow-wow. Alger's furious and wants Patience to give Christian whatever he needs to stop the continuing leaks. Seems Tubs-O-Lard hasn't been able to get it done, and the Administration has had to scramble more than once to undo the damage. Cutting the Resisters off is now priority numero uno for Alger. He even went so far as to put it on National Emergency standing."

The hairs on Bruce's neck stood at attention. He needed to go home and tell Liz so she could get everyone offline right away. While all Bruce could think about was how to get out of there, Byron scoped out the bar. Libations were delivered and Byron took a long and thirsty sip.

Bruce hadn't heard a word recently about Jessica's disappearance and he'd made it a point not to ask too often so as to avoid seeming overly interested. But it had been several days since he'd last brought it up, so he pushed ahead. "Heard anything lately about that woman at Faith, the one they caught copying papers?"

"Not formally."

"For whatever reason," Bruce said, "an awful lot of troubles come out of Hillcox's department. Everyone knows he's not up to the task. It's a wonder Alger keeps him on."

Byron drained his drink. "Yeah, it really is. To tell the truth, he never impressed me. Funny you should bring up the girl. I overheard a couple of guys today saying that guards had found her in an old copy room scanning classified documents. Apparently, after a rough interrogation, she vanished. You can guess what that means. Cruel as it may sound, it makes sense. You can't keep a traitor like that around, no matter how hot she was. You wanna hear a good one?"

Bruce nodded, so as not to talk.

"Word around Faith is that Hillcox had a thing for her."

Of a sudden, Byron lost interest in the conversation and in Bruce. Byron shifted his gaze to the mirror across from them to check himself out, his self-admiration allowing Bruce's grief-filled features to go unnoticed. Ensuring that his hair was in place, Byron flashed himself a camera-ready smile. A curvaceous blonde alone at a nearby table saw his grin in the reflection and assumed it was directed at her. She rearranged her dress in obvious invitation, Byron's finely honed sexual antennae picking up as he stood.

"Sorry bro, but it seems the night's entertainment beckons," and without a goodbye, he was off.

"Enjoy," Bruce called to his retreating back. He paid the tab and hurriedly departed.

Liz was on her computer when Bruce returned. He sat down opposite her.

"They have Jessica," he said without expression.

"Who?"

"Faith."

"You know this for sure?"

"I do. There's more. Alger is throwing everything they've got at Christian to ensure he puts an end to the Resistance's ability to transmit on the Shadow Web. As of today, it's their top priority."

Liz grabbed her sat-phone and texted Josh, "Betsy's daughter cut her first tooth," code for 'Everyone go dark at once!'

"We've gotta get Matt out of here."

Matt had been absent from Faith for five days. In this time, Christian would undoubtedly have learned of the relationship between Matt and Jessica and dispatched his enforcers to bring him in. It was time to move.

It was past curfew, too late to risk being on the roads. An hour later, at ten o'clock, Liz told Matt to pull together his false papers and pack a light bag. He feared the worst but asked nothing. At seven the next morning, Liz backed the car out of the driveway, Matt prone in the backseat. When they crossed into Maryland, Liz told him he could sit up and she explained everything. Gutted, he didn't speak the rest of the way. When they pulled up to Manny's warehouse, the shell-shocked young man tonelessly said goodbye and trudged off to the loading dock where Manny awaited with instructions.

Twenty minutes later, Matt was at the wheel of a delivery truck, filled with athletic gear, headed towards Cleveland. With luck on his side, he breezed through the checkpoints, arriving at the Beachwood store by early afternoon. Per Manny's directions, he put the keys in the drop box and disappeared into the streets.

For the second time in five days, Liz and Bruce relocated, this time to a safe house in the northeastern part of the city.

49

Eight a.m.

LIZ IMMEDIATELY made her way to Eric's office. What she needed to say could not wait.

He looked up as she put her finger to her lips. She picked up a felt-tipped pen and paper and wrote, "I have to get to Portland ASAP."

"Why?," he scribbled back.

"Shadow Web's no longer safe. Need to talk in person."

They traded looks. Knowing one another so well, they could read each other's minds.

50

Ten a.m.

ERIC EMPTIED his pockets, set his jacket and shoes on the conveyor, and after a thorough wanding, the security guard waved him through. A sign announced, "You have entered the Department of Faith of The United Christian States of America. May God Be With You."

He walked beneath rows of massive photographs of Christian that filled the soaring space, each one suspended from the ceiling by heavy gold chains. The blow-ups were of Christian ministering to the masses, or standing alongside former politicians and world leaders with whom he used to have a relationship. The display had been psychologically en-gineered to heighten feelings of impotence and subservience in those who visited Faith.

In the center of the lobby, a gilded case held a well-worn Bible atop a pillow of royal purple. The label read:

Secretary of Faith Christian Hillcox's First Bible.
Presented to Him by his Father at the Age of Six.

While the Bible was indeed Christian's first, this particular good book came not from his father, but from his first grade teacher at Victory Baptist Elementary in Pearsall, Texas. In point of fact, anyone who knew Mason would roar with laughter at the suggestion that he'd ever had a biblical thought in his life unless one considered "Men what lay with men are faggots" to be scriptural.

Eric sensed the evil surrounding him. It wasn't hard to do. Uncertain he could pull off what he had come for, he was nonetheless determined. Riding the escalator to the top floor, he was faced with a stern portrait of the secretary, its Mona Lisa-like eyes following him, increasing his apprehension. The remaining wall space was filled with framed 'historical' documents interspersed with gilded plaques bearing Scripture, each verse cherry picked as proof of the forefathers' Christian intent. He thought back to the day, thirteen years earlier when, a week before the National Museum of African-American History and Culture opened, he had come to this very office to interview the managing director. It had been a hopeful time, one that suggested the country might be at the start of reckoning with the sin of slavery. But that was not to be. Were it not for the gravity of today's situation, there was nothing on earth that could have brought him back to the nefarious devolution of this building.

He noted the cameras pointed at him, pasted on a smile, and entered Christian's outer office, nodding to Lurleen.

She spoke into the intercom, "Eric Mansour here to see you."

"Send him in."

Christian stood behind his desk, his hand outstretched, "If this ain't a surprise. Never thought I'd see the day you'd come to my lair."

"May I?" And Eric sat. "You continue to think I'm not on your side, sir, when nothing could be further from the truth. Like my network's name, we believe in giving viewers the truth and in that vein, I have an idea I think you'll like."

"I'm all ears." Christian leaned back, his expression cynical.

"How about we put together a production to tell Faith's story? Call it "Secretary *John Christian Hillcox's Soul-Saving Gift to The Territories.*" Shoot it somewhere near Portland, using locals as actors. Keep it simple, keep it real." A master of his facial expressions, Eric gave nothing of his concern away. This had to work.

Hillcox muscled himself upright. "I declare, t'aint what I expected from you. Cain't b'lieve I'm sayin' this but I like the idea, indeed I do. Could it be you've come 'round after all? What say I put you together with Jeremiah York, head a Faith's TV an' Brandin '? See what the two of you come up with."

"That would be great."

Christian got Jeremiah on the line. "One o'clock today," he told Eric. "Two floors down."

"I'll be there. This'll be great. You'll see."

Further polishing the apple on his way out, he called back, "By the way, nice place you got here!"

Eric met with York after lunch. It would be an hour-long piece and they'd shoot in Troutdale, sixteen miles east of Portland. At both beginning and end, TBT's remaining Portland anchor, Rick Stubbins, would read a statement from

President Alger on the importance of ignoring all news unless it came from the State.

That afternoon, Liz sent a coded interoffice memo to Stubbins: "If you get a chance, would you check on my cousin Ben? My Aunt Ruth hasn't heard from him since the earthquake even though he lives nearby. Understandably, she's in a panic. If he's okay, please let her know."

Stubbins replied immediately, "I've seen Ben myself. He's fine and will get to her as soon as he can. Meanwhile, I'll make sure she knows. Best."

51

Three p.m.

PAPERS WERE fanned out across the oak table in Faith's conference room as Christian prepared the commencement speech he was to give Wednesday morning at The Talmudic University of Florida. Summaries of completed legislation were spread across the surface, there to jog his memory, reminding him of the enormous number of bills the 121st Congress had already passed. There was nothing in his oration that would speak to the graduates or their futures. Invigorated by the inroads he'd made outside The Grotto last Saturday, and also looking forward to the coming TBT documentary, the self-congratulatory words flowed until he was interrupted by a knock on the door.

"Who is it?" he snapped, his irritation evident.

"Zeb."

"C'mon in then," he barked.

Zeb Alperstein pushed open the door. Named Zebulon after one of the Twelve Tribes of Israel, Alperstein was born and bred in Brooklyn's Crown Heights. Despite being raised in the Hasidic enclave, Zeb reached adulthood as the only one of nine children to have developed a sense of religious skepticism. After graduation from a local Jewish day school, he went on to Yeshiva University in Manhattan, a 'modern' Orthodox institution disdained by most Brooklyn Chabadniks. In his freshman year, he changed his major from Pre-Med to Poli Sci. The times he tried to talk politics over Shabbat dinners, his father would, in no uncertain terms, end the discussion, "Leave it alone, Zebulon."

Four years later, his parents' concerns about him evaporated when he told them he'd accepted a job with Health and Human Services in D.C.. It didn't take them long to realize that Zeb could do a lot more good working inside the government, advocating for Israeli and Jewish issues, than he could have had he become a doctor like his father and grandfather before him.

An ambitious young man, he climbed the ladder within D.C.'s rarefied ranks. In no time, he had mastered the nuances of political survival. No matter the reigning administration's politics, a chameleon-like ability made him a favorite of Democrats and Republicans alike. As a lifelong bachelor, his marriage was to his work.

Back when Alger was a congressman, he had chaired a subcommittee for HHS. It was then that he noticed Zeb, not only because of his keen intelligence, but also due to his appearance. Up until then, he had never been around this kind of Jew, and he found his dress and facial hair bizarre, cultic even. At that time, Zeb had maintained his Orthodox dress because it set him apart. He dropped the costume shortly thereafter, but when it became evident that the Republican Party and its Christian Zionist wing were on the rise, Zeb read the tea leaves and resumed his Hasidic dress. When Alger assumed the presidency, he remembered Zeb as the only Jew he knew who fit the biblical narrative, so he appointed him ambassador to Israel. Since Israel remained one of the UCSA's few foreign delegations, Alger put them under Faith's umbrella, inside Christian's building, one floor below. Zeb was as well positioned as a Jew could be.

For the first time since he began to work in government, Zeb wrestled with the promotion. Obvious to him were Hillcox's, and thus the entire Administration's naked manipulation of the Jewish people. Theirs was a feigned love, one that was completely transparent, but only to those paying attention. They traded on the Jewish fear of persecution in order to accomplish their biblically motivated goals, and they did so with great success. With the enormous sums of money that CZOA and similar ministries provided Israel and Israel-loving politicians, a Faustian bargain was struck—one that had lasted over thirty-five years. Payment, however, was soon to come due.

Coupled with the undisguised anti-Semitic remarks that Alger and Hillcox traded, words often spoken in Zeb's presence, working for them proved repellent from the get-go. For Zeb, though the impetus for political expediency was gone, he decided it was wiser to remain inside the tent and know what was going on than to be outside and ignorant.

"Good afternoon, Mr. Secretary."

Zeb was the last person Christian wanted to see. He didn't have the will or the energy for him. A more honest truth was that he found him repulsive: his dirty hair, long, scraggly beard and side curls, the same greasy suit he wore day after day. If times were different, he'd request a more presentable Jew, but the game of biblical chess was complex, and Zeb knew it better than most. If nothing else, he convinced the hardliners in Israel that Alger was one with them.

Christian put on a welcoming smile. "Glad you stopped by, Zebulon. You're a much needed tonic on this gloomy day. What brings you here?"

Zeb took a seat. "I've just returned from Jerusalem. Something happened during my visit that I found deeply disturbing."

"What thing?," the challenge in Christian's voice clear.

Zeb had come today determined to resign, but he immediately lost his nerve. Surrounded by the power Christian represented, Zeb was overcome by feelings of impotence. As shaken as he was by what he had seen, the fear he felt here and now reduced him to silence, diminishing him in his own mind. On the spot, he changed what he had planned to say.

"While the Israelis are relieved we've joined them in finally putting an end to the farcical discussion of two states, I myself had a near miss on Thursday. I was in East Jerusalem when a suicide bomber blew himself up not far from me, killing a family of five, along with himself."

"Hah! You don't gotta tell me about assassination!"

"Unreported in Israeli media was that the bomber turned out to be a Hasid," Zeb added.

"I heard 'bout the bombin'," Christian said. "Didn't know it was Yid on Yid."

Zeb recoiled.

"S'pose I oughtn't say words like Yid or Hebe in front-a you. I'll try to watch it."

In truth, it wasn't so much the bombing that had bothered Zeb. What ate at him was what his life had turned into: the people he shilled for, and for what Israel itself had become. He could no longer bear to be a part of it.

What he dared not tell Christian was that he had visited a settlement that abutted a centuries-old olive grove. The ancient trees had been in a Palestinian family for generations. The Israeli government looked away, as usual, when settlers destroyed the grove in order for the settlement, Har Tala, to expand. When Zeb asked a trio of settlers what had happened to the Palestinian farmers, a bearded Jew with a Brooklyn accent scoffed, "Farmers? Feh. You mean the filthy arabosh, the human waste who stole our land? They scurried back to their terrorist nests is what happened." The Israeli spat onto the dry ground, turned his back, and stalked off.

For reasons he did not fully understand, Zeb returned that afternoon. From one hilltop over, he spotted several tents pitched next to a spring beyond the now barren field. He looked down to see an Arab woman doing laundry, surrounded by young children playing in the dirt. Suddenly, reports from a rifle rang out and Zeb watched the woman and children fall to the ground. Turning in the direction of Har Tala, he saw a settler shoulder his weapon and disappear.

Lurleen entered the conference room, returning Zeb to the present. She cleared a place in front of them and set down a pot of freshly brewed coffee and a platter of pastries. The treats thankfully diminished the expectation of conversation. Watching crumbs collect in Zeb's beard, Christian looked away in disgust. Wolfing down the sweets, Christian thought nothing of own piggishness.

"Zeb, now that you're here, it's me what's got somethin' ta say. You been loyal to our shared biblical goals, but I been thinkin' how lately, you've gone weak on Zi-on." He paused. "Muslim chatter's at a high, an' all it'd take is a couple of A-rabs settin' off a dirty bomb or three an' we'll have ourselves a nucular beginning of End Times. While that's our goal, we're not quite ready."

Zeb sipped his coffee so as not to answer. If he did, there'd be no stopping him. He couldn't keep the recent killings out of his mind, all the while Christian cited Ezekiel, "'*I will take you from the nations and gather you from all the countries and bring you into your own land.*' Get ourselves a coupla-twelve thousand more Hebes over there an' the King will return."

Previously, Zeb had seen Christian's messianic zeal as crazy talk, but he'd never taken it seriously. What he knew now, though, was that those in power today had both the will and the means to end the world. Then and there, seated across from Christian, Zeb committed to the notion that not only would he escape, but that once he did, he'd do everything in his power to help bring the lot of them down. First, he'd have to figure out how.

52

Oregon, May 30

AS THE GROUP circled down the backside of the coastal mountain, they covered as many miles in a day as the terrain and weather permitted. Surviving on berries, greens, and small game, they filled their containers whenever they came upon a stream. At day's end, they'd build a fire and make camp, huddling together more for connection than warmth. The going was punishing, so much so that two of them didn't make it. A young woman, who early on had provided Ned great solace, fell into a deep hole, and when the most experienced climber among them threw down a rope to rescue her, the ground beneath gave way and he too disappeared into the void. Having become as close as family, the loss touched each of them deeply with a kind of pain that, so far, only Ned had experienced. None of them would know the fate of their own families until, and if, they made it home.

They hiked up and over great uprooted old-wood trees, detouring around crevasses so deep they seemed to reveal the earth's core. Drenched from intermittent downpours, they slipped and slid, suffered cuts, gashes, twisted ankles and bruises, but still they progressed.

Along the way they came upon others, people who resembled ghosts more than human beings, and, like a snowball, their band of survivors grew. As macabre as the situation was, and despite his grief, Ned was surprised to feel a certain lightening of spirit. While he would never recover from his loss, no longer did he want to die. In fact, he very much wanted to live and do what he could to pay back a world that, prior to the quake, he had worked to destroy.

Another lifelong trope of Ned's was upended when early on, he learned that Ben was a Jew. Up till then, Ned had viewed Hebrews exclusively as Jesus rejectors, as the people who caused His death. But here and now, in this devastated landscape, he stood as one with Ben, understanding that what he'd been taught about Jews from childhood on had only and always been lies. Yes, Ben Aronson was possessed, but possessed with grace, intelligence, and compassion. Mere hours into this existential journey, Ned held Ben close to his heart, believing in him over any idea of God.

There came a collective gasp when, at last, they reached the road. Great slabs of concrete thrust their way upwards towards a mocking, sun-filled sky. Scarcely recognizable as the cars and trucks they used to be, vehicles lay flattened like jumbo-sized tin cans. Some held drivers and passengers, frozen at the moment of death, impaled by steering rods, smothered by airbags, flattened into blood-smeared pancakes of flesh and bone. Dogs, half dead, limped across the fractured pavement. It was a scene to surpass any Hell that Dante ever conjured.

The final leg of their journey found them on the outskirts of Portland. Though corpses littered the ground in varying states of decay, the able-bodied still fought against the odds to assist the wounded. In the end, it was the heroism they witnessed that kept the group going. As it made its way towards the city center, Ned came upon scene after scene of compassion, each one moving him in ways his former religion never had.

Travelers began to peel off at their respective crossroads, each one looking to pick his or her way down the ravaged streets in search of loved ones, even as they prepared themselves for the likelihood that they would find neither home nor family. They neared the plaza and what remained of The Grotto. Ben asked the others to hang back while he went ahead to assess the situation. As he moved through the clusters of people, his thoughts tracked back to the morning of May 30, when he and Josh had had coffee together inside The Grotto to discuss the Resistance's next steps. The meeting happened to take place on the day before Ben would leave for a brief, but much-needed couple of days to himself, hiking the trails above the coast.

And so it was with incredulity that he looked up to see Josh before him, the same look of disbelief on both of their faces. In something of a daze, they spent a few moments trading stories. That was when Ben learned that Christian had named the earthquake Delilah, that the president told the nation it was a minimal event, and that the federal government had done nothing besides sending in teams of proselytizers, just as Ned had predicted.

53

Christian's Soul-Saving Gift
to The Territories

ERIC AND LIZ put together a script in short order. It centered around the secretary's enduring belief that all sinners should have the chance to choose eternal life.

At 6:00 a.m. on June 4, Liz and Eric boarded a small government jet. Jeremiah York was already there, eagerly awaiting them. The crew sat in the back of the plane. Once he and Liz settled in, Eric handed York the draft for final approval. He sped through the forty-seven pages, and beamed, "This is terrific! Exactly the story Christian wants told."

"We're happy with it. And Liz is a great director. Wait till you see."

TBT's team had cast the documentary with locals from Troutdale, the characters running the gamut from young to old and black to white. Asians, gays and transsexuals, each selected to play to the stereotype the Washington elite believed represented the region. These day-players signed their releases, relieved to get the cash.

A local crew member met them at the Troutdale airfield and drove them to set where Liz went straight right to work blocking the action. Eric stood on the sidelines with York, ready to begin his charm offensive. Liz began to shoot the first scene in the distance when Eric started in. His easy smile and evident confidence made Jeremiah feel a ready closeness. Eric sensed the shift and led the conversation as planned.

"You know, I don't generally share what I'm about to say, even with close friends, but there's something about you that makes me think you'll understand. And not judge me." York felt that something special was opening up between the two of them. He had few real friends and none nearly as charismatic as Eric, so he answered, "I would never judge you." And he meant it.

"Good. Here's my story in a nutshell. I used to be pretty wild-ass – sex, drugs, alcohol, you name it, I did it. The night I woke up in a jail cell surrounded by the lowest of the low, I had something of a revelation. I was smart enough to understand that my behavior was a poor substitute for whatever it was that I lacked. Mother-love, father-love, who knows. I needed help and if I didn't get it, my future didn't hold anything good. As I saw it, I had two options: religion or rehab. I went with God and the choice turned my life around.

"I don't know if the secretary said anything to you but I was something of a leftie journalist during those years—you know, save the world and all that—and knowing that has made it difficult for him to see me as I am today. I only hope that our work here will make him realize I'm fully onboard with him."

"God's truth, I wouldn't worry. He mentioned his concerns but as soon as you came up with *Soul Saving*, he seemed to relax."

"I hope so."

Skillfully, Eric shifted the focus to Jeremiah, his interest in him flattering. "How did you come to Jesus, if you don't mind my asking?"

"Like you, I suppose. Different behavior, same outcome. Sexual addiction has always been a problem for me and I succumbed at the wrong time, with the wrong woman, in the wrong place. You see, I'm married, with five children."

"No way. You're not old enough!"

"I married young. Way too young. Should have waited. Sowed my oats. Anyways, one afternoon my wife Georgina went out shopping for a couple of hours. She'd only just arrived at the mall when she felt a headache coming on, so she turned around and came home. I didn't hear anything until she opened the door to our bedroom and, there I was, *in flagrante delicto*. With Tish, her best friend."

"Oof!"

"You can say that again."

"Without a word, Tish swept past Georgina, and immediately after, Georgina called the children home. She helped them pack, and told them to wait for her in the van, her plan being to leave for Nebraska and her parents. That was when I fell at her feet, swearing on the Lord I would never cheat again. A devout woman, the marriage covenant is as sacred to her as anything, so she allowed me one last chance. I've behaved since that day, not that it's been easy. Like now when I look at your girl over there," he pointed to Liz. "You can't tell me you don't have thoughts."

Eric let out a long, low whistle, "Thoughts? Fact is, I've got plans. I'm thinking to assert myself on her tonight. She doesn't have a clue."

York raised an eyebrow. Oddly, knowing that Eric would have his way with her helped. "With all my heart, I say, go for it, man. But only if you share every last detail."

Liz saw them tittering away, reassured that Eric was making headway. As Director, she was more focused than she'd ever been in her professional life, the goal being to finish the day early. At three o'clock, she called out, "Cut! That's a wrap for today. There's not much left so we'll finish tomorrow. I want everyone on set at 6:30." Approaching York, she explained, "What with travel and the time change, the D.C. crew is pretty wasted. I have a couple of scenes left to shoot here and, other than my interview with Secretary Hillcox, we're done. We'll be finished here by noon tomorrow. If it's okay with you?"

"Fine with me," and he dirty-winked at Eric. "I blocked off three days for this so it's not a problem." Liz walked away and York whispered to Eric, "I got you your lay-over," both of them chuckling at the juvenile double-entendre. "You got it 'coming,'" and again, they chortled like frat boys. "Assert your headship man, it's your right."

"Jeremiah, I'm just spit balling here, but there are a few hours of daylight left. I'm wondering if Liz and I should try and get to Portland to lay eyes on our studio. No one's complained but I get the impression they're holding back. What do you think?"

"Not a bad idea. In fact, it could up your status with Hillcox. Since we lost our UCSA headquarters, he's wanted someone to come out and check on the station. As I'm sure you know, TBT plays an outsized role in our communications strategy. Be careful and make sure you're out before dark. Word is, that's when the natives get restless." York made a quick call, then delivered the good news: a government helicopter would take them to Portland and back. He told Eric where to meet the chopper and, after sharing one last prurient look with Eric said, "I'll see you both on set at 6:30."

On his way to the Motel 6, the only Troutdale accommodation still open, Jeremiah thought with pleasure about the bond he'd cemented between TBT and Faith. He was even more excited by the friendship he'd started up with a man like Eric.

As they neared the city, what Liz saw below brought her to tears. The destruction was more extreme than any war zone she'd covered and she had covered a lot. Coincidentally, the pilot found the same makeshift landing pad Christian had used and, after a short walk, they stood outside BEST's back door. Built in 2008 to withstand earthquakes, the building had held up well. The exterior's cracked facade gave them pause, but once inside, they were comforted to see that the interior was fully intact. The space was not only safe, it buzzed with activity.

Josh rushed to greet her, "Liz! At last!" and he pulled her in close. Overcome with emotion, neither spoke, tears pooling in Liz's eyes, threatening to spill over.

She clasped Eric's forearm, "This is the man I've been telling you about."

He held out a hand, "Eric Mansour."

"Liz has told us so much about you. We're honored to have you on the team."

"Don't be ridiculous. I'm the one who's grateful. It took a lot to convince this one here to let me in. She's one hard-headed woman."

Liz exclaimed, "You people are wonders. There are no words for what we saw on our way in. What you're going through . . . ."

"You do what you have to. At least we're not living under Alger."

"I'd love to keep talking but we've a lot to cover and not much time, so let's get cracking."

Ned joined them and Josh said, "This is Ned. He might be our most valuable resource. He used to work at Faith but he's one of us now."

"That's a story I want to hear," Liz said, "but we'll save it for another day. I hope you don't think me rude."

"Not a bit. Follow us."

Portland being Portland, there were solar panels on many buildings, the drugstore's headquarters being one, meaning they had electricity. And science being science, researchers had created a gel-filled sponge that, once submerged, filtered out dangerous contaminants, giving citizens potable water. The technology was so extraordinary that even after toxic spills into the Bull Run Watershed and Columbia South Shore Well Field, the city had enough to drink.

Prior to Delilah, the first floor of BEST's headquarters served as the company's flagship drugstore, but to locals it was best known for its lively retro lunch counter. After the earthquake, Chad Bergstrom, BEST's CEO and a major Resistance supporter, turned over the building and its adjoining warehouse to Josh and Ben, both of whom he greatly admired. While volunteers distributed the headquarters' vast stock of non-perishables and medications from a door that opened onto the alley behind, Josh, Ben, and Ned ran strategy up front.

As the foursome progressed through the space, Josh looked at Liz. "We've gone dark like you asked. While I get it, I have to say it worries me. If we stop putting out our reality, trust me, we'll be forgotten. Are you sure it's the right move?"

"It's the only move. And it's temporary. We can't afford for Washington to find out what you're up to."

Josh and Ben filled them in. Liz and Eric were heartened to learn that, despite the earthquake, the Resistance was far more robust than they'd imagined. And when Josh told them about Ryan and the Cascades Control Center, they felt the first stirrings of hope since the takeover.

Greatly fortified, Eric explained the need for them to leave after such a short time together. "We've got York where we need him and don't want to give him any reason to suspect we're other than we appear."

"Smart. It's no time to get sloppy. At least we had the chance to bring you up to date."

They said their goodbyes and Liz and Eric headed out. On the way back to the helicopter, they heard a rustling in the shadows, bringing them to an abrupt halt.

"Who goes there?," asked an unseen voice.

Eric nudged Liz behind a bush. "Who are *you*?"

A uniformed man showed himself, rifle in his hand. "Lieutenant Selwyn here. Department of Faith, Curfew Enforcement. State your name and business." He lifted his rifle .

"I'd put that gun down if I were you. It so happens that I'm head of TBT. A little network you may have heard of?" Slowly, so as not to startle him, Eric took his card and signed pass from his pocket and handed them to Selwyn. "Seems we have the same boss."

Selwyn immediately backed down. "Apologies, sir. I wouldn't have stopped you but for orders. You understand." That was when the soldier spotted Liz's heel. He kicked at the bush, Eric's eyes focused on the gun .

"Now, now. What do we have here, Mr. Broadcast Man?" He used the tip of his rifle to urge Liz from the bushes. "Seems you feel the need to hide this, shall we say, lady of the night. Makes me think our boss wouldn't look too highly on your extracurriculars."

"Don't move Liz. He's armed." Looking hard at Selwyn, Eric snapped, "How dare you? This is my colleague, Liz Boorman. Also here at the Secretary's behest. She's hiding because men like you are hardly known for treating women well."

Selwyn shone a flashlight on Liz's papers, contritely lowering the gun when he saw they were also legitimate

Greatly chastened, he grumbled, "On your way then," and melted away as quickly as he'd appeared.

The rest of the trip was uneventful. In Troutdale, after checking into the motel, Liz and Eric spent the next few hours reviewing what they'd learned.

When the sky began to lighten, York looked out his window to see Eric in yesterday's clothes creeping along the balcony from Room 206 to 207, and he smirked.

At two o'clock that same afternoon, Eric, Liz and Jeremiah boarded the plane bound for Washington. Five hours later, two fast friends and a woman disembarked from the plane.

54

June 6

AFTER CHRISTIAN delivered his address at Talmudic University, he shook a few hands, gave a brief comment to the press, and made his exit. Landing in San Antonio later that day, he hurried home to spend the night in seclusion at Second Coming, ensuring that neither Dwight nor anyone else knew he was in town.

Early the next morning, John Christian Hillcox climbed into the cockpit of his private jet, The Messiah. Having kept his pilot's license current, he made the decision that from now on, he'd fly himself from San Antonio to Hood River. He should have done so from the start, but that was in the past. As he rose above the city, climbing higher, then higher still, it seemed he'd never felt closer to Father God than he did now. And that mattered.

55

June 7

THE FOUL-SMELLING woman in the ill-fitting housedress edged toward her 'friends' outside The Grotto when, from out of nowhere, a member of the Pastor Brigade stepped up, blocking her passage. His nametag read 'Lieutenant Chaplain Elwood Brickell, UCSA Department of Faith' and, dressed as he was in solid black, the uniform punctuated only by the UCSA silver cross, he projected dominance.

"As I live an' breathe, if you ain't the living vision of godlessness."

While Christian appreciated the authority the pastor projected, the fact that a member of his own organization had the potential to expose him and destroy his mission was unthinkable. Trapped by a situation of his own making, Christian chose to remain silent.

"I'm talkin' to you!," Brickell snapped. "Didn't your mama teach you manners?" He backed the impoverished woman against a slab of concrete and held her there at the point of a gun.

Silence.

"I'll tell you this, sweetheart," he snarled. "No one's comin' to save you. Only Jesus hisself can do that."

Silence.

Brickell's cheeks burned red. That this disheveled, desperate-looking woman dared disrespect a man of his stature enraged him, and he did not deal well with anger. In an exaggeratedly and mockingly slow meter, his voice spiked as with vigor he sneered, "Mebbe you cain't hear, so hows 'bout this. Can . . . you . . . read . . . my . . . lips?"

The volume with which he spoke rose in direct proportion to his ire. Christian cast down his eyes and stood stock still, trembling for fear that someone would recognize him. So far today, Brickell had been shunned by everyone he'd approached, and he was in no mood for the disrespect coming from this malodorous mutant.

"'An' on the Eighth Day, God created you as a joke,' eh?," Brickell cackled, his casual cruelty meant for those nearby, satisfying him in a way that ministering did not.

The tenor of his voice, coupled with his wild gesticulations, drew attention their way. Ned glanced over to see the sort of man that, were he still at Faith, he would have dispatched. After a hard look at the pastor, he searched the woman's face to see how she was holding up, when it hit him like a ton of bricks. He'd know that face anywhere. Instead of a pitiful deaf-mute, Ned found himself looking at none other than the Secretary of Faith. In drag. Alarmed, he rushed to get out of sight—and fast, before Christian spotted him.

He sidled up to Ben and Josh and casually led them to the perimeter. "That woman over there, the one the Pastor is harassing—that's the Secretary of Faith as sure as I'm Ned Burroughs." Ben turned his head to look, but Ned stopped him cold. "Don't draw attention this way. What the hell is he doing here? This is unbelievable!"

"Are you sure it's him?"

"One hundred percent."

"Holy crap!," Ben exclaimed quietly. "What is *he* doing here? And for Christ's sake, why is he dressed as a woman?"

"It can only mean they're putting enormous pressure on him to flush us out."

"Ned, you've got to get outta sight. Now! If you recognize him dressed like he is, he'll know you at first glance." Heeding his advice, Ned ducked behind a nearby wall and watched. Josh issued his pre-established whistle and the Resistors dispersed.

The pastor had gotten nowhere with the vagrant. About to leave, he roared, "You revolting freak! If you think life on Earth has treated you poorly, just you wait for Eternity, when you will burn!"

That was when Brickell noticed Christian's whiskers. "Good God, you're a man!"

Christian pulled back.

"That's right, get away from me, you twisted freak!"

Ned took a certain pleasure in the Secretary's shame, but the sense of his own dishonor was the more powerful. After all, he had served in the very department that had hired this pastor, a man who took it upon himself to demean the desperate and in the name of his God. Since he couldn't change the past, a new energy surged through him. He would do whatever he could to stop these monsters and help rid the world of this human stain.

Shaken by the encounter, Christian stood stock still, waiting for Brickell to go. Josh's eyes, trained on Christian, signaled for the others to return. Once he explained the situation, but before Christian started to move their way, one of the Resisters exclaimed, "That woman! She's been here before. Anyone else remember? She passed around a thermos of coffee."

"Fuckin' A," another answered. "You're right! The cross-dresser who couldn't talk. You're saying *she's* the Secretary of Faith?"

"One and the same," Josh answered quietly. With the realization that Hillcox had been there before, and more than once, it was clear that Christian had come to spy. That he had not sent an employee spoke to the urgency of his mission.

On the spot, Josh determined that if it was information Hillcox wanted, information was what he'd get. As Christian drew near, Josh spoke out, "Everyone, listen up. I'd planned to hand out your marching orders today but I've decided to wait until Tuesday. By then we'll know for sure whether we'll be getting the outside help we need. Without it, as you well know, we're finished."

As if on cue, Ben picked up, "We'll meet here Monday afternoon at one. Till then, we'll do our best to get back online." Seemingly discouraged, they immediately dispersed, each of them going their separate ways.

Buoyed by what she had learned, the deaf mute turned and trundled off, Josh trailing from a safe distance. When the ponderous woman reached her destination, Josh watched as she boarded the chopper. When he could no longer see the helicopter, Josh returned to the plaza with the plan that, going forward, they would post a sentry at the helipad twenty-four hours a day to alert them when Christian returned, as they fully expected he would.

With luck, thanks to Ned's discovery, a grand disinformation campaign had just begun.

56

Hidden Assets

UNDER THE ANODYNE-sounding name, Event Planning Inc., Stefan Vargova developed his proprietary next-generation software, Image Screen Planning, or ISP. Vargova had figured out how to circumvent the most sophisticated security walls, even those of the military, by taking over enemy screens, seamlessly replacing reality with photos or footage of the client's choosing. When first designed, he realized that if the software fell into the wrong hands it would be catastrophic, so he kept the program to himself. If not for the collapse of America, he would have left it on the shelf, possibly forever. But after Alger's inauguration, he joined the Resistance and didn't think twice before offering it to Josh. When the time came, Vargova told them, they would switch it on and the Alger administration would no longer see reality. Instead, their screens would display weapons-free landscapes, urban or rural, replete with people, vehicles, or animals moving about, depending on the setting.

So fortified, if BEST was the brains of the Resistance, the Control Center was its beating heart.

57

June 9

AFTER LUNCH, Ben pushed back his chair to face Ned.

"Ned, Josh and I have been going back and forth, wondering whether or not you'd consider returning to D.C. and Faith. Then we realized it's not our call. You're the one who'd be going and taking all the risk. So let's talk."

Until that moment, neither Josh nor Ben had realized how much they needed him to say yes, how vitally important it was for him to be on the inside. Ned's expression was impossible to read for all the feelings swirling in his head, so when his answer came, it surprised them.

"I've actually been thinking the same thing. I'm ready. In fact I need to do this," he said with great confidence.

"I know these people, their fears and motivations. And when I walk in the door, I can only imagine Hillcox's hysteria, thinking I'm his own personal resurrection, God's chosen risen from the dead."

They couldn't help but titter at the vision.

"Here's the thing, Ned. We have word that an attack on Portland is imminent, which is why the time for you to go is now. With you on the inside, we'll learn when to expect them."

"I'm ready."

"You're sure?"

"Absolutely. Just give me my cover."

"Okay. When you see Hillcox, indulge his excitement. Once he's calmed down, explain to him that you and your family had taken a drive inland in order to connect with one of the Christian communities scattered across the state."

"Hillcox is well aware of them. Fact is, he sees them as eventual partners."

Josh continued, "It was providence that you were away from Portland when the quake hit so that not only were you spared, but these good people took in you and your entire family. It was so easy, so right just being with them, you could have stayed much longer. You'll know how to play it. Schmaltz it up as you see fit.

"Anyway, you couldn't stop thinking how, after such a purpose-driven blow to the West Coast, you'd be needed more than ever at Faith. You left your wife and children behind, rather than trying to arrange travel for so many. You hitched to Boise and from there, flew commercially to D.C.

"In reality, you'll fly east on Ryan's jet from the Control Center and land here," and he brought up a map on his computer, the cursor atop an airfield just outside of College Park, Maryland. "From there, it's a short walk to the Green-Yellow Platform where you'll catch the Branch Avenue subway to Fourteenth and Harvard. Take the bus to Metro Center. After that, you're good."

"When do I leave?"

"This afternoon."

Taken aback by the immediacy, Ned felt himself waver.

Ben saw the flash of uncertainty cross Ned's face. "Seriously . . . if you're not up to this . . . ."

"No, I'm good. I just need a minute to wrap my mind around how fast it's happening, that's all. I'll go pack."

"Not necessary."

Ben handed him a beat-up canvas bag, the UCSA logo printed on the exterior. Inside were clothes and various toiletries. He showed him the false bottom underneath which several burners and a SAT phone were hidden. "Hide these well when you get to your apartment."

58

June 10

ALGER HAD CALLED another pre-church Cabinet meeting. Christian went first to his office to pull together a set of papers detailing Friday's terrorist explosions, one in Indianapolis and the other in Atlanta, both resulting in mass casualties. He hoped to redirect Alger's attention from Portland to the growing threat the Resistance posed to the rest of the country.

Interrupted by a knock on his door, he called, "C'mon in."

He looked up, the miracle of Jesus hisself before his eyes! Ned Burroughs before his eyes! Ned, alive and in the flesh. Christian exploded from his chair.

"What the . . . How on earth can this be? 'Less my mind is playin' tricks on me which, these days wouldn't surprise me none, I am lookin' at none other 'n' Ned Burroughs! We took you for dead, boy!"

"Yes, sir. It's me and I'm very much alive."

"Alive? Why yer a livin' miracle, is what you are! A miracle if ever there was." He looked up, "To God goes the guh-lory!"

Ned had captured the Secretary's notice prior to his departure for Cannon Beach by way of a report he'd put together for Dixon. In it, he had parsed out and listed every chapter and verse in the Bible that dealt with God's will when it came to disasters, no matter how obscure. Since Delilah, Christian had called upon Ned's findings nearly every day.

With an equal measure of emotion and devotion, Ned regaled him with the prepared tale, all the while Christian reflected on how like God it was to have spared—no, to have saved—this man, and brought him back to Faith. In what seemed to him a living Bible story, he made the snap decision to elevate Ned to his Aide-de-Camp.

❖

MEMBERS OF THE Cabinet filed in. Christian arrived last, his gut roiling. When he closed the door, Alger looked up and tersely addressed the room.

"As if I don't already have enough on my hands! Last night, protesters in Missouri burned an effigy of Jesus!"

"The photos were taken down right away," Jones said, the only one courageous enough to speak. "I doubt . . . ."

"I WILL NOT STAND FOR THIS! The entire world is seeing our Savior on fire." He turned his fury on Christian. "I want these images scrubbed! Every last one! Take care of it!"

The room fell silent. No one had seen the president this angry.

Christian's eye began to twitch. "Yes, sir. Of course." To be called out in front of everyone was bad enough but far worse, he didn't have a thought as to how to handle yet another breach. All he could do in the moment was to obfuscate. "We could shut down the rest a' the country's internet access, but I fear that would trigger a mighty uprisin'. I'm near to puttin' the ki-bosh on Resistance postin's for good. In the name of all that's holy, I swear to you, all's I need is another coupla-few days an' you'll have all what you need."

For once, what he said was not a complete lie, at least Christian hoped it wasn't. And it appeared he had successfully dialed down the tension. "I'll get it done, sir, you have my word."

Then Christian proceeded with his news, "Mr. President, somethin' of a miracle happened a few minutes ago. Call it a message from the Lord on High. One a Faith's finest, point a fact, Dixon's second, was on vacation at Dixon's place on the Oregon coast when Delilah happened. We never heard from him so we were forced to accept he'd gone to God. Then who should walk into my office jest b'fore I come here?" He gestured towards the door. "Ned! Come on in." Unshaven and dressed in yesterday's clothes, Ned entered. "President Alger," he announced with pride, "we thought he was dead, but God intervened to raise up Ned Burroughs."

Alger didn't give two donkeys about Christian's holy intervention. Furthermore, he was enraged that Christian dared invite an outsider to a confidential meeting. His hand shot out, "How dare you Christian? And you, you, "pointing at Ned, "leave this room immediately!"

Christian gasped, taking the slight as it was meant, personal and denigrating. He had offered something extraordinary, and Alger's abrupt dismissal cut straight to his insecurity.

The president looked at Riggins. "What's the plan for The Territories? Does anything stand in the way?"

"Sir, we've been ready." He directed a long, lean finger at Christian. "We've been waiting on him."

Alger studied Hillcox. "Do you understand that the future of this country is in your hands? Remember, you are only here because I gave you the opportunity. Which I can just as easily take away. I've had enough of your stalling. You have seventy-two hours to assure us that their lies will never again get out. This meeting is adjourned," and he stormed out, leaving Ned in his wake.

59

Four Fifty-Five p.m.

CHRISTIAN FOLLOWED Ned into the backseat of the town car. "Drop us by Clyde's," he ordered.

There was no time to lose. He spoke sharply to Ned: "Have Andrews to ready my plane. I've business to attend to. I'll be back t'morrow night."

"Yes, sir," Ned replied. Christian looked past him like he wasn't there, his slow and tortured breathing attesting to the cumulative substances in his system.

"Won't take me no seventy-two hours neither," he muttered aloud to himself. "Alger's 'bout ta go after The Territories . . . thinks they're weak from Delilah. Soon's I get my intel, it's a go. "

It was Ned's first day back, and already things were in play.

Traffic was backed up. "Let us out here." Christian told the driver. Once the Lincoln turned the corner, Christian said, "Get us a cab." He would keep this final trip a secret, at least until he returned with the goods. The taxi pulled up to The

Watergate and rather than get out, Christian tossed Ned his keys, "Get on up to my place. Unit 1211, alarm code 316."

The biblical numerology was so blatant, it was difficult for Ned to keep a straight face.

"In my linen closet at the end a the hall, there's a brown bag on the shelf b'low the towels." Ned was half out the door. "Hold on!" and he handed Ned his heavy gold bracelet, diamond studded pinkie ring, and Rolex watch. "Leave the jewl'ry in my top drawer. Make it snappy."

Knowing he'd find the dress and wig inside the bag, Ned unzipped it anyway. Not only was the costume there, but so too were several bottles of prescription pills. When Ned returned to the idling taxi, he passed the tote to Christian and started to get in. Christian held his palm up. He slipped Ned a wad of cash. "Git yourself to the office an' keep the place runnin'. Don't tell a soul I left."

"Not to worry, Mr. Secretary. I'll take care of things. Godspeed."

Ned stopped at his apartment before heading back to Faith and texted Josh: "Grandma's on her way."

"Can't wait to see her. Any idea how long she'll stay?"

"Just the day."

60

June 11

THE HALF-HOUR helicopter ride from Hood River to Portland was punishing. Blades whirred angrily above, suggestions of God's judgment filling Christian with more dread than he'd known. His head throbbed. How he longed for a Xanax. "Gotta stay on my toes," he said aloud, the rotors drowning his words. No longer a mentor to the president, he instead felt at his mercy.

In his well-worn disguise, the dress better suited for the day's warm weather, he arrived a minute before ten. When the gowned and bewigged deaf-mute stood among the familiar faces at The Grotto, she had no idea that they knew who she was. Or that everything she was about to hear was designed to deceive.

Josh and Ben sprinted up. Josh announced. "I've dreaded this moment ever since we began our fight. There's no way to sugarcoat it." He swallowed hard. "It seems everything's fallen apart."

Those gathered acted as if the air had communally left them, while at the same time Christian's pulse quickened.

Ben stepped in. "Our access to the internet remains compromised. Even worse."

Christian's ears perked up.

"Without the beginnings of a workaround, there's no way to get the word out. Additionally, no one will know if and when we need military help. It's become clear that we won't be seeing our way back online. We tried our best, but it's time to face facts. Our fight is over."

Christian was baffled. It was his job to destroy their access to the internet, yet he'd had nothing to do with it. Nevertheless, he would report it to Alger as his own accomplishment.

Josh stepped up, his anguish raw, tears at the ready. "We probably always knew we wouldn't slay the dragon. We did our best, but in truth, we never had a chance, not with the power we were up against." He went silent, passing from person to person, shaking a hand here, sharing an embrace there, exchanging a few well-chosen words, all to extend the charade. Then, as they had done in the past, Josh and Ben faded away. The remaining insiders stayed put, acting out their shock and despair while Christian silently rejoiced. With their communications in ruins and no one coming to save them, he would return to Washington the conquering hero. After this, there would be no stopping him. Tomorrow, The Territories, thereafter, Dominion.

After the dirty woman pushed off, the mood turned jubilant. It was no small feat having duped the mighty United Christian States of America. While no awards would be given, Josh and Ben had delivered two superb performances. Consummate actors as well, the supporting cast were every bit their equals.

61

June 12

FAITH'S JET BUMPED down the runway. It was one in the morning when Niles McDaniels, the head of Christian's Secret Service attachment, met Christian at the bottom of the airstairs. He was less than happy.

"Mr. Secretary, you can't keep skipping out like this. We had no idea where you were. Haven't reported you, but if you give us the slip one more time, we'll have to. After all, it's our necks on the line if anything happens. You, of all people, oughta know there are plenty of folks wanna do you harm."

"Niles," Christian leaned in close, "keep this between us, okay? There was a lady involved. I finished with her, God's truth. There'll be no more disappearances."

McDaniels chose to accept what he said, and moments later Christian's limo appeared and whisked him away.

Christian returned to Washington a much different man. Not only would he be able to give the president the news that the Resistance was finished, but *Soul Saving* had debuted to critical acclaim on all three networks during the flight back.

Settling in the next morning to revel in the documentary's review in The Christian Times, he couldn't keep from brooding over who really had stopped the Resistance's ability to transmit. It made no sense. For a split second, he wondered if Riggins was the responsible party, in which case Alger would have no more use for Christian. No, that was his paranoia speaking. Instead of worrying, he should look at what had happened as a gift. There are times in life to accept His favor and this was surely one of them.

But later that afternoon, doubt found its way back in, albeit for an entirely different reason. Christian had never fully shaken the thought that there was more to Mansour than he let on. No matter that York sang his praises and that Mansour had come through with *Soul Saving*, something still didn't sit right. The truth was, he didn't trust Eric. Never had. It was a gut feeling and his gut was rarely wrong.

He looked up Eric's address, pleased to find that, like him, Eric also lived in Foggy Bottom. Christian decided he'd stroll on by that very evening. Edgy as he was, he needed the relief that comes from action. Not only that, but the adrenaline come from spying had taken root, at least it had for now.

Eluding security, he left the building on foot. It was a beautiful June evening. He arrived across from Eric's historic pink row house at twilight and quickly concealed himself behind a thicket. Raising his binoculars, he zoomed in. The lens was so powerful, it seemed like he was right there, in the room with Eric and his family. The dining table was framed by a wide bay window, and it showed him, his wife, and three children at dinner. Christian watched them talk, laugh, interrupt one another, a glimpse of the life that had eluded him as son, husband, and father, and he felt a surge of envy.

Once they finished eating, Christian watched Eric clear the table, then head to a room in the back of the house, presumably the kitchen, where he and his wife did the dishes. The children scattered to other parts of the house. When husband and wife returned streetside, their laughter ended in a warm embrace. What Christian would never understand was how a man like Eric, a man without zeal for the Lord, had more in life than he. Inexplicable as it was, it left room for the bottomless ache that, as always, he forced aside.

That was when he spotted a familiar-looking woman approach the house. At nearly the same moment, a man arrived from the opposite direction. It came to him at once that the woman was Elizabeth Boorman, from TBT, and he remembered the man as someone he'd seen in the studio at SHOX the week before, when he'd gone there for an interview.

Why were these two meeting at Eric's house, and at this hour? Instinctually, he snapped a photo. Didn't this prove he'd been right about Eric all along?

Christian would get him alone in his office at Faith the next morning. He could hardly wait.

62

June 13, 7:30 a.m.

FOR THE SECOND time in a week, Eric approached the secretary's outer sanctum. This time, two armed guards stood sentry. He was chilled by how quickly the public had become inured to the constant and ubiquitous military presence. However, history had proven time and again how easy it was to instill fear. Once burrowed into the body public, it was nearly impossible to ignore the drumbeat of constant propaganda. Such was the way of the authoritarian state.

Today though, Eric smiled as he showed the soldiers his papers and they waved him in. Such was his anticipation of praise for the documentary, that he seated himself across from the Secretary and exclaimed, "Isn't the response to *Soul Saving* incredible?"

"Mansour, what went on at your home last night around nine?," Christian tapped the standard manilla folder on the desk in front of him.

Alarm bells clanged, shattering Eric's sense of well-being. "I'm sure I don't know what you mean."

Christian pulled out the photo he had taken and slapped it on the desk in front of Eric, "By chance, you were seen hustlin' Elizabeth Boorman an' a man I know to work at SHOX inside your house."

"Journalists with proper papers? I don't see the problem," he replied coolly, trying to erase the fear from his face. "Are you spying on me?"

"I prefer to call it 'keepin' tabs.'" Christian's eyes bored into Eric's. "Ya wanna know what I really think? You an' these individuals were meetin' for a not-so-kosher reason."

"Much as I hate to disappoint you, Christian, have you stopped to consider the simple answer? With your recent budget cuts, we've had to double up. We're down a cameraman so I asked Liz to my house to meet a less costly hire. We did it at my house in order not to cut into the work day."

"An' iffen I look that up?," Christian shot back.

"I can't stop you."

"I'd hoped we were past this Mansour—the lies an' such."

"As I've offered before, feel free to go through our devices. You'll find nothing but that we're one-hundred percent loyal to the State."

Christian leaned in, the pores on his face large and shiny in the bright light. "Say what you will Mansour, but I believe you're workin' for the other team. An' that you an' your Gal Friday are playin' at some mighty treasonous stuff."

He saw Eric tense and went in for the kill. "I'll git proof. I'm talkin' days, not weeks."

"Mr. Secretary, TBT is your network. We've done every single thing you've asked." He rose, trying to retake his dignity. "Unless there's anything else, I have a station to run."

Now Eric understood why the guards were there. As he crossed through the outer door, he expected to be wrestled to the ground and cuffed, surprised when they let him pass. Ducking into the nearest men's room, he locked himself inside a stall and sat on the toilet. The ceiling camera missed the near breakdown he had. Seconds later, the outer door swung open and, holding his breath, he lifted his knees and held them high. Hillcox's soldiers looked in and, seeing no feet beneath the doors, stormed out. Eric rested his feet back on the floor, gasping for air.

Thirty minutes later, far from the building, Eric called Liz, burner to burner, "He's on to us."

"Who?" Liz asked.

"That son of a bitch, Hillcox."

63

Nine a.m.

"MR. SECRETARY, your time is up. Do you have what I asked for?" The president, anticipating another plea for more time, looked ready to explode. But for the first time since early on, Christian stood up, smug with accomplishment.

"It took me more time 'n I'd hoped, but I got all what you asked." All too aware of the communal disdain for him, he paused, taking the time to look at each man's face. He was going to enjoy this.

"Y'see, I been playin the spy, goin' to Portland disguised as a woman." Around the table, hands covered mouths and bellies shook at the thought of Christian in drag.

"As the Lord would have it, day b'fore yesterday, I stood cheek to jowl with the enemy, heard 'em wailin' 'bout how they won't never get back on their dark web. Squallin' away how without it, they won't be gettin' the outside help or weapons they need. Otherwise put, they seem to know we're comin' an' cain't do nothin' ta fight back."

Christian shot a glance at Riggins, gratified to see his eyes flash with a fiery jealousy.

"Yup, they're finished. If you ask me, I say, the time's ripe. Go on ahead. Take 'em out."

"Thad, can you back this up?"

"I can, Mr. President. As you well know, I've been unable to issue a go-ahead until I knew for certain that all Resistance comms were disabled. We cannot afford for our 'skirmish' to be seen around the world," his fingers held in air quotes. He sneered openly with eyes that burned into Christian's. "I mean c'mon man, this war should have been long behind us!"

Christian looked right back at him, his only answer a satisfied smirk.

For Alger, Christian had finally delivered, and that was what mattered. "Thad, what Secretary Hillcox did, he did at great personal risk, which is more than I can say for you." Those present sat in stunned silence. Never had anyone heard the president chastise Riggins.

Patience broke the tension. "I say, here's to the great and holy United Christian States of America! Blessings go to you, Christian."

Bickle popped in: "From sea to shining sea!"

"Here, here!," the others chimed in.

In this moment of great consequence, Alger gave the order. "Riggins, set the occupation in motion."

The validation coming from his peers washed over Christian, but it was nothing compared to the relief that came from Alger once again holding him in high esteem.

As they exited, Riggins' caught up with Christian. "I hope you're satisfied now that you had your little moment. But it's time you move aside and let the real men take over."

President Alger heard not the words but moreso the contempt with which they were spoken, and said sharply, "Thad, we owe a debt of gratitude to Secretary Hillcox. I shouldn't have to say this, but I expect the two of you to work together and with respect."

Christian walked off, but not before shooting Riggins one last victorious smile.

That same morning, Ellison Mann arrived at Zeb Alperstein's home. He had come to believe there was a decency in the ambassador, something sorely lacking in today's Washington. Keenly aware of the Secretary of Faith's close working relationship with the Ambassador, he took his time before he dared to approach.

Over the past few weeks, the men had traveled similar moral journeys, if for very different reasons, Mann's beginning when he witnessed the savagery of Jessica's murder, and Zeb's ending with his recent trip to Israel. Passing one another in Faith's hallways, they sensed a commonality through their brief but pointed glances. As the days and weeks passed, Zeb became desperate to speak with him, to learn if he was right, that Mann really was a fellow traveler. Screwing up his courage, he invited him to his house so they could talk freely. The eagerness with which Mann accepted was greatly encouraging.

After trading formalities in the front hall, they proceeded to the living room. "Thanks for coming, Ellison," Zeb said. "You seem like a good man."

"As do you."

The dance began, Ellison sending up the first balloon.

"I'm relieved to be here, just the two of us." This hardly seemed the time for small talk, so he dove right in. "I don't know about you, Mr. Ambassador, but I'm finding it more and more difficult to stay between the lines, both personally and at work. And as I'm sure you've noticed, the lines continue to narrow. I've been a widower for over two years. Raising my sixteen-year old daughter Alyse alone is not only difficult for the usual reasons, but I wake up in a cold sweat most nights for fear she'll do something, the smallest thing, that gets her noticed. The times are challenging, if you get my drift."

Zeb heard the subtext and cautiously picked up. "It wasn't all that long ago when things were different. There was a trust among professionals in Washington up until, well, until it all changed. Ellison, can I trust you?"

"Nothing will leave this room. You have my word."

Pacing, Zeb began and once he did, the floodgates opened. "Extremism is extremism, no matter the religion. My role used to be to diminish tensions. Now I see right-wing Jews acting as crazy as a certain segment of Christians, and I think you know who I mean. Meanwhile, these very Christians resemble the farthest of the far-right Muslims whose ideology they so disparage. Diplomacy used to be our guide. It made the job worth doing. But when Alger appointed me Ambassador to Israel, it didn't take long to see how dark he'd go. Now, every week is worse than the one before because, while the endgame for Alger was always domination, Hillcox truly believes he was chosen by God to end the world, Book of Revelation style. I'm telling you, the man is batshit crazy. The way things are going, he'll get us there sooner rather than later."

Mann nodded in agreement and that was all Zeb needed.

"I won't do it anymore. No longer will I help Hillcox further a messianic vision that can only result in humankind's destruction. I should have resigned the moment Alger won, but I was in so deep career-wise, I wouldn't admit to myself that working for a man like him was something I'd regret the rest of my life. If you leave here today and report me, so be it. At least I'll have spoken my conscience."

It was Mann's turn. "This is my conscience speaking. Three weeks ago I watched Hillcox, that supposed man of God, murder a young woman, after which he sodomized her lifeless body."

"Wh . . . what in the world are you saying?"

Mann put his hands up as if to erase the memory. "What I saw was the most evil, the least godly thing one human being could do to another, and I broke. Since then, I've been searching for the courage to escape. A courage I believe you just gave me."

These days, because anything could happen, they agreed it would be wise to find a way to get to the west coast as soon as possible. Both being connected through different channels, they quickly figured out how to do so in ways that would cause no alarm. With the Canadian border closed to Americans, Mann would pull strings to get Alyse and his sister on a flight to the French island of St. Pierre, off the coast of Newfoundland. Sending Alyse away would be the hardest thing he had ever done, but there was no other way to ensure her safety.

For his part, Zeb had access to a government jet. When he returned to work that morning, he went straight to Christian's office to suggest that he and Mann fly to Oklahoma City, where a virulent anti-Semitism had taken hold. Zeb made the case that if ignored, Israel would quickly lose confidence in Alger and his Administration.

"You're right to address this, Zebulon. I'm blessed to have you lookin' out for me." Christian's attitude towards Zeb often flopped around like a fish on the deck of a boat, according to his need and mood.

Six hours later, Zeb and Ellison boarded Faith's plane for Oklahoma City, carrying briefcases that held official documents, along with two overnight bags, the linings of which concealed newly obtained false identity papers.

When they arrived, they took a taxi to a downtown hotel and checked in. They stayed in their rooms only long enough to change clothes, and for Zeb to shave off his beard and side curls. Exiting the hotel by a rear door, they walked a few blocks, hailed another cab, and made their way back to the airport. From there, they flew commercially to Bend, Oregon, where Zeb rented a helicopter under his assumed name.

What they would do when they arrived in Portland, they didn't know. They would figure it out in due course.

64

Spectacle

UPWARDS OF TWO hundred thousand citizens filed onto the Mall, filling the area from the Reflecting Pool to the Capitol steps, a sea of believers come together to share their love of God. Today was "The First Annual Presidential Rally for Faith." Mammoth screens projected the pre-celebration entertainment: upbeat, joy-filled Christian-pop groups.

At 1:00 p.m., Alger mounted a platform twenty-five feet above the Reflecting Pool and looked out over the crowd. Flanked by his Cabinet, three rows of select members of the House, Senate, and Supreme Court filled the stage behind him. After an extended period of applause, Alger gestured to Peacock who, with great flourish, pressed a button, releasing seventy-five feet of opaque sheeting into the water below.

The crowd roared with excitement at the unveiling of this, the nation's most fundamental of monuments: *Jesus Rising*. His arms outstretched, the statue of Christ was framed by the marble structure of the Lincoln Memorial, the statue's size and siting designed to obscure the sixteenth president, as Christ looked eastward across the Mall toward the Capitol.

The sounds from the inspired crowd were deafening, Christian absorbing the energy as he stepped to the mic. "And there, He Rises! Our Savior takes His rightful place in this, our sacred city." He waited for the din to subside, then continued. "You know that as a lifelong Christian, an' your Secretary of Faith, my mission has only and always been to fight for His Truth! It is why I stand before you today, here in this most sacred of American places ta pledge, 'Never Again'! Never Again will we be forced from the public square. Never Again will His light be hidden under a bushel. Together, as one, we have succeeded in fulfilling His destiny!'"

Hundreds of thousands of voices came thundering back, "Never Again!"

Peacock caught Christian's eye, reminding him that Bickle was waiting in the wings. "Without further delay, it is my honor to bring on the greatest Vice President ever to serve this nation, God's emissary, Ron Bickle!" The men shook hands, and as Bickle faced the public and raised his arms in the V of Victory, Christian made his way down the stairs, Bickle's words ringing out, "Yeah, He hath delivered!!"

Christian reached the bottom step where a beaming Jeremiah York stood waiting. "What a show! We continue to outdo ourselves!" They began walking, Jeremiah, buzzing with excitement. "And how about that documentary?"

Christian's face darkened, "York, I unnerstand you got yourself into a friendly relationship with Mansour an' his girl when you were together in Oregon."

"Indeed I did! It was most enjoyable."

"They ain't what they seem, an' you can take that to the bank." He led him further away from the revelry. "It is my strongest belief that they are Resistance. High up too."

York could not have been more astonished. "Eric?" He couldn't believe it, wouldn't believe it. To think that he, who prided himself on his ability to judge a man's character, a trait that had contributed to his rapid rise in government, could have been so badly duped, it was unimaginable. He thought back over his time with them and found no cracks in their behavior. Until he remembered their afternoon jaunt to Portland. What if they hadn't gone to check out TBT? Could Hillcox be right, that the documentary had been a ploy and Eric and Liz members of the Resistance? In a perverse way, it made sense. But that he was so easily taken in? If so, Christian had fallen for it as well.

"You let a fox in the henhouse, you damned fool! You make a plan an' meet with 'em, an' you do it right away. Get me proof." And then he stalked off.

Shaken by the depth of their possible deception, York left the Mall resolved to get to the bottom of things that very evening. If what Christian said was true, aside from the growing anger he began to feel towards a man he had come to see as a friend, he felt a stab of fear for what might happen should Christian one day need a scapegoat, and pin it all on him.

65

Eight p.m., Dupont Circle

LATE IN THE DAY, the skies over the Capital turned dark and threatening. The atmosphere was heavy with moisture, and when the skies let loose early in the evening, they did so with fury. The storm was so savage as to make even the most devout shudder in fear. Thoroughly drenched, Eric and Liz arrived at York's chosen restaurant to find him sitting there, dry and contented, in a corner booth.

"Look at the two of you!" he exclaimed, as the duo peeled off their dripping rain gear. "I got inside just before the heavens let loose." He motioned to the waiter, "Take these things and hang them so they dry out." He looked at Eric, "Can't have you catch your death of cold on your way home. Doesn't look like this will let up anytime soon."

They settled in. "It's good to see you," he said, Liz's antennae immediately sensed the lie in his words.

"Seems a good time to build the ark, that is, if it's not too late," Eric chortled.

"Hah! Good one. But hey, let's forget about what's going on outside and enjoy ourselves." York had acting skills of his own, easily keeping up a friendly banter, the purpose of this dinner hidden from view.

"Have either of you been here? It's tremendous."

"First time for me," Liz forced a smile. "Thanks for the invite."

York didn't answer, instead he looked at her hard. There was something different about him. She suppressed her concerns hoping it was his stress she was feeling. After all, everyone had problems of their own. This didn't have to be about them.

"The food is outstanding. I recommend the lamb." He passed a plate of chorizo-stuffed dates to Eric, while Liz nibbled on a warm olive.

"Thanks Jeremiah. Glad as we are to try the place, we're happier still to see you."

Excluding select tables in the better establishments, a recent order mandated that restaurants seat customers close together so as to encourage eavesdropping.

"It's difficult enough to get a table here, much less this one. I prefer privacy," and he pointed to the other diners seated elbow to elbow. He snapped his fingers and the waiter reappeared. York flashed his Select Pass. "Get these good people a couple of drinks." He turned to Eric. "You did a terrific job and I wanted to thank you in person. The response to *Soul Saving* is off the charts. Even the president is thrilled."

"Terrific. We're pleased with how it came out. Again, I want to say how much we enjoyed working with you. Hopefully, there will be other opportunities."

"What would the two of you say to documenting next month's King of King's Heritage Festival in Raleigh?"

"We'd love to," Eric answered enthusiastically.

They ordered and while they waited for their food, Eric and York fell into their customary patter. Relegated to the sidelines, Liz sat back to observe.

What neither knew was that York had phoned TBT-Portland that afternoon under the guise of settling the invoice for the helicopter. He reached the receptionist, a new hire who didn't know to cover for them.

"TBT Portland. Allison Merrick speaking."

"Allison, this is Jeremiah York from the Department of Faith. I'm finishing up the allocations for the shoot last week, and I need to know whether to bill your office or the documentary for the chopper Eric and Liz took from Troutdale to Portland when they came to check on the station."

"Eric and Liz? That's odd. I know for a fact they haven't been here. My boss said just yesterday that he hasn't seen them since before the earthquake."

York rustled some papers to hide his indignation. "Must be my mistake. I'll go ahead and bill it to Faith."

Allison left the studio five minutes later, not thinking to leave a note about the call.

Dinner arrived, and they began to eat. "Eric," York said, in between bites, "I never asked: How did you find your studio in Portland? You didn't say anything, so I assume everything was okay?"

The hairs on the back of Liz's neck stood at attention.

"There was some minor damage to the exterior and they lost a truck, but all told, they were lucky."

There it was. The big lie resting right there on the table between them.

York maintained his cool, even with his near-blinding rage threatening to explode. Eric, a man he had taken into his confidence, along with Liz, were traitors, exactly as Christian said. His cell vibrated. "Excuse me, I'd better take this," relieved that the distraction might help conceal the darkness fast overtaking him. With phone to ear, he listened, expressionless, "On my way."

"That was the Secretary. Some highly classified information regarding the Resistance just came over his desk and he needs to discuss it with me in person, right away. Said it won't take long. Seeing as we've hardly had any time to catch up, how about we meet up at Johnny's Half Shell say, in forty-five minutes?"

"Sounds like a plan," Eric answered.

York motioned to the waiter, "Put the whole thing on Faith's tab." He turned to Eric and Liz. "See you shortly."

Torrential rain slanted across their faces as Liz and Eric made their way the few blocks to Johnny's. The streets were quiet, the storm's ferocity having sent even non-curfewed Washingtonians home for the night. As little as either wanted to be out in this, they could hardly turn down a chance at what they might learn about Christian's unexpected call.

Eric and Liz crossed Connecticut Avenue a couple of blocks below Dupont Circle. The streets shone with water, making it difficult to see. Midway across the multi-laned thoroughfare, a truck appeared from out of nowhere, accelerating fast. Eric grabbed Liz's hand in an effort to pull her out of its path, but he never had a chance. As they swerved, so too did the truck, plowing into them both. The driver stopped, reversed gear, then backed over their bodies. Shifting back to Drive, the vehicle picked up speed, turned the corner and disappeared.

Except for a clap of thunder and the hammering rain, all was quiet.

As their bodies lay lifeless on the street, Bruce was in a nearby bar comfortably seated across from Byron, listening to him prattle on about five-foot-ten Daphne, his most recent conquest. Just when Bruce thought he could take no more, Byron's phone sounded.

"Lord have mercy," he grimaced, ending the call. "Something bad went down a few blocks from here. Terrorists drove a truck into two people from TBT. Both were killed outright."

Bruce paled.

"Freaks me the fuck out. Coulda been us. These animals, they despise us and now they've turned violent here in D.C." He stowed his phone. "Everyone is to shelter in place," he sighed, clearly frightened, "except for me. Thing is, when you're dealing with Muslims, Spics, and Darkies, you can spot 'em. Not always so with Resisters."

"Did they say who was hit?"

"The station head, Eric Mansour and his second-in-charge. Gotta say, my friend, I'm not feeling so brave at the moment. But I hafta go. I'll text when it's safe for you to head home. Until then, stay put."

"Be careful, buddy," Bruce managed. "It's a war zone out there." That Bruce could speak at all was a testament to his instinct for survival. At that instant, it came to him that he was the sole remaining member of their cell.

"For realz." Byron slapped a hundred dollar bill on the table and left.

Minutes later, before any police or emergency vehicles were on the scene, SHOX cut into their programming, "Breaking News." Bruce watched with alarm as Byron shouted into the wind-buffeted microphone, "Minutes ago the Resistance delivered a well-calculated blow to the nation's sacred press right here in the capital. Waiting until the victims were mid-crosswalk, terrorists cold-bloodedly ran down TBT head, Eric Mansour, and his longtime producer, Elizabeth Boorman. Both were dead on impact."

He put a hand to his ear, listened for a moment, then added, "We have just learned that Resisters had planned to pin the assassination on the Administration." How Byron, or anyone, could know that so quickly, he didn't say.

Bruce was frozen in place.

"The drivers unwittingly dropped a calling card on the pavement, one that is known to authorities. While this is so far the only clue, closed circuit camera footage will aid in identifying the evil-doer. Whether this is an isolated incident or there will be others tonight, we cannot know. Anyone who is out should shelter in place until Homeland Security gives the all clear."

Haunting music accompanied the dark, rainy street in the background. The cameraman pulled in close for a pan of the mangled bodies, Bruce forcing himself to watch. That was when he noticed there were no emergency vehicles on hand. It wasn't until minutes later that the police and EMS showed up, and when they did, despite the fact that this was a hit and run supposedly carried out by a hostile enemy, no yellow tape was put in place, nor was anyone searching for evidence. As the chyron, "Take Immediate Shelter," crawled across the screen, Byron added, "If everyone cooperates, no one else need get hurt." Medics loaded the bodies into the ambulance as the rain continued to wash the blood away. It occurred to Bruce that the folks at SHOX knew what had happened before the police did. It made no sense. Until it did.

Frozen no longer, he grabbed his backpack and dashed from the bar. He removed the SIM card from his phone and tossed it down a sewer grate, the river of water washing it away. For him, the need was not to shelter in place but to get the fuck out of Dodge.

Thanks to Eric, he had plenty of cash. Pulling a SHOX cap from his pack, he slanted the bill downward to hide his face. Keeping to the shadows, he made his way to Union Station where, using his false I.D., he bought a ticket for the first train bound for Cleveland. There being no direct route, he chose the earliest to leave. All told, with a transfer in Pennsylvania, it would be a six-hour journey, one that was sure to try his dwindling courage, but he would chance a longer trip if it meant getting out of D.C. right away. The fifteen minutes until the train's departure were the longest of his life, particularly with so few travelers out, and the UCSA Police stomping loudly throughout the terminal. Even the restrooms offered no protection. He saw four armed guards enter and drag out a cuffed and screaming woman.

At last he boarded. As soon as the train left the station, uniformed men started down the aisles barking, "Papers! Have your papers out for inspection!" Bruce could scarcely breathe for fear of the well-muscled soldier who, seat by seat, passenger by passenger, advanced towards him.

From the car ahead, an officer shouted as an elderly Black man ran from him towards the back of the train. A second guard grabbed him, then calmly waited for the sergeant who had stopped at the now-abandoned seat. He searched around and underneath, until he found the book the Black man had thought to hide. Ripping off the homemade cover, he held it up for all to see: Ralph Ellison's *Invisible Man*, one of the tens of thousands of banned and burned books. "Boy, you're under arrest!" Left unsaid was that it was less the communist tome than it was the color of the old man's skin that so incensed these men. Together, the soldiers manhandled him unashamedly past Bruce and beyond.

A third officer stopped at Bruce's seat. Thinking to engage him in a manner he hoped would read as collaborative, Bruce stole a glance at his nametag, "Glad they got him, Lieutenant Frasier. Can't have filth like that on our trains," and he handed over his papers, hoping Frasier wouldn't notice the tremor in his hand.

"Attorney, are you now? That's a sweet gig." By this time, Bruce could only nod, so unnerved was he. He agonized until the red, white, and blue stamp, the symbol that would tell soldiers down the line he'd been cleared, dried on his pass, and his heartbeat slowed to a gallop. Eyeing him one last time, Frasier intoned, "May the Lord shine his countenance upon you, Mr. Adams."

"All glory goes to God, " Bruce replied.

Hours later, he changed trains without incident. The inspections began again and this time, were more deliberate. Passengers who displayed questionable papers were pulled from their seats and shoved to the back, protesting loudly.

At this point, exhaustion overtook Bruce and he nodded off, awakening an hour later when the train came to a stop. The moon waxing gibbous provided enough light to illuminate the sign from what used to be a state park. Beyond a forbidding iron gate, searchlights fixed to the top of a tall concrete wall swept the landscape. Moments later, Bruce watched soldiers offload dozens of shackled passengers from the rear of the train. Men, women, and children were poked, prodded, and ultimately shoved through the maw of what looked to be some kind of internment camp.

A couple of hours later, Bruce disembarked in Cleveland deeply shaken. He proceeded to an out of the way spot inside the terminal, fished out a burner from a zippered pocket in his pack, and texted Matt, "Here." Spotting a map stand, he took one and traced his finger to the location Matt texted back.

Exiting the station, he made certain no one was following, then walked the short distance towards the former Rock

and Roll Hall of Fame, its iconic glass pyramid now display-
ing an overly-large UCSA flag. A familiar voice from behind
said, "Don't turn around. Walk straight ahead like we're not
together." They proceeded down 9th Street. Fifteen minutes
later, Matt passed him to open a steel door on the backside of
a now-defunct men's clothing store. Once indoors, he yanked
Bruce in, threw the lock, and pulled the door shut. Matt led the
way up two flights of lightless stairs into the dank and moldy
space he now called home.

Matt finally spoke, "Wow, man, Liz and Eric," greatly
emotional. "I saw the headlines. I'm so relieved you made it
out."

That things had gotten to this, Bruce thought, looking
with sorrow at his friend.

"Do me a favor and stay clear of the windows. I can't afford
for anyone to know I'm here."

Bruce sank onto the linoleum floor and when he began to
describe what he had seen from the train, Matt lowered himself
alongside him.

"All those lives," Bruce shuddered. "I think it's the first
time I took Alger's regime all the way to its end game. Yeah, I
made it out, but it sure wasn't how I wanted to."

Their recognition of this new phase held them in silence.

"I have no idea what I'm doing now that Liz is gone. All I
know is that I have to get to Portland."

"I'm still plugged in enough to have gotten word that
Manny left a truck for you a couple blocks from here with instructions for the next leg of your journey. They'll be under the
passenger seat along with the registration and key."

"Is it okay if I spend the night with you?"

"As if you have to ask."

"Thanks, man."

They set to work planning a route that would take Bruce west along roads with the fewest number of checkpoints. These specific byways were surveilled daily by Resistance cells across the country. Even so, it was always possible that independent militia groups would throw up their own.

Matt handed over a new set of false documents and a prepaid phone. Bruce paused before speaking, "I hesitate to ask, but do you have any interest in joining me?"

"I wish I could, I really do, but," he sighed, the weight of all that had happened near to heartbreaking, "but I'm hollowed out. First Jessica, now Liz and Eric," his voice trailed off. "I don't have it in me. I hope you don't judge me."

"As if I would. To be honest, I don't know if fighting back even matters."

Matt shrugged in reply, a shadow of the man he used to be.

The next morning, as Bruce prepared to leave, Matt said, "Promise you'll be careful."

"We all thought we were. What I can say is that I'll do my best. When this is over, I'm coming back for you. That I promise."

"I'll hold you to it."

They embraced and sooner than either wished, they were on their own again, sustained by the affection that bound them.

66

One Night and One Day

THE DRIVE WAS easy, pleasant even. With no clouds in sight, and the open road ahead, Bruce felt a sense of freedom he had not experienced since before the election. He was stopped once, and that time, quickly waved through.

Ten hours later, Bruce pulled into the corner of a parking lot in Cedar Rapids. He shut off the engine and stashed the keys above the visor. Crossing the street, he went inside the Red Robin and ordered four burgers per Manny's instructions: a Southern Charm, one Burning Love, and two Black & Bleus. Bruce kept his eyes straight ahead until his number was called. Then, according to plan, he followed a man in a red cap out of the restaurant. He walked behind him up the street to a silver Toyota Camry and they both got in. After a short ride, the fellow Resister let him off at an airfield, speaking his first and only words, "Wait here." They shook hands, and soon after, Ryan's Gulfstream touched down and Bruce climbed on board. Three and a half hours later, the plane landed on an old Forest

Service tarmac six miles southeast of Portland. Relieved to have made it this far, Bruce set off on foot into the woods.

He spotted a band of travelers at a bend ahead and called out to them. They stopped to wait but the closer he got, the edgier they became.

"He doesn't look right," he heard a woman say. "Check out his clothes. No way he's from around here."

He tried to tell them how wrong they were about him, but he was a stranger and that was all that mattered. Still, thinking it would be safer to travel with others, he fell back and followed from a distance. They walked along the broken trail and when it became impassable, they pushed through the tangled brush, climbing up and over the earthquake-exposed boulders until they made their way back to some kind of path.

As the going became more difficult, he caught up with a woman who had a handicapped toddler with her. Clearly spent from carrying him, she had stopped to rest. Bruce took a chance. "Ma'am, if you would let me, I could carry your son for a while."

She eyed him warily. It had become natural to distrust everyone, but her arms ached so, she knew she couldn't continue. She let him talk.

"I get it. You don't know me. In your shoes, I'd probably feel the same. But believe it or not, I'm more afraid of all of you than you should be of me."

Her silence encouraged him to continue.

"My name is Bruce Bauman. Days after Alger's inauguration, I joined a cell in D.C. At the time, I was already employed as a cameraman at SHOX News, it having been the only position I was offered after graduation. It turned out to be a good thing because days after Alger won, I was in a good position. I joined a cell in which my job was to get close to their top anchor, Byron Stepford. He had access to the stories they didn't air–in other words, the important stuff. Whatever I learned from him, I would pass on to Liz, my cell leader and she'd share it with the Resistance."

A wave of grief stopped him for a moment. "A few nights ago, Liz was assassinated along with the last remaining member of my cell, leaving me on my own. Figuring I was next. I took off and made my way here."

She took a long, hard look at him. She had known a beloved fellow Resister named Liz Boorman, and hoped against hope that that was not who he was talking about. She hadn't heard about the assassination, but then again she hadn't been in touch with anyone since before the earthquake. This guy Bruce seemed like he was telling the truth. Besides, her muscles were screaming with every step. There was no choice but to accept his help, so she decided to take a chance.

She told him her name was Elodie and that she was married to a man who was high up in Portland's Resistance. She had taken their son, Jason, to Denver to see a medical specialist the day before the quake struck, and since then they'd been working their way home, with Elodie being rightfully anxious about whether or not she'd find her husband alive.

There was something about her earnestness and the way she cocked her head when she stopped to listen that reminded him of Jessica, and he had to use everything at his disposal to force the memory aside.

After a time, she left Jason with Bruce and went ahead to the group. A brief discussion ensued and she returned to say they would hear him out. They caught up with the others and, after a rigorous interrogation, the hikers voted twenty to three to let Bruce join them.

Night settled on the darkening woods. They built a fire and made a meal of their combined provisions. Justified or not, there was a feeling of security among them. A communal exhaustion set in, and soon, all were asleep.

The next morning when they emerged from the woods they found themselves facing a highway so fractured that, more often than not, they were forced off-road. Nevertheless, with so few miles to go, the anticipation of reaching the city became palpable. The hours ticked by and their spirits rose and fell according to conditions. Bruce and Elodie were no longer the only ones to carry Jason; everyone took a turn. The bonds among them had strengthened and as they neared the end of the trek, their faith in one another was undeniable, their society strong.

When they neared the city, they were overcome by the scale of destruction. Elodie led her compatriots to the ruins that were now The Grotto, openly weeping at what she saw. When several of the Resistors saw her, they ran to her, tears running down their faces. Clearly a beloved member of the community, they gathered her close and rejoiced. She introduced them to Bruce.

"Did you say his last name is Baumann? I've heard that name," someone said. Aren't you a member of Liz Boorman's cell?"

"I was," he choked out. "But she was assassinated Friday night. Along with Eric Mansour, the head of TBT. That's why I'm here. I knew I was next."

The words dealt a tremendous blow to them all. Even as the finality of Liz's death sank in, Elodie scanned the crowd in the fast diminishing hope that she would find her husband alive and well.

It was then that a man emerged from the shadows. Like a fantasy come to life, he stepped up to embrace his wife and son. It was Josh, her dear Josh. Incredulous, all she could do was hold him tight and weep for whatever joy might remain.

67

Come Together

YEARS BEFORE the pandemic, Zeb had attended a health conference in Portland, and his thoughts traveled back to that time and skyline, now so altered. As for Ellison, he recalled the thriving metropolis that had stood over a network of rivers when he had come there to evangelize many years ago.

The videos that continually aired on state television bore no resemblance to the massive destruction they faced. Having been cogs in Alger's machine, they were horrified at the lengths to which the government had gone to lie about the gravity of the disaster.

In trusting Mann, Christian had revealed the location of the Resistance's meeting place, and that is where the two men headed. When they reached the plaza, they hung back to get the lay of the land until all of a sudden, Zeb gasped. From twenty feet away, he recognized Bruce, a cameraman he had seen many times at SHOX. Why was he there? It had to mean that the government had tracked them: that they had eyes everywhere. There was nowhere to hide.

"That guy there!" and he pointed to Bruce, grabbing Ellison by the arm, pulling him back. "He works for SHOX!" His instincts told him that it was wiser to approach Bruce before Bruce saw him. Shorn of his beard and side curls, and dressed in street clothes, he should have a minute or two to talk before Bruce recognized him. He signaled Ellison to stay put.

"Don't I know you?" he asked. Now it was Bruce's turn to panic. Josh registered the alarm on Bruce's face and rushed to his side. He looked at the person causing Bruce's distress and, instantly, it hit him.

"You're Zeb fucking Alperstein! The UCSA's Ambassador to Israel." Shit, he thought. That Hillcox's kapo was here had to mean they hadn't fooled Christian after all.

Zeb looked Bruce in the eye. "Former Ambassador. As of yesterday."

Taking advantage of Zeb's confusion, Josh led him to a spot where they could talk more freely. Zeb motioned Mann over and when Bruce saw a second official head their way, he whispered, "Jesus, that's the Under Secretary of Faith."

Josh's mind spun out at a thousand miles an hour. To think the Administration had also sent Faith's Under Secretary beggared belief that their appearance was innocent. However, they needed to find out for certain.

"Name's Josh and for now, that's all you need to know." With a whistle, he could summon his comrades to his side, which was more than these two could do. At least that's what he hoped.

"Seems we're at an impasse," Zeb said.

"We're listening."

Zeb didn't want to lead, so instead he looked at Bruce, "When did you leave Washington?"

"It's not for you to ask questions here. Make your case." Bruce snapped.

"I appreciate your caution. I know how it must look. But if you can put aside your disbelief for a second and listen . . . ."

"We're all ears."

"We left D.C. yesterday and, unless Bruce here is with the government, Hillcox thinks we're in Oklahoma doing his business. Once he finds out we're not, he'll connect the dots and send out the dogs." Ellison stood quietly by.

On instinct, Bruce offered, "I left D.C. a couple of days ago. Let's just say I was a wanted man."

Ellison started to take off his backpack, Josh and Bruce ready to pounce. He reached inside the canvas bag and when, instead of a weapon, he pulled out a sheaf of papers, their affect changed. "Here, take a look," Ellison said.

Josh leafed through the pages, handing them one by one to Bruce. Each showed a different drone shot of the region, superimposed with longitudinal and latitudinal grids. The first was of BEST's, the second of the Grotto, both circled in red. Josh knew immediately that he was looking at classified maps of UCSA targets.

He looked up. "How did you get these?"

"Grabbed them on my way out," Ellison said. "Figured I might as well go for broke."

"Any idea of their timeline?"

"No, only that it's soon."

"It doesn't really matter. We have a man on the inside. Do you know Ned Burroughs?"

"Dixon's assistant?"

"He's working for us now"

"That's impossible. He and his wife and kids were vacationing on Cannon Beach when the earthquake struck and disappeared with all the rest. I'm afraid you've been played."

"No, Ned is very much alive. He lost his family, but luckily for him—and for us—he was hiking in the hills above the coast when disaster struck. Let's leave it there for now. Suffice it to say he's one of us and is in fact back in D.C., officially serving as Hillcox's second."

Ellison and Zeb traded looks. This was a stunning turn of events.

Despite this piece of good news, there was clearly something troubling Ellison.

"Is there anything else?"

"There is. Bruce, did you happen to know Jessica Stapleton?"

Bruce's heart plunged. He nodded weakly. "Why do you ask?"

"I watched Hillcox interrogate her." He took a breath. "I saw him torture her to death and then rape her dead body."

"My god," Bruce stammered, falling back against the crumbling wall behind. "So it is true. He did murder her, that sick son of a bitch." That she had died was bad enough but the anguish in knowing how was unbearable. Hell was real all right, it's just that it was here on earth. Real, and perpetrated by men who masqueraded as saviors.

68

And on the Seventh Day, We Rest

GENERAL ISAIAH POLK faced the president. He looked down the length of the table in the Situation Room, its surface littered with half-eaten sandwiches, bowls of greasy chips, and half-empty jars of jelly beans. Riggins busily scribbled notes while the General spoke, the Cabinet members and ancillary staff scrutinizing the plans.

"As you see," Polk's uniformed arm stretched toward the screen on the wall behind him, "our images show no movement in The Territories whatsoever." Vargova had blocked the USCA satellite drones from seeing the transfer of weapons.

Riggins had chosen Polk to lead the operation. The detail with which the General approached the mission confirmed him to be the right man.

"Absent an army to stand against, it's unnecessary to mobilize more than one regiment. With Hillcox's intel," and here the General's laser-like eyes bored into Christian's, "our efforts going forward will be directed towards clean-up."

Christian's uncertainty grew. What if he were wrong?

"But because I come from the 'can't be too careful camp,' Mr. President, I'd like to put the Reserves on High Alert. The last thing we need are sleeper cells outside the theater of operations going rogue."

"Agreed. Wallace, do you have anything to add?"

Alger's press secretary stood, "Coverage of the event, of course, goes to SWBN. My forward staff will set up a safe zone in the center of Portland and remain there until I give the order to go live. Two reporters, minimal crew. The fewer, the better. Less chance for leaks."

Jim Wilson, Head of Counter-Insurgency Psy-Ops, interjected, "Before the first strike, the media will blanket the airwaves, reinforcing the threat the Resistance poses, that Homeland Security has tied every bombing to them. "

Riggins jumped in to remind the room that the operation remained under his control. "Shall we get back to brass tacks, gentlemen? Run through the plan once more, General."

"Drones will drop bombs on targeted buildings to ensure their complete devastation, fighter jets immediately following for broader destruction. With Delilah having softened them up, it's safe to say that whoever remains will cave quickly." He nodded to Grant, "SWBN will of course be live, showing people running for cover as chaos takes over. While all of this is happening, commentators will hammer home the danger that Resistors have continued to pose to the rest of us."

"Next, ground troops will enter the city and sweep up anything still moving, and finally, fighter pilots will fan out, up and down the coast, from Seattle to San Diego. Doubtful as it is, should there be areas where they put up a fight, we'll simply send a little more love their way.

"Equally important, the savagery and speed of our victory will send a message to terrorist cells outside the region, signaling that there will be no safe harbor. No matter what, no matter when, if they attack, we will find them."

Riggins interjected, "Mr. President, understand that the ease of the operation does not diminish its importance. The plain truth is, the enemy is so obscenely over-matched, Operation Cleanup will be over in lightning speed."

Christian's glazed mind spiraled inward, his heart thundering. Here he was, the catalyst to the coming dance with the Rapture, yet he was filled with foreboding. All he could think was that if he hadn't destroyed their internet, then who had? He looked from Riggins, with his bluster, to Polk and his determination. It was all so muddled; nothing made sense. The Resistance had no army, no weapons, no internet. He had heard them say exactly that, had seen and felt their dismay. Yet here he was in a cold sweat and all he could do was to dig into his pocket for more of the only support left him.

It was far too late for him to silence the demons. By now, they owned him, their mighty claws sunk deeply into the cortex of his brain, their fiery limbs wrapped round his being. Sounds from a thousand ghouls clanged inside his head, leaving no room whatsoever for reality.

"A cool head, that's what you need," the always joyful voice of Arna-Geddon submitted. "Here you are, the only man since the Lord created the universe, called by Father God to bring on the glory an' yore feelin' scairt? I say, screw that bunkum!"

Eska-Tology, Choirmaster for the Doom and Gloom Chorus, hissed snakily at Arna, "Why you lyin' sssssssunofabitch. Faggot here best get hisself fuck outta town, an' I mean lickety-split."

Christian, a decades-long, if clandestine, fan of sixties music, shivered as a chorus of pre-pubescent boys sang out;

Well, we'd rather see you dead, Pastorman
Than to let you ruin all our plans
You better keep your head, Pastorman
Or you won't know where we am.
You better run for your life if you can, Pastorman,
Get away from this land, Pastorman,
Catch you as you know we can,
That's the end-uh
Pastorman

When Christian came to, all eyes were on him. With no way of knowing what to say, the rote preacher in him took over, "An' *their portion will be in the lake that burns with fire, an' on the first day.* Leaves us five days for cleanup. An' on the seventh, we rest."

"Amens" ricocheted about the room. "Here! Here!," Patience called. So accustomed were they to Christian's sermonizing, they had no idea how close to the edge he was.

Polk cleared his throat and the men turned back to him. "The attack begins Monday at three a.m. Pacific Standard Time, an hour when the heathens are either sinning or asleep."

The president bowed his head, "With God on our side, on Monday afternoon, His Kingdom shall rule the entirety of this nation."

"As He wills it," Riggins added, looking at Christian, his words devoid of good will.

That was the moment when the nation's man of faith let loose a loud, sulfuric fart.

Conversation came to a halt as, man to man, they looked to one another, some tittering, others reeling from the stench. As repulsed as Riggins was by Christian's lack of dignity, he vowed to himself that once the war was behind them, he would no longer feign civility towards this fraudulent boor. Not only that, but he intended to share his thoughts and concerns about Christian with the president.

Christian waved at the air. Half in, half out of his mind, the truth was he didn't give a good goddamn. All that mattered to him was the battle taking place in his mind.

"Psssssssssst! It's Eska again. Get the fuck outta here! Far as you kin. If it falls apart, it'll all be on you."

"Don't go on lis'nin ta him," Arna parried. "You know what you heard."

Eska, Arna, Eska, Arna, whom to believe?

With the cumulative amount of chemicals chasin' round inside him, it was near impossible to know what was real, but in the end the instinct for self-preservation prevailed.

"Mr. President, ahem, I, er, I mean, we got ourselves a problem. Um . . . ah . . . a coupla two week ago I scheduled meetins' with Goldfein an' his ministers over in Jeruuz-salem. Fer this Monday point a fact. Iffen I were to cancel now, it might could look real bad for us, happenin' as it'll be on the day we're droppin' bombs on them that's sposed to be our own. To my mind, that's when we most need ta show our solidarity."

While troubled by Christian's affect, Alger considered his words. His administration was five months into its rule, and during that time he had concentrated solely on national issues. What Christian said brought home the importance of the UCSA's relationship with Israel. Also, politically speaking, his base expected him to satisfy the biblical imperatives he'd promised during the campaign. Reminded of why he had named Christian as Secretary of Faith, Alger conceded.

"I'll allow you to leave the country, unusual as it is, considering we've based our timing on your word. I agree you should be with Goldfein, but I'll expect you home no later than Tuesday night. We have to assume that the International Red Cross will demand an inspection of at least one of our facilities and that they will do so quickly. Reputationally, we have no choice but to allow it. If past instances are anything to go by, we will know beforehand which site they plan to visit. When you return, it will be your job to oversee the eradication of incriminating evidence, then to populate said location with common criminals, making it appear to be an ordinary prison."

For Riggins, it had all changed. He couldn't be more delighted that Christian would be out of the country. With Christian an ocean away, Alger was sure to attribute the victory to Riggins. While moments ago he'd vowed to treat Christian with the disdain he deserved, he was now the first to speak for him.

"Secretary Hillcox is on target. When it comes to the Holy Land, we should always defer to him."

"That's settled then. Christian, before you leave, make sure you read your new second in."

Christian was struggling, his mind a blur. Digging nails into fleshy thighs, he willed himself to speak.

"Yesssssssir. Ned'll handle things. I fly out Sat'rday night so's not to interfere with their holy day an' I'll be back at my desk Wednesday mornin'." His words had become unintelligible, but by now no one paid him any attention.

Half an hour later, he was fast asleep in his office, his head lolling, and a steady line of drool tracing a path from his mouth to the desk blotter.

69

A Play In Two Acts: June 21

CHRISTIAN CLAMBERED up the jet stairs to the aircraft that would ferry him across time zones and an ocean to a land soon to serve as respite or refuge. Winded and beset by chest pains, he swallowed the little white heart pill and settled in, keenly aware this could be his last journey as a government official. On the other hand, it may well herald the prophetic ascension he'd always recognized as his destiny. And his due.

When the plane began its ascent, the pilot circled the city in a nod to its esteemed passenger. Looking down on the monuments, Christian pondered the educational toll assessed by a godless Congress that, in 1962, drove God from the schoolhouse, the result of which was the indoctrination of far too many lost generations. Only since he effectuated a complete educational overhaul did textbooks finally read true. Today, students were taught that the Washington Monument soared to the heavens in reverence of the country's founding as a Christian nation. And that Lincoln, his given name a tribute to the Bible's first monotheist, sat sagely in his seat, not because he had eliminated slavery, no, far from it. The statue of the great man was a tribute to the role subservience plays in the Bible. The Civil War had had nothing to do with the white man's ownership of the Negro, but instead and only with religious freedom, as derived from the Bible—that darkies as well as women were put on God's green earth to serve and obey. In future years, students would learn that Operation Clean-Up was the nation's conclusive battle for Christian Dominion. From now until Planet Earth's inevitable end, American children would be taught what President Alger and Christian mandated during this, the only true iteration of our country.

Overtired and emotionally depleted, Christian stretched out on the freshly made-up bed. As the hours and miles passed, aside from awakening a couple of times for pharmacological replenishment, he spent the night in the world of his subconscious and oh, what a world it was.

Faces and figures, wildly distorted, flew in, flew out. Visions of Darlene, of Mason, of blood. Blood everywhere, crimson-red, coating every surface. Blood, bloody blood.

Act I

"Drink me," squeals a kelly-green servant, a figure in a not-so-wonderful wonderland, tray in hand. He offers Christian-the-Manly-Man a sparkly glass of Chartreuse, a teasingly green liquid. Christian greedily snatches the vessel from the manservant's silver-green platter and thirstily drains the brew. Shrinking down to the size of a mouse, his skeleton flattens like that of a rodent, and he follows the also-reduced critter through a narrow space beneath a door, the door to his bedroom at Second Coming. Tiny Christian shimmies on up the leg of a bedside table in time to see his ghastly, ghostly transparent father and his once-upon-a-time, also-dead-but-still-gloriously-fleshed-out wife as they furiously rut away, the translucent Mason thrusting in and out as Darlene moans in painful ecstasy.

Blood and Semen, Blood and Death, Blood Brother, words set in green-tinged crystalline bubbles, dance gaily about the lovers' heads.

Act II

Brobdingnagian-sized J.J. saunters by, coming to a hard stop when he spies the wee Christian crouched beneath a prodigious mushroom. Cradling Mother Dar in his arms, a satisfied purr issues from her mouth. J.J. sets her down, then vigorously flings the Bible at his eensy-weensy brother-not father, barely missing him and his 'shroom. The book falls and click, click, click, its pages turn as if by magic—or God—to Genesis. *Lot's daughters became pregnant by their father* glowing large upon a hedge, the words a most carnivalesque neon green, the rutter-ers, dead center.

Enter, the Queen of Hearts, "Uncle John! Uncle John!" the monarch's tenor voice roars, as a great white stallion, bare of back but with the face of Satan, thunders past. In an uncharacteristically deep and booming cry, Mother Darlene sounds, "No, 'tis I, Lot." And Jumbo J.J., brother-not-son, savagely hisses venomously at Mouse Man, "A man so barren as you—my mother, your wife—she birthed a child of your father's seed, the pity being you found out."

Along slimes a harlequin-green caterpillar, a ring of smoke encircling its head, he-she-it caustically chanting, "Your brother. Your son. Your brother. Your son. Your brother. Your son. Your s-s-s-s-s-s-shame."

Act III

Strappingly virile men draw near. Wicked are they, for they taunt and sneer and cackle like brutes, whereupon another chalice of green, always green, this one of the lime persuasion, appears in Christian's hand, the Queen's deep voice commanding, *"Drink Me!"* and so, of necessity, he obeys and drains the glass dry. Of a sudden, the wee Pastor-Not-Secretary morphs back into a man of human proportions, a once-upon-a-time lamb beside him, dead at his feet, feet soaked scarlet red with blood. An upside-down sign flashes, "Wrong lamb. Bloody, bloody wrong."

Forsooketh, forsaketh, forsaken.

When the plane touched down, the first sign of daylight bestirred the righteous Hebrews. Their Sabbath behind them, it was Sunday, the day before America's Final Awakening. Christian rose from his berth in the fitted-out jet, the bed-linens tousled and damp. Vibrating from the night's terror, he tried his best to slough off the augury, then he showered, shaved, and dosed up.

70

June 22

LLOYD KRUEGER, anchor of SWBN's *Tomorrow Live*, the primetime show that immediately preceded Charles Korteen's *God is Good*, startled when a UCSA officer slammed a document on the table in front of him, the release that reporters covering Operation Clean-Up were required to sign.

I hereby agree that any and all information regarding or relating to Operation Clean-Up, including without limitation communications, videos, pictures and other descriptions and accounts thereof, are the exclusive property of the United Christian States of America, and that I shall not use, publish, or broadcast any such information other than on Spread the Word Broadcasting Network (SWBN). I agree that any violation of this agreement will subject me to capital punishment, and I hereby waive any right I may have to trial or appeal.

Kreuger readily agreed to the terms. Upon signing, he received one hundred thousand dollars in danger pay, all in crisp UCSA bills. Hell, he thought, he'd sell his mother for the opportunity to participate in the most consequential battle in American history.

He and Korteen set to work assembling a skeleton crew of videographers and livestream experts essential to the production, each of whom signed an identical non-disclosure agreement, and received a smaller, though still substantial, bonus.

By nightfall, Krueger, Korteen, and the scant crew are winging their way to Portland to await instructions.

71

June 23

TRANSPORT AFTER transport bumped down the runway at a hastily constructed airstrip on the eastern side of the Cascades. Buoyed by one another's enthusiasm, the warriors deplaned to the sounds of a full military band, Generals Isaiah Polk and Jerry Mulholland standing by. The day was picture-perfect, the bluest of skies glinting off the water's surface. Volcanic cliffs framed the lakes' glacial waters, stands of blue-green firs waving from above, their scent intoxicating. The troops marched along the cliff's edge until they reached what used to be the state park's campground, which is where they set up base. Formerly a haven for hikers and city-dwelling week-enders come to commune with nature, the park, like all public preserves, it was shuttered two weeks into the Alger presidency. Many of the isolated parklands had proven ideal for military and other government purposes.

United States soldiers had fought and died for their country around the globe, but not since the War Between the States would the military target its own citizens. The challenge of the moment was to fire up the troops for the brutality that lay ahead by putting a different face on an enemy who looked and sounded like themselves. If anyone could accomplish this, it was Polk and Mulholland, both of whose reputations for exacting military strategy were matched only by the coldhearted cruelty with which they had always carried out their missions.

The first evening, Polk spoke to God's Warriors in an outdoor arena nestled among the pines, from atop a stage large enough to have once held a community orchestra. He let his eyes travel slowly over the troops, giving each soldier the illusion he was looking at him. His aide de camp handed him a cordless microphone, and then, his resonant voice boomed out across the open space.

"As I welcome you tonight before this, our homeland's most significant battle since Confederate troops fired on Fort Sumter, it is important that you recognize what an honor it is for you, the select, to play this critical role in our nation's history. You have trained hard and, militarily, you are ready. But regardless of how prepared you think you are, the ways in which you handle the psychological component of what's to come will determine how quickly we wrap things up.

"I speak in particular to the ground troops. You will go hand to hand with an enemy who might look and sound like you, or like people you know and love—your mothers or fathers, brothers and sisters, your friends. There will be moments that you will clutch, question yourself, wonder if killing them is the right thing to do. My simple, unequivocal answer is yes! Yes, it is right! Yes, it is just! Yes, it is God's will!

"Do not, for one moment, let the enemy's physical appearance play mind games on you, for that is none but a trick of Satan. As Warriors for Christ, you must go into battle assured that every man, woman, and child you target is the Lord's sworn enemy, evildoers who, given the chance, would murder you in cold blood. Understand that as we gather here, there are Resistance cells across the country preparing to bomb more malls and churches, schools and airports, places your wives and children, your mothers and fathers go. I tell you this so that, in the heat of battle, not a one of you will think of these people as countrymen! Or that they live and worship as we do!"

Almost as one, a ferocious roar came back at the General, loud enough to make squirrels scamper away in fear and birds flee their nests. When the noise subsided, the hoot of one solitary owl pierced the air.

"Imagine your exultation when you feel the Devil's soul slip from their godless bodies." He paused to let the vision sink in.

Polk pretended to search the men's faces, then he bellowed loudly, "What must we do?"

Prompted by placards which platoon leaders hold high, the warriors howled, "Destroy them!"

"Who?"

"The godless terrorists!"

"When does the bloodletting begin?"

"Mon-day! Mon-day! Mon-day! Mon-day!"

The sounds they made were otherworldly. Satisfied, Polk held up a hand to quiet them. "Drones will pave the way: too high for the enemy to register. After sowing this first round of death, fighter jets will follow with broader strikes. At the same time, air transports will deposit ground troops at Portland International. Those of you who make it into the city by foot or by tank will have the glory of going face to face with any survivors, flooding the streets and administering the final and conclusive blows."

On cue, two soldiers walked across the stage, unscrolling a banner that ran the width of the platform. *WE SHALL RAIN FIRE AND BRIMSTONE; THEY SHALL FEAR THE NAME OF THE LORD.*

Polk raised his arms to the heavens, "Believe on your God and His glory shall be ours."

As the sun set on the eve of battle, the soldiers reassembled for a final address. General Mulholland took the stage, his voice lit with the fire of righteousness, "Fellow warriors, in a few short hours, our battle begins. Our mission is just, it is simple, and we shall prevail. Tomorrow is the day we shall eradicate the nation's spiritual enemy for all time. Yes, tomorrow will be a day most biblical.

"To begin this holy journey, I have invited Chaplain Healy to lead us in prayer tonight."

Healy mounted the platform. Straight-laced, he was a more youthful version of the Brigade's Storm Vorderseit. The sky retained enough light for him to see faces, if not the features, of those in the front rows, and from the first word his plea hit the mark: "Oh Lord, bless these men so that they are strong in Your vision. For theirs is a struggle not against flesh and blood, but against the Master of Darkness himself. Clad in Your armor," and here he looked up, "they shall need no more. With the belt of truth buckled around their waists, the breastplate of righteousness in place, their feet fitted with the readiness that comes from the gospel of peace, Your shield of faith shall repel each and every arrow of Evil directed their way."

The forest went quiet, as still as the atmosphere in the eye of a hurricane.

Most of the men were young enough to remember the time when they held their mamas' hands, but the sounds that came from their throats that night were so visceral, so bloodcurdling, that any doubt Polk and Mulholland might have vanished. Were it another era, the sounds in these Oregon woods might well have been set in an arena hundreds of years ago during the time of The Crusades. Their war cry resonated for miles to the east, while to the west, the granite mountain blocked their howls.

If the Resisters could hear their sound and fury, they would throw back their heads in laughter, as they looked around at their own technologically superior might.

72

UCSA TANKS lumbered up the planks onto Air Force Globemasters. At one-thirty in the morning, the moon illuminated the way as infantry boarded personnel airlifts bound for the one usable runway at Portland International. Their mission divine, hearts full and excitement high.

Three hundred miles southeast of Portland, the transports lifted off, their initial altitude concealing them, but when the first drone rose above the mountain, it triggered the Cascade Control Center's system, at the same time a piercing alarm on Ben's SAT phone startled him out of a deep sleep. He rocketed from bed and raced downstairs to the darkened main floor. This is it, he thought, the moment none of them had let themself fully believe would come. In near darkness, he nearly crashed head-on into Josh.

"It's happening!" Ben shouted. Hastening to the desktop, he punched in a code and pressed send.

Hope and dread had come together in the dead of night, in a city devastated by Nature, and a country destroyed by Man.

Bruce materialized. "Jesus, let this work," he said prayerfully, following Josh and Ben to the motherboard where, independently, they checked and rechecked the system. No matter how prepared they were, everything they'd practiced before was a dress rehearsal. This was not a drill.

They watched Vargova's scrambler begin to transmit its delusory signals to drone operators in Nebraska.

"Look at that arc!" Josh cried. "It's perfect! Heading straight for the target!"

The men saw the first USCA drone explode, its fiery particles filling the screen, then a second later, another evaporated in mid-air, Josh, Ben, and Bruce loudly cheering.

At that same time, manufactured video began streaming to Mulholland and Polk at base camp, and to the Situation Room in the White House. What Alger, Riggins, Polk, and Mulholland saw was a fraudulent feed of UCSA bombs letting loose, one after another, blowing Portland's landscape to smithereens. Thanks to another feature of Vargova's software, Josh, Ben, and Bruce were able to watch Alger's and all the others' reactions in real time.

Riggins leapt from his chair. "Huzzah! Blast 'em to the bowels of Hell!"

A feeling of euphoria filled the Situation Room. All it had taken was a savage bloodletting.

A tight grin crept across the president's face. The others looked on, their hearts filled with the sanctity of their offensive. "I didn't think it would be this easy," Alger said. He turned to Riggins: "Must we still bring in the ground troops?"

"They're on their way, so yes," Riggins replied. "Besides, there'll be some few survivors. It's critical we finish off whatever's moving."

"After that, order them to take the entire coast," Alger exclaimed. "This land is ours, all of it!"

On the other coast, Josh declared, "Beautiful, simply beautiful."

"Goliath doesn't know about David, but David knows about Goliath," Bruce added.

❖

CHARLES KORTEEN and Lloyd Krueger were set to go live from the roof deck of the Ritz Carlton, the tallest building in the city to have withstood Delilah. The USCA had notified Riggins, Polk, and Mulholland that the hotel and its surrounding area were to be treated as a Safe Zone, so as to broadcast the battle live from there. The journalists were about to sign on, when a Resistance drone dropped a small explosive onto the rooftop, vaporizing the men and turning the top floors to dust. There should have been greater concern in the Situation Room when the SWBN monitor went blank, but Alger and the others were focused on the military feed showing on the main screen. Thrilling to the sight of fires blazing out of control and citizens running helter-skelter in the streets, Alger and his generals didn't notice the failure, so completely engrossed were they in the swiftness of their victory.

Reality could not have been more different. Having destroyed the UCSA drones, heat-seeking surface-to-air missiles launched from their positions at the Command Center. As they locked onto the government's F-45s, each hit sent the young pilots to their deaths, flaming debris falling on the countryside below.

Bickle called out, "Jiminy Cricket! He hath shown us the Way!"

Riggins spoke into his headset: "Polk, it's going great guns! When your troops arrive in Portland, have them start clearing the area until we can get our people there to begin the reconstruction and resettlement. We just got ourselves some of the finest land in the country!"

"Yes, sir."

When the first Globemaster's wheels eased onto the runway, Ben radioed Command, "Don't take out the tanks until they're all on their way into the city. That's when we'll go live. Show them the reality of their 'victory' in blazing color. Initially, they'll be so confused, it'll take time for their minds to assimilate what's real and what's not. Once they comprehend what's happened, they'll see how royally fucked they are."

"Beautiful," Josh said. "Simply beautiful."

The AFVs made their way down the ramps and God's Ground Army began their journey into the city. With news of the rout, the soldiers were relaxed, assured of the easy conquest ahead. The tanks rumbled forward as quickly as the terrain permitted, a recording of the National Choir ringing out inside each one:

He has sounded forth the trumpet that shall never call retreat;
He is sifting out the hearts of men before His judgment seat;

Oh, be swift, my soul, to answer Him: be jubilant, my feet!
Our God is marching on.

To a man, the soldiers put hand over heart, and raised their eyes to the heavens, so significant was the moment and the mission.

At mile one, the UCSA's screens went live. The first tank exploded and after that, the next, and the next, and all the others after that. Those in the Situation Room went silent. As Ben had predicted, the visual transition from fakery to reality was so seamless that their brains, having been immersed in the imagery of irrefutable victory, were incapable of reconciling what they now saw on-screen. These men running the country were, after all, just men. For several minutes, they retreated into their individual silos, not one of them able to make sense of two such vastly different scenarios.

Riggins snapped to and rushed the screen. "No! No! Go back! Go back to how it was! This is not real!" But there was no going back.

What they'd seen as a complete rout had instantly and un-imaginably transformed into their own apocalypse, a twisted terror suffusing every heart. When the last tanks exploded, Alger reengaged, and though helpless to affect a thing, he began to shout, using the kind of language the Devil employs. With Christian out of the country, he turned his fury on Riggins, "Fuck all, Thad. You okayed this! I promise you, heads will roll!"

Amidst the chaos, Ned slipped out unnoticed. He quickly made his way upstairs through the White House and out the employee door. He flashed his badge at the guard and crossed over to Lafayette Park, bending down to retrieve the satellite phone he had hidden beneath a bush on his way in that morning. He texted Ben, hardly able to type for the shaking in his hand, the words, "Morning has broken," flying into space.

For a moment, Ben could scarcely take in the magnitude of what they'd seen on-screen, and now, here was Ned confirming what for so long has been an unfathomable dream. He fired off a text to Vargova and Ryan at Control, all fear of detection gone.

Josh and Ben awakened everyone in the building and brought them together onto the main floor, where Josh climbed atop a stack of wooden crates to exuberantly proclaim, "In the past hour, we stopped the greatest military power on earth! Congratulations to all of us, and to everyone across the country who fought to resist, each in their own way, large or small! Under the most difficult of conditions, we risked our lives for the sake of humanity. While we can't know what lies ahead, we can take pride today in knowing that we rewrote a major chapter in history. We proved once again that, in the end, good can prevail. This is a moment for celebration."

Bruce popped the cork on a bottle of Aurore Brut, the sparkling wine that BEST used to sell, and raised a glass of the bubbly high. "To life!," he cheered, "And to the United States of America!"

73

One-Thirty p.m., Israel Standard Time

STRETCHED OUT ON a poolside chaise, his pale girth gleaming with sweat, courtesy of the unrelenting Israeli sun, Christian summoned the waiter. "Boy, I'll have a large ice tea." Bringing his head in closer, he added, "Without the tea. Fill 'er up with your best bourbon instead."

Discreetly, he palmed the server the equivalent of one hundred UCSA dollars in shekels and winked, the implication obvious as day; this stays 'tween us. He can't afford for his security detail, standing several feet behind, to know he was about to imbibe the devil's brew. But honest to goodness, his nerves were so on edge that a goodly amount of liquor would go a long ways toward calming him down, today of all days.

Pocketing the money, the accommodating waiter walked off. That's when Christian noticed a none-too subtle sniggering come from close by. He glanced down the row of loungers to see a group of comely young women, pointing to and laughing at him, their scorn prompting not so much anger as it did the age-old sting of shame.

Brandishing their sexuality like a weapon, they notice his regard and rather than feel embarrassed, they brazenly looked back. He sat upright and pulled the hotel robe across his white whale of a belly, muttering to himself. "If you hoors knew who I am, you wouldn't be mockin' me. Barely a strip a cloth to cover yer nether parts, yer filth on show for all t'see."

He would excuse not a lick of their behavior. Nonetheless, their derision unsettled him, not the least because he felt nothing for them sexually. Red-faced, he looked away.

As if he sensed Christian's unease, the waiter reappeared with a tall glass of liquid escape. Before long, the drink mixed with the drugs in his bloodstream, and finally at peace, he fell asleep. Within moments though, he was jarred awake by the harsh ringtone he'd assigned the president. He stood unsteadily, then moved far enough away so that no one could overhear. "Mister Prezdent?"

An explosion of panicked cries made clear to Christian how wrong he'd been. Dead wrong.

"H'lo? I cain't hear you!," he shouted into the phone.

"Lord, save us!," a voice comes back. Then, "They've destroyed us!"

"H'lo? H'lo?" Christian hollered.

Strangled in their fury, Alger's words assaulted him. "You ruinous jackass. That I ever believed in you! Do you have any idea what you've unleashed?"

Christian spoke over him, "You're breakin' up, Mr. President. H'lo? If you hear me, I don't seem to have serv...," whereupon Christian ended the call, shoving the phone inside the robe pocket, where it whirred and whirred and whirred.

He hurried into the hotel, his detail following close behind. From poolside to elevator, elevator to penthouse, Christian's nerves buzzed with a dread the magnitude of which he had never before experienced. He was freelancing now. As his mind spun out in a thousand directions, he wondered that he had been such an easy mark. But there is no use going over that. He had to move, and move fast. His head cleared; danger will do that to a man. He was all action now.

Outside his suite, he turned to his minders, "Boys, I gotta take a phone meetin'. Go on to your rooms 'til I call for you." Though accustomed to his requests for privacy, this was Israel after all, and so they hesitated. But orders were orders and so they obeyed.

Alone in his room, Christian threw the bolt on the door and set to the task at hand. Although Alger knew that the UCSA had no control over the international airwaves, Christian expected that amidst the chaos, he hadn't yet thought that far. At the moment the president was surely focused solely on the truth that they'd been bested by a supposedly fatally doomed group of people, and all of it based on Christian's word. Once Alger couldn't reach Christian, once he realized that his humiliation was being broadcast across the world, his wrath would know no bounds.

Christian switched on the TV as he began to throw together his belongings when suddenly he stopped, frozen in place. On BBC News, a reporter was saying, "In the UCSA's failed attempt to take over what remains of the old United States, the Resistance continues to dominate. In fact, what is taking place, in the areas known as The Territories, is nothing less than a rout of biblical proportions, the underdogs coming out on top! What we're seeing is extraordinary, unbelievable. We'll stay on the story as it develops."

If Christian knew one thing, it was that viewers in the States weren't seeing anything like this. Instead, they'd be watching canned imagery of a glorious victory, likely narrated by Thaddeus Riggins.

He thought back to the moments when he'd stood among the group outside The Grotto, heard a young man say, "We won't be seeing our way back onto the Shadow Web." How he'd initially intuited that it couldn't be. But pressured by Alger as he was, he recklessly chose to believe that the Resistance could indeed no longer access the Shadow Web and had offered it up to the president as his own accomplishment. What he could not fathom was how in the Sam Hill those wretches, still firmly in Delilah's death-grip, had acquired the kinds of weapons they were using. Furthermore, how had they known exactly when and where the UCSA would attack?

The chyron 'Modern-Day David Repels Goliath in Stunning Defeat' scrolled across the screen, gutting him as he stood not far from the ground where that actual biblical battle had transpired.

BBC International Affairs reporter Gillian Roberts interrupted. "In further breaking news, President James Alger has severed all internet communications between his nation and the outside world. The UCSA is now an electronically walled-off state, its internet completely shut down. With me is Clive Battersby, BBC's Financial Affairs expert."

"Thank you, Gillian. This is an extraordinary development, one with long-term implications. While Alger has imposed an information blockade to keep Americans from learning of the UCSA's ignominious defeat, the economic fallout in sealing themselves off from the world threatens to trigger a major recession across the pond. Thankfully, since they've become so isolated, financially and otherwise, the impact should remain local to the UCSA. Except of course for the handful of countries like Israel, Russia, and a few others who continue to do business with them. In the end, the blackout could be a short-lived solution, that is if citizens find the necessary work-arounds, something that very much remains to be seen. Also important to note is that these actions are the mark of a ty-rannical government in decline. It's hard to believe that we're talking about a nation that, until six months ago, was the greatest power on earth."

"What a fascinating turn of events, Clive, one we'll continue to monitor closely."

What Battersby didn't understand was that there would be no workarounds. Still in control of the largest and most powerful military on earth, Alger would continue to control the citizenry through propaganda, oppression, and sporadic acts of homegrown terrorism. Add to that the threat of capital pun-ishment for anyone caught trying to circumvent the shutdown. He could maintain an iron grip on the country for a very long time. Truth would remain fantasy, and fantasy truth, no matter the cost.

As for Christian, he no longer gave a good goddamn about Alger or any of them. Switching off the television, he set to the business of vanishment.

Dropping his swimsuit to the floor, Christian unzipped the carry-on he'd brought along. He grabbed the black trousers and white shirt from within and quickly threw them on. Next, he fixed in place a wiry beard, yarmulke, tallit, and tzitzit. Last of all, he pinned a pair of side curls to his beard and lifted the tall, flat-topped black hat from its separate carry case. It took but a few short minutes for Christian to transform himself from a mildly sunburned, porcine American into an inconspicuous Haredi Jew. After taking one last look in the full-length mirror, he wrapped his fingers around the handle of his wheeled bag. Leaving his phone behind, he quietly opened the door and poked his head out. The hall was empty. Exiting the room, he noiselessly rolled the small suitcase along the carpet to the service elevator, directing it to the loading dock. Only when he felt the car begin its descent did his breathing return to normal. Unnoticed, he exited the hotel through the loading dock and, once outside, moved along, blending into the crowd with ease. Making his way through the narrow alleys of central Jerusalem, the unremarkable man trudged eastward towards the Old City. Within the space of eight days, he'd morphed from a Cabinet Secretary into an earthquake-battered hag, back again into a Cabinet Secretary and finally, into an unidentifiable Orthodox Jew wheeling a bag across the same ground upon which Jesus once trod.

Boutiques selling Hermès scarves and Italian leather goods gave way to souvenir shops and souks peddling everything from spices to Judaica to hijabs. He continued on when suddenly there came a bloodcurdling explosion from a storefront just ahead. Christian hustled across the street as fast as his corpulence allowed and looked around to assure himself he was out of harm's way. Shattered tiles, splintered pieces of wood, shards of glass, any one of them potentially lethal, had exploded outward from what seconds earlier had been a busy hair salon. Sirens blared and emergency vehicles converged from every direction. Greatly shaken, he hastened along, huffing and puffing, periodically glancing behind until at last, he arrived in front of a free-standing dwelling deeded to one, Yehudah Michelman. He had purchased the home with cash as a safe house twenty years earlier, back when he and Darlene were at the height of their empire. Those were the days when there was no reason in the world to think he might ever need to go into hiding. Yet the inner darkness that dogged him his entire life had taught him it was important to always have an out.

The house was as nondescript as he currently was. Its modesty had originally appealed to him, both for its inconspicuousness and the neighborhood's Haredi Jewish makeup. After all, these were the holiest of Israelites, the ones doing the work necessary to help achieve Christian's goal of taking back and repopulating all of biblical Zion. As a bonus, if he stood just so, he could see a sliver of the Western Wall from the corner of a second story window. At the time, the view alone signaled that God had led him there.

Once inside, Christian drew the curtains, unpacked his bag, and removed the plastic coverings from the furniture. He turned on the television, relieved to see that the carnage he had only just barely avoided had pre-empted America's disaster.

On screen, local Jerusalem reporter Schmuel Levy was live outside the Queen Esther Beauty Salon in the heart of the Old City, flames licking at the adjacent buildings. "Still unknown is who is behind this latest act of terrorism. What we do know is…." He pressed his hand to his earpiece and listened closely to the voice inside, "Wait. Hold on. We have just learned that so far, nineteen women are dead inside the salon. As of now, we have no other information. For security reasons, there seems to be a further blackout on the story. With nothing more to report at this time, we'll return to our coverage of 'The American Reckoning.'"

Christian switched off the set. He had escaped two disasters today, one large and life-changing, the other normative, almost mundane, and he did not want to hear or see more about his abject failure regarding the first. Emotionally and physically depleted, it struck him that, for the first time in decades, there was no one around to see to his needs. If he wanted to eat, he would have to go to the store himself. But first, he would attend to his addiction, and that was easily dealt with. He had traveled to Israel with an ample stock of sedatives, benzos, and other anti-anxiety medications, and when his cupboard ran dry, he knew a man who knew a man.

Heavily dosed, he sat slumped in an armchair, luxuriating in the soon-to-be sensations of floating. Of blessed numbness. Before the drugs took him too far under, he pulled an un-registered phone from the carryall next to him and punched in a phone number, one he'd had the foresight to ink onto his forearm before he'd left the country. While he waited for the only man at Faith who put Christianity above personal or political gain, Christian began to feel a lightening. He was safe, anonymous, and out of reach. In fact, he could stay hidden here for as long as he chose. After enough time passed and the world forgot about him, he would be free to facilitate his lifelong biblical goals from the very lands deeded by Father God Himself!

Ned's phone rang. He was back in the Situation Room, having returned there so as to be physically present at the moment these men learned of their defeat. He picked up on the first ring. "Burroughs here." When Christian heard Ned's voice, his nerves further eased. He was as good a man as there was and with that first "Hello," Christian knew he could trust him with his life. Which was exactly what he'd done the day he'd welcomed him back to Faith.

"Ned, s'mee." The same chaos from before came back at him. The Generals, Cabinet members, and Alger were currently suffering through the earlier videos of the obliteration of the UCSA's drones and fighter jets. Christian would have been far more concerned had he been able to think clearly. He did have enough awareness to ask, "Can you step away?"

The noise and confusion in the Situation Room made it easy for Ned to leave unobserved, once again. He walked down the hall at a purposeful but unhurried pace telling Christian, "Stay on the line till I get a little further away." Considering the frantic nature of what he had just been a part of, his tone remained conversational, not a hint of worry in his voice.

Ned was a true friend, Christian thought, the only one he had. It took a few more seconds for him to gather the courage to ask the only question that mattered, "What're they sayin' 'bout me?"

Ned took the next steps of his pre-planned exit. It was business as usual as White House officials and staffers went about their day, as out of touch with reality as everyone else dependent on UCSA media. He rode the elevator to the ground floor, and almost as if he were invisible, exited the building.

"Mr. Secretary, are you inside your safe house?"

Christian stood, sputtering, hardly able to speak. "How in God's name d'you know 'bout that?"

"You don't remember? You told me all about it that day in the cab before you went to Portland for the last time."

Christian broke out in a cold sweat, his hand gripping the phone hard. How could he not remember? More importantly, why in the world had he told him?

His voice still measured and tranquil, Ned continued, "I would think by now you would have realized how completely you've been manipulated."

The enormity of these words was staggering. Christian fell back into the chair.

"What a pompous monster you are, thinking you own the truth. I lost my wife and seven children in the tsunami, watched helplessly as they were swept out to sea. I doubt you are capable of understanding, but it was then that I lost faith in your higher power. Not to mention in a government run by murderous theocrats. What happened in Oregon proved to me that your mythical God is nothing compared to the whims of nature. It also made me realize that my role in administering the arbitrary destruction of this once great nation was a far greater sin than anything described in your so-called holy book. Since, shall we say, I saw the light, my only real pleasure has been to work with the Resistance to foil your plans."

Christian gasped, his breath physically leaving him. His mouth made the gaping motions of a dying fish, and when he tried to speak, nothing came out.

Ned looked back at the heavily fortified People's House, his voice still calm and even. "I surmise from your silence that you're surprised. Well then, imagine my astonishment the day I recognized you dressed as a woman at The Grotto. It shouldn't take much for you to figure out the rest," Ned chuckled. "It was almost too easy."

Ned crossed through the park, still talking. "You and Alger, you gave it your best, but in the end you're no match for us. We're strong, we're united, and we are a coalition of US citizens and other countries committed to Alger's and your destruction. If you have the time, you might want to call your President and tell him it's best he surrender. He can't imagine the totality of what we, and the world, have in store for him.

"The consequences for you, on the other hand, will be rather more immediate, which is why I recommend you try to reach him without delay. You see we—and by we, I mean The Resistance—know precisely where you are. That same day in the cab, you also shared the address of your Israeli refuge, which I passed on to Zeb, who, by the way, is also one of us. Mr. Secretary, my last bit of advice to you is that you make a swift escape. If you can, that is."

Ned climbed into an unmarked van on the southwest corner of Lafayette Square, the first leg of his return journey.

At the same moment, the sound of boots stormed up the walkway to Christian's front door. In that instant, the eternity between awareness and a battering ram, Christian raced for the back door, but even with Father God looking on, he wasn't fast enough.

The End